Set Free

Also by the author

Set Free

Anthony Bidulka

ISBN: 978-0-9952292-1-1
ebook ISBN: 978-0-9952292-0-4

Bon Vivant Books

Cover design by Kelly Nichols
Edited by Roxanne Alcorn, BCAI, Word Superb

Acknowledgments

For me, Set Free represents embracing new opportunities, turning dark into light, seizing control, and reasserting my love for the craft of writing. None of this would have been possible without the support of numerous people, friends, family and colleagues, too numerous to mention by name even though I would dearly love to. Thank you.

Certain specific aspects of this book would have been lesser than without the help of these people: Roxanne Alcorn, Kelly Nichols, Mary Clark, Rhonda Sage, Neil Plakcy and, most of all, Herb McFaull. I also want to say thank you to the great many people who participated in an online poll several months ago, voting on a title for this book. I valued your input and exuberant interest. Although the winning title was *Book of Lies*, I hope that once you read this book you'll see why I settled on *Set Free*.

As always, I am indebted to booksellers, book reviewers, supportive media and most of all, my readers. You have made life as a writer more rewarding than I could have ever imagined.

Dedication

For Herb

PART I

Chapter 1

Excerpt from the novel Set Free, *by Jaspar Wills, bestselling author of* In The Middle.

I would have packed less if I knew I was going to die.

Travel-worn, I waited for my ride, carry-on and small, battered suitcase at my feet. The atmosphere was chaotic, the air stifling. Marrakech airport is not the kind of place you loiter for long. Not unlike an ant hill, if you aren't scurrying about, you either need assistance or you're dead. You either haul ass or someone is going to do it for you. Familiar with the drill, I gamely accepted being harassed by an endless parade of locals, all of them anxious to do something for me—anything at all—for a hastily negotiated, wildly inflated price.

After failing to see my name—or anything vaguely resembling it—on any of the placards being waved in the air by a throng of waiting chauffeurs-for-hire, I settled on a reasonable wait time. Forty minutes seemed just right. It was long enough to give the driver I'd arranged for a chance to show up if he'd been unexpectedly delayed, but short enough for me to maintain a semblance of patience. If he never showed, half an hour was a bit on the chintzy side, whereas three-quarters of an hour was playing the fool.

At minute forty-one I gave up. No one was coming to meet me. I grabbed my luggage and headed for the exit.

"I can help with your hotel." The voice belonged to a pleasant-looking young man, Arabic. At first he'd tried French, but quickly converted to near-flawless English when he saw the dumb look on my face. He was wearing a typical costume for Moroccan men: lightweight white djellaba, with a matching pillbox-style hat (I'm guessing he wouldn't have appreciated the description) and a pair of well-worn black leather babouche slippers.

I pulled out a slip of paper on which I'd written the name and address of my riad and handed it to him.

"Yes," he said with a confident nod, at the same time reaching down for my suitcase. "Riad Hadika Maria. Derb Zemrane Hart Soura. I know it. Come with me." He carried the bag instead of using the rollers.

It happened that easily. Nothing about the man—a boy really—hinted that something wasn't quite right.

The things I love most about visiting new places—the mystery, the unfamiliarity—are the very same things that can make it exceedingly dangerous. Everything you trust about the world is suddenly in question. How was I to know I wasn't being taken to my hotel? How was I to know that, instead, I was simply being taken?

Chapter 2

I'd left home at 8:00 p.m. By 6:30 the next morning I was in London. From there, Air Portugal took me to Lisbon, then Marrakech. In less than twenty-four hours, I'd left behind one world and begun my adventure in another. My plan was to be in Morocco for sixteen days: ten for work, the rest pleasure. I didn't know about the other plan. The one made by someone else. The one that would bring my life to an end.

The official languages of Morocco are Arabic and Berber. Oh shit, right? The unofficial third language is French. Better—sort of.

Despite my life as a traveler, I'm a steadfast, uni-linguist American who figures I'll somehow get by. And usually I do. In preparation for the trip, I'd boned up on as many key francophone expressions as I could stuff into my head and loaded my iPhone with a killer translation app. I'd done this kind of thing before. From Amsterdam to Zanzibar, I've proven to be exceptionally skilled at combining phrase book jargon, a friendly smile, and hand gestures to get me pretty much anything I want.

Landing in Menara Airport that day was a happy reminder of why my love affair with travel had endured. It's the heady rush of finding yourself somewhere completely new. The dizzying unfamiliarity. The euphoria of being on foreign soil. It's like voluntarily ingesting a mind-altering, body-shuddering elixir you can never get enough of.

That first step off an aircraft is beyond thrilling to me. I may as well be a space traveler making first contact with an alien planet. My brain sizzles with stimulation. Accomplishment and heady delight overcome me before I've even had a single experience. It's as if I've won first place in the game of life, and my prize is about to reveal itself.

I dutifully made my way through customs and security, surrendered to the aggressive jostling of the luggage carousel hordes, and finally inched my way into the arrivals area. Every fiber of my being was thrumming with anticipation. Not until that very moment did I allow myself to acknowledge the truth. I'd grown desperately thirsty over my lengthy, self-imposed dry spell without travel. Even with all that had happened back home, everything I'd left behind, I had to admit something: I was over-the-moon, idiot-grinning happy.

Huh.

Happy.

I'd forgotten about happy.

Given my extensive experience, people often seek my guidance on travel to foreign destinations. The best piece of advice I can give is this: slow down, stay in the moment, bask. By far, the easier choice is to become overwhelmed. But why waste energy trying to escape the unknown? Embrace it.

As I pushed my way through the swarming airport, pretty much every sense jumped into hyper drive. Smell was the first to detonate. Must and dry mold. Spice. The tannic scent of unrelenting heat. The pungency of travelers thrown together from every corner of the world, mixed into a heady stew of humanity. The unmistakable fragrance of ancient civilization, of a place where lives have been lived—some well, some not-so-well—for centuries. Of generations briefly colliding, then moving on, one disappearing to make room for the next, each bound by fate and circumstance to leave behind a residue, like motes of dust from a beaten carpet.

The sights, sounds, even the way the air tasted on my tongue, was a tonic. Discovering old ways of life inspires new life within me. In an instant, I'd gone from being a passenger on a commercial aircraft to an explorer navigating a grand adventure in a mysterious land.

The icing on the cake? No one knew who I was. In recent years, anonymity had become a rare luxury. Here, in Morocco, I was awash in it. I could finally revel in the simple pleasure of being left alone.

As a boy, I'd been fascinated by ant farms, doggedly intent on constructing one of my own. Several ill-fated attempts later, I mastered the craft, using an extra-large mason jar. There are two key elements to remember when creating an ant colony. First, it's a good idea to place a soda can in the center of the jar. The can acts as an obstruction so the ants don't dig their tunnels in the middle and lamentably out of sight. Second, while holes in the jar's lid are important, it's vital they be smaller than the actual ants.

On mother's orders, I kept the glass-sided realm in my bedroom. I spent countless hours mesmerized by the deceptively haphazard, seemingly disorganized miniature world moving at triple speed. Marrakech airport was just like that: a million scrambling bodies, each intent on their own purpose and oblivious to yours. If you weren't careful, the tide would grab on, swallow you whole, and take you places you didn't want to go.

I knew where I wanted to go. A moderately-priced B&B I'd found on Expedia called Riad Hadika Maria. It was very near the Medina, the walled old part of the city where I'd planned to spend most of my time. Before I'd left home I'd arranged for an airport pickup. Not that I'm incapable of navigating my own way around a strange city—I was simply following the second piece of advice I give would-be travelers. How do you guarantee a positive start to your trip? Have the first big decision—getting to your hotel—already taken care of. A bit of what I like to call "peace-of-mind insurance."

But, as we all know, insurance doesn't always pay off.

The plan was a good one. After all, where better to find an American hostage than an airport? And as far as someone to grab, I was a pretty fine choice. Alone. Traveling light. Even though I'm a big guy in good shape, I generally give off a non-threatening vibe. And I'm easily engaged, a trait I've had to cultivate because of what I do. If given the choice, I prefer blending into the background, but that hadn't been possible for me in a long while.

I'd studied a simple map of Marrakech, mainly the zone immediately surrounding the Medina. I'd thought myself generally acquainted with the area, yet within five minutes of leaving the airport, I barely knew up from down.

I like maps. Simple, old-fashioned, impossible-to-refold paper maps. The kind with a North-South indicator, red and black squiggles for roads, green blotches for forests, blue ones for water. They provide a sense of familiarity with a place without stealing away the thrill of being there for the first time. Nowadays, online maps can show you your neighbor's backyard swimming pool, the location of every Starbucks within walking distance, and pretty much every bump in the road between here and there. I can see how these kinds of maps, with their absurdly high level of detail and information, offer comfort and introduce ease—but for me, they destroy the ecstasy of discovery and surprise.

"How far to the hotel?" I asked the driver in what I felt was a conversational tone.

Despite his earlier affability, once we were in the car—him and my suitcase in the front seat, me in the rear—the young man who'd solicited me in the airport had fallen into determined silence.

"Not far," he finally mumbled.

"How long will it take to get there?"

"Not long."

Approaching an impressive structure of red brick and stone, I tried again. "What's that place?"

Silence. I guessed he wasn't into playing tour guide.

I waited several seconds before making another attempt. "Are those the walls of *Jemaa el-Fna*?" I thought I'd win him over with my worldly knowledge of local landmarks.

"Be quiet."

And there it was.

Only two words. But they told me plenty.

I was in danger.

Chapter 3

When I was a child, my parents were not the type to issue dire warnings. They never said, "Don't answer the door if you're home alone," or "Don't get into cars with strangers." They were more the type to suggest, "When you meet someone new, say hello and introduce yourself. Ask questions. Don't just talk about yourself." To them, the world was a friendly place.

Parents aren't always right.

By the time I wised up to the fact that my driver and I were not bound to become best buddies and I was in a dangerous situation, it was too late. I demanded he stop the car and let me out. He disagreed with the suggestion, a point made abundantly clear when he used his free hand to point a gun at my face. I guess I should have asked a few more questions when we first met.

"Sit back," he ordered.

Our eyes met in the rear-view mirror. I'd like to say his were malevolent and oozing with murderous intent. But they weren't. They were just eyes. Dark. Moist. One noticeably larger than the other. I wondered what he saw when he looked at mine. Surprise? Anger? Fear?

The gun was sufficient motivation to do as he asked.

Nothing about my life to that point had prepared me for this moment, unless you count having watched too many action movies. In no way was I a tough guy. Not in a beat-their-brains-out, knock-them-down, blow-them-up, or any other kind of way. Even if I'd had a gun, I wouldn't have known what to do with it. The only fights I'd ever been in were with my wife, Jenn, and those always turned out the same way: with me flat on my back, in a headlock, in about three seconds tops. Metaphorically speaking, of course.

Don't let the movies fool you about how easy it is to be a hero. Or worse, give you unreasonable expectations for your significant other's performance in dire circumstances. Most of us, no matter how many hours we've clocked pumping iron at the gym, mastering tai chi, or watching UFC, would be at a loss sitting on the cracked leather back seat of a stinking hot car barreling down an unfamiliar street in an African city with a pistol kissing their face. Fodor's definitely doesn't cover this.

I wasn't a complete idiot about what was happening in this part of the world. I'd done my research. One needn't look too far back in history to find reasons to practice caution. Scores of unhappy Moroccan rebels had taken part in Arab Spring revolutions. Activists were regularly staging mass protests calling for government reform and constitutional amendments to control the powers of the king. In 2011, seventeen people—mainly foreigners—were killed in a bomb attack on a Marrakech cafe.

And the problems extended far beyond local and continental politics. There'd been plenty of tension between this country and mine. As recently as 2013, Morocco canceled joint military exercises with the United States when Washington decided to back the UN's call to monitor human rights in Western Sahara. Instead of seeing the move as supporting its people, Morocco saw it as an attack on its sovereignty. Apparently they don't like that kind of stuff around here.

Sitting back, trying to calm my nerves and figure out what the hell to do, I stared out the window. A blur of traffic swept across a backdrop of earthen-hued buildings hunkered low beneath sun-bleached sky. Despite my best efforts, fear began to take hold, menacing, snarling, clawing. In the past, whenever I'd been scared, either I knew it was coming—like on a roller coaster or visiting a haunted house on Hallowe'en—or it appeared suddenly. This fear was different. It began as a pinprick, somewhere in the back of my head, then grew like an exotic flowering tea bud, blooming as it steeped, suddenly expanding to many times its original size, invading my brain until it consumed me. Only when I was fully diseased with dread did it carry out its merciless endgame, communicating the very real possibility that I might soon be dead.

The rumors of what happens in the moments before you die proved untrue for me. I didn't see my life passing before my eyes. I saw faces. A procession of the people I cared for most. My mother. My father. My brother James. His quirky, funny wife. My twin nieces for whom the word precocious was invented. I began to concern myself with how worried they'd be when they first heard the news that I'd never arrived at my hotel. That would only be the beginning. Mom would cry…

Screw that!

I couldn't sit back and let this happen to me. Okay, I was a writer, and yes, a nerd, and I might suck at most sports. But I work out. I look after myself, eat healthy. I could be forceful if I needed to be. And boy, did I need to be.

"Where are we going?" I demanded to know, pulling myself up against the front seat. I was close enough to smell the driver's heavy cologne, barely masking the acrid scent of perspiration.

Again with the gun.

My last words were stupid ones. "You can't shoot me and drive at the same time!"

When I awoke, the first thing I knew was why I'd been asleep. It hadn't come naturally. There was no mirror in sight, and my hands were bound behind my back, but I didn't need them to know there was a giant lump on my forehead. It might have been the size of an asteroid for all its throbbing intensity, radiating pain into every nook and cranny of my skull.

Without moving, I tried to figure out where I was. I'd been tied up, gagged, and laid out on a floor. The space was small, dark, perhaps a storage room. A single window—little more than a narrow opening near the ceiling—let in just enough light to coax black into muted grey.

Wincing from the wound, I pulled myself up so I was sitting with my back against a wall. Everything hurt, not just my head. The worst of it originated from somewhere on the left side of my torso. My eyes moved to the spot, the effort triggering excruciating jabs of pain. A small splotch of red penetrated the fabric of my shirt: a pathetically inconsequential clue as to what had just happened to me, and what was about to.

Chapter 4

When considering taking a trip, does anyone factor in the possibility of dying? Figuring out how many pairs of underwear to pack, selecting the right swimsuit, making sure you've got all the relevant travel documents—do people think to themselves, even fleetingly, *I may never come back*?

Maybe some people. Nervous flyers. Chronic pessimists. An article I once read estimated that every year, two hundred people die on cruise ships, and about the same number in plane crashes. In the United States alone, there are over forty thousand automobile-related deaths annually. Travel is not for the faint of heart.

On the day I left for Morocco, pulling khakis from the closet and stuffing socks in my shoes, I never gave my lifespan a second thought. I've traveled all my life. My parents were—still are—travel enthusiasts. Some have gone so far as to describe them as modern-day gypsies. Even when my brother Sam and I were very young, they'd regularly bundle us up and whisk us off to faraway places.

My first travel memory goes back to when I was five. It was a family trip to Africa. I don't remember exact details of how we got there or how long we stayed, but I do remember seeing an elephant up close; so close I could smell its breath. I remember being surprised by how the Zambian scrublands looked nothing like where I imagined Tarzan would hang out, and spending hours enthralled by a family of baboons as they picked insects out of one another's fur (an action my brother and I imitated with great hilarity for months afterwards). All the while, Mom and Dad would take trillions of pictures and fill copious journals with their observations, a habit I picked up and continue to this day. Ever since that first magical, mystical, long-ago adventure, I get antsy if there isn't at least one planned trip in my future. Fortunately, when I grew up, I found a way to turn my travel addiction into a career.

Although my primary reason for being in Morocco was
work, it seemed a waste of a perfectly good foreign country not to
pad the itinerary with some personal recreation. Then again, for a
guy like me, the two are rarely mutually exclusive. The only
downside was that Jenn was staying home.

Generally, work trips are not holidays. But every so often,
whenever life allowed, Jenn would tag along. God knows we both
needed to get away. We needed time together, somewhere far away
from what our day-to-day lives had become. But the law firm she
worked for was struggling—eternally—and Jenn was perpetually
working killer hours. She'd convinced me the trip would do me
good. Getting back to work would do me good. Being on my own
would do me good.

How did I get so lucky as to score a woman like Jenn? There
was certainly nothing special about me when we met. I was an
English major, with aspirations of writing the great American novel:
how original. I'd never had a real girlfriend before. Not because
none would have me, but because all my free time and attention
were spent chasing literary inspiration in whatever far-flung
destination my habitually starving bank account would allow.

Jennifer Flanders, on the other hand, was remarkable. The
first time I laid eyes on her was at a campus pub. My buddies and I
were drowning our sorrows after some no doubt less-than-stellar
performance on the soccer field. She was our enabler. Yup, my wife
was a shooter girl.

From there our love story is standard stuff. Not to us, but to
pretty much anyone else who hears it. I pawed her a few times that
first night. She soundly rebuffed me. The next morning I was
royally hung over, but nowhere near enough to forget how
completely enamored I'd become with this goddess. I vowed to do
whatever it took to find her again. Admittedly, that wasn't much of
a vow—in order to go on making enough money to stay in school
and keep ramen noodles on the table, Ms. Flanders had to keep
showing up for work. And when she did, I was there. As a paying
customer she was obliged to pay me a middling amount of
attention. That led to me downing a shockingly stupid number of

shooters over the course of the next few weeks, until she finally agreed to go out with me.

I confess: my first round of attraction had a lot to do with the deadly combination of a certain tank top and tequila. But the heavenly creature that showed up at the off-campus diner we'd agreed to meet at was something else altogether. The hair was still blond, but now in a way that made you think Laura Linney, not Tara Reid. She walked with the poise and confidence of a sophisticated, grown-up woman. And there I was, still the nerdy manling, sporting flaming-hot cheeks, a wrinkled plaid shirt, and a dopey smile. Content to sit there and watch her for the rest of my life, I almost forgot to say hello.

If they're talking to another girl or somebody's mother—and they're not complete idiots—when asked what they find most attractive about a girl, most guys will go with something like: sense of humor, intelligence, sparkling eyes. Suddenly I was beginning to comprehend how maybe some of those responses weren't utter bullshit. Jenn had all of those things and more, and they were turning me on to the highest decibel level. Only dogs could hear how much I was into this girl.

Over the next three hours, with tea for her, two beers for me, and something that may have been burgers and fries but I don't remember because I never took my eyes off my date to actually see what I was eating, I learned everything I needed to know about Jennifer Flanders. About how she was from a small town, the first in her family to pursue a college education, on scholarship. About the pressure she felt to prove to everyone she'd left behind that she could succeed. I knew right off she needn't worry about any of that stuff. She was pretty much the smartest, most capable person I'd ever met. She just didn't know it yet.

Jenn asked and I told her stuff about me too. Mostly middle class boring stuff and how I lived and breathed writing and travel. I told her about the few pieces I'd had published, all in local print rags no one ever read. She seemed genuinely interested.

We slept together right away. It's just what college kids do. We didn't call it love, at first. But I did get the distinct impression

that if Jenn hadn't been feeling something close to what I was—
freakin' smitten—she would've said her goodbyes at the door of the
diner that night and that would have been it.

Seventeen years later she's still kickass smart, steaming hot,
married to me, trying to make a name for herself at a law firm that
doesn't deserve her. Me, I'd done some much-needed growing up. I
was a committed slave to writing and travel. And I'd just made the
decision that would end my life.

Chapter 5

I was tied up, gagged, hurt and alone, locked in a dark room. I didn't know exactly where I was. Yet all I could think about was whether my credit card would be charged for my full stay at the *riad*, because I hadn't canceled within the required twenty-four hours of my failure to arrive. What was wrong with me?

Finding a comfortable position in the small, hot room was impossible. The air was stagnant and smelled of mothballs and decay. I had no idea what time it was or how much of it had passed since I'd been taken and beaten into unconsciousness. Like everyone else, I'd stopped wearing a watch a couple of years back, relying solely on my iPhone. But my phone—along with the rest of my belongings, except for the clothes on my back—was gone. How long had I been in here? It couldn't be days, I quickly concluded. If I'd been out that long, I'd feel woozier and my face would itch with stubble.

With nothing to look at, and nothing to listen to—the place was like a tomb—I was left with what was going on inside my head. Even that seemed a fool's game. Try as I might, I couldn't manage to focus on anything of importance, instead always coming back to fretting over the cost of that damned *riad*. Whenever my mind dared veer into the deep dark place that was reality, it snapped away like an elastic band, not wanting to deal with what was there.

I was on the verge of falling asleep when I heard the noise. A muted, low grumbling coming from somewhere below me. My first clue telling me I was in a room above another. There was either a basement beneath me, or I was on a second floor or higher. I strained to hear, to identify the sound. The lack of any other stimuli made it easier to concentrate.

Voices.

People. There were people in the building.

Were they here to save me or hurt me?

Should I thump the floor with my feet and scream bloody hell through my gag? Or should I remain deathly quiet?

The garbled sound continued. At least two people were having an exchange. Probably in a language I wouldn't understand. Were they talking about something important? Were they talking about me? Time passed. Whatever the discussion was didn't seem to lead to someone coming for me. I didn't know if I should be disappointed or relieved.

The conversation continued so long that I began to nod off, the muffled chatter a bizarre lullaby. It reminded me of falling asleep to the sound of my parents talking in the living room, their voices low, sometimes stifling laughs, always cognizant of their slumbering sons. Desperate, I grasped onto that pleasant memory. I eventually found myself easing into a drowsy recollection of my final conversation with Jenn, the day I left Boston.

It had been snowing for two days. Winter: a time of year I'd always loved for its coziness and the fact that a string of bad weather always seemed to inspire a blitz of good writing. Until now. I didn't love winter anymore. Or summer. Or autumn. Or spring.

I'd gone outside earlier to shovel a skiff that had accumulated on the driveway. My bag was packed and sitting by the front door. I was hungry, but decided I'd grab something quick at the airport. I didn't want to put Jenn through the trial of a drawn-out farewell meal, sitting across from each other, food sticking in our dry throats as we tried to make light conversation.

"The yard guy should be here on Monday to take care of the leaves." We should have done the raking ourselves, but we'd waited too long. Too many other things going on. Now it was winter and I was going away.

"Okay." Jenn was on the couch in the living room, feet tucked under her, laptop perched on her right thigh—a favorite position.

I walked over and switched on the lamp nearest her. Left on her own, she'd go half blind before thinking to turn on a light. One of her peccadilloes.

"Thanks," she said, looking up briefly, a distracted look bothering her pretty face.

Conversations move much quicker when sentences consist of one word or less. It had been like this for weeks. Ever since the trial, and the long, frigid fallout that came after it. It was as if we'd somehow managed to live through a nuclear blast, and now we were waiting to find out if we'd survive or die from its poison.

I dropped into the armchair closest to where she'd set herself up in a nest of work. "I don't have to go."

"Of course you should go. We've talked about this. Why are you bringing it up again now?"

She was right. We had talked about it. Made a decision. My cab was five minutes out.

"It feels wrong, leaving you here alone."

Her eyes rose from the computer screen, the line of her mouth tight as wire. "Nothing's going to happen." The words barely slipping through.

"I know that," I said quickly. "That's not what I meant."

"What did you mean?"

Yes, Jaspar, what did you mean?

"I want you to be okay."

"I think we both know that's not going to happen," she said, her expression turning her into that person I wouldn't have recognized six months ago. "Not right now. Maybe never."

I let out a breath, doing my best to ignore the acidic bile eating away the walls of my stomach. The feeling was always there now. I had to concentrate to keep it from making me physically ill.

"Jenn, we can't let this happen to us."

She sighed. "It's too late, Jaspar. It's already happened. It's not like we had any say, any control. We didn't do this. It did."

"Not all of it." The biting words leapt from my mouth, even as every fiber of my being warned me to keep them inside.

She looked away. Eyes back on the screen. I knew what she was trying to hide. Anger. And guilt.

"I'm sorry, Jenn. I shouldn't have said that." I was only half convincing. "You're right. We've talked about this. I just don't want you sitting here for the next two weeks being miserable."

I pushed myself to the edge of my chair, closer to her, wishing I could be the bigger man, wishing I could reach out and touch her. Wishing I really wanted to. Like I used to. Such a small thing, a simple move, so effortless, so pleasurable. So impossible. "You're right," I said, my voice sounding like a stranger's. "It happened. We're damaged. We had no control. But that was then. We have to change this. That's what this trip is about. I'm trying to make a change…"

"Jaspar, it's okay," she assured me, eyes back up and nearly—*nearly*—on mine. "I told you that. I think what you're doing is good. It's the right thing for *you* to do."

An accusation? "For *me* to do. But not for you, right?" God, I hated feeling this way, sounding so pissy and defensive.

"What do you want from me? I told you to go. I told you it's okay with me."

"Tell me you're going to be alright while I'm gone." I needed this.

Now it was my wife's turn to swallow a deep breath, and force truth down my throat. "I won't be."

Chapter 6

Zero to sixty. Suddenly everything changed. Darkness turned into blinding light. Silence into uproar. I was ripped from uneasy sleep, fingers digging into my armpit, hauling me to my feet. My eyes watered. My ears burned from the barrage of unintelligible words being screamed at me with such ferocity I thought I might lose my hearing.

Two men had blasted into the room. One of them, slender and young, stood back, near the door, saying nothing. The other, much older, was creating all the commotion. They were both dark: hair, complexion, eyes... hearts? Arabic if I had to guess. The language the same. Once I could keep my eyes open for longer than a second or two, I could tell the older man wanted me to do something, and was growing increasingly frustrated the longer I didn't comply. He yanked the gag from my mouth and yelled some more.

"What? What is it?" It felt good to be rid of the sodden, dirty rag, to use my voice again.

He screamed back at me, dotting my face with stinging spittle.

"I don't understand what you want me to do!" I shouted back, meeting loud with loud, anger with anger.

More yelling.

"What the fuck do you want?" I roared back, the savagery in my voice, the uncharacteristic swearing, surprising even me. Unusual circumstances call for an unusual response. My glare moved from the older man to the younger, quieter one, with the dim hope he might understand English. No such luck.

After more bawling me out with no change in my response, the old guy shouted an order at the young one. In response, he left the room, returning seconds later with a wooden chair. He shoved it behind me and, with surprising gentleness, pushed me down into it. The touch of his hand on my shoulder, its unexpected tenderness, filled me with optimism. I searched his face, desperate for something more. I was badly in need of compassion, comfort. I needed to believe I wasn't about to be killed—or worse, tortured. But the young man would not look at me. He had a job to do. He wanted to do it and then get the hell out of there.

I felt something being shoved into my chest. I looked down.

Oh, God.

Now I knew what was happening.

The young man murmured something. I think he was encouraging me to take hold of the item. The old guy continued to bellow unintelligible instructions.

It was a newspaper, *Assabah*, an Arabic-language daily.

I was about to have my picture taken. Not just any picture: a proof-of-life picture. The newspaper would display the date, proving to whoever saw the photograph that, at least as of today, I was alive. Anyone who's read a book or watched a movie about kidnapping would know what was going on. I'd been kidnapped—which wasn't breaking news—the kidnappers had made their demands—which remained a total mystery to me—and, in return, negotiators would have asked them to prove I was still breathing.

My mind raced to consider what they could be asking for. Did they expect a big payday out of the pockets of a celebrity? Had I been foolhardy to think I could come to Morocco and no one would know who I was? With the internet's proliferation around the world, I should have known that not even here in Northern Africa could anyone remain anonymous.

Maybe this is what these guys did for a living: hung out at airports, grabbing the first public figure or rich person they recognized. The Moroccan version of Somali pirates, but instead of tankers and yachts, they went after people with fame and fast cash.

I could never have imagined something like this happening to me. Of course I'd aspired to fame and fortune. Who doesn't? Especially writers of a certain ilk. But, deep down, I never truly believed I would become someone who might be kidnapped for money. Nothing about how Jenn and I started out would lead me to such an outlandish conclusion.

By the time we had finished college, Jenn and I knew we wanted to be together forever. She was from Phoenix, I was from Portland. We decided the best thing was to start our joint lives somewhere completely different. May as well piss off both sides of the family instead of just one.

Being the more marketable of us, Jenn led the charge. We ended up in Boston, where she'd been offered a decent internship. I was still keen on writing for a living, but keener on eating, so I took an entry-level position at a bank that offered reasonable hours and wage and little else. That was fine with me. A dead-end career allowed me time and energy to devote to my real passions: travel and writing.

For a while it was the perfect life. We were young and in love and having adventures in a new city. Every six to eight months we'd somehow scrounge together enough cash and vacation days to head off somewhere exotic and cheap. I'd come back with renewed inspiration, and Jenn would return with renewed energy to dive back into what was turning out to be a dirge of a career. The pay was crap and the caseload staggering. She adored every second it—especially her work in family law. The messier the better. Something about bringing logic and reason to situations of high drama and irrationality turned her on. In my spare time, I'd write articles about our experiences and eventually started selling a few to local newspapers and travel magazines.

Then came baby.

We started out reeling in shock from the latex industry's epic failure, and ended up rejoicing in the considerably more epic result. Our lives were busy, Jenn working long hours developing her career, me trying to create mine. But none of that mattered when we brought home six pound three ounce Michelle Catherine Wills.

It took about half an hour before we were calling her Mikki and canceling plans so we could stay home and spend every waking moment with our new daughter. At one point during the transition from unencumbered hipsters to homebodies, smarting from the loss of our freewheeling pre-baby life, a wise young parent explained parenthood to me this way: don't see it as giving something up, but as willingly exchanging one thing for something you want more. I got it.

Along with our bundle of joy came a serious discussion. In the end, with Jenn's income potential being greater—and less fictional—we concluded that I would stay home with Mikki until she went off to school. Ironically, this somewhat unorthodox arrangement turned out to be the biggest boost of my writing career. First off, we were blessed with a really good baby. She started sleeping through the night by five months, and when she was awake, she was mostly content to burble and gurgle and smile. We couldn't travel like we used to, but I had more time than ever to write. Once I had my stay-at-home-daddy routine down, I began submitting short pieces to magazines and anthologies. With some regularity, I came away with small checks, big accolades, and even an award or two.

Adjusting to our lack of freedom and flexibility to take off for a week to backpack in Europe, explore a desert, or hike a mountain range—adventures which had heretofore fueled my travel writing—I tried my hand at writing pieces that focused on Boston's robust tourist industry. Turns out I had a flair for that sort of thing. I soon landed regular gigs writing columns and reviews for a handful of local newspapers, a monthly glossy or two, and even a high profile national magazine. It wasn't quite what I'd hoped for in terms of a writing career, but I was an adult now, making adult decisions, and doing what I needed to support my family. Best of all, I was raising a great kid.

Some of the credit for what happened next goes to my parents. Still avid travelers, in love with their granddaughter and wanting to spend as much time with her as possible, Mom and Dad invited the three of us to join them on a trip to Australia. There was no way we could have afforded a trip like that on our own—even if we'd wanted to, which we weren't exactly sure we did.

Mikki had just turned two. I know. We've all suffered through long flights with the unholy screeching of an unhappy infant scraping out the insides of our skulls. Jenn and I swore we'd never be one of those couples, dragging baby along on a trip with no regard for how it would affect others. But my parents can be very convincing. Before we knew it, we were on a flight to Sydney, baby in tow.

To offset our concerns, I'd pored over the internet for tips on how to best prevent a two-year-old from driving fellow passengers, hotel guests, or tourists to self-immolation. What I found was that there was astonishingly little guidance to be had. Since I couldn't find it, I made it up and hoped for the best. Several weeks later, I penned an article unimaginatively titled: "How to Travel with a Two-Year-Old and Survive."

The title may have been insipid, but sometimes in-your-face clarity is exactly what's called for. The article was a massive hit for the magazine that published it, having succinctly served up information that its demographic of well-heeled, well-traveled, well-read YAWKs (young adults with kids) were desperate for. This led to a commissioned series of related articles. There were nearly endless permutations of the theme: tips for traveling with children of various ages by various transportation modes to various destinations. Suddenly, my career was on fire.

By the time Mikki was enrolled in first grade, I was signing my first publishing contract. The book would present all my articles under one cover, accompanied by photographs and quippy narrative from me.

Although not a major blockbuster, the book did become an immediate bestseller in several key markets. More importantly, it became the impetus for Jenn and me to shelve our original plan. With Mikki in school, instead of me going back to the bank, I would attempt to make a living—or something close to it—from writing. Jenn was still working hard at the same firm, but now making more money since being taken on as a partner. With Mikki needing less of my attention, the timing couldn't have been better.

Six years later, lightning struck. Well, no, I take that back: it wasn't lightning, it just felt like it. Lightning hits you out of the blue, no matter where you are or what you're doing. In my case, I wasn't exactly standing out in a rainstorm with a metal-tipped umbrella, hoping to be zapped—but I wasn't inside hiding, either. I wrote a second book.

In the Middle was a (mostly) fictionalized account of an everyday guy who takes a year-long leave of absence from regular life to travel the world. An early reviewer described the book as "gut-wrenching, side-splitting, surprisingly heartfelt, a must-read for anyone wading through the mess of midlife." When the New York Times called it "the *Eat Pray Love* for middle-aged men and the women trying to love them," sales exploded.

In the Middle hit every major top ten list and was a New York Times bestseller for over forty weeks. Just like that, I was famous. My life had changed. Instead of spending my days making lunches for Mikki and late dinners for Jenn, I was flying cross country doing radio, TV, and internet chat show interviews. Whenever fatigue or homesickness caused me to balk at the crazy schedule, my no-nonsense agent with a knack for hyperbole would remind me to "make hay while the sun shines, because the wind is picking up and the clouds are coming."

The more promotion I did, the more requests that followed. Apparently I photographed well, had a semblance of charm, was likeable enough, and managed eloquence and good humor under pressure. I'd done publicity for my first book, but it had never amounted to much beyond the local market. In due course the public interest had died off, and the book slipped and then disappeared off lists and bookstore shelves, quickly followed by the media attention. Event opportunities dried up like popsicles in the desert.

This was different. The frenzy began to feed off itself in a way that was inexplicable to me and my permanently-grinning agent. Before I knew it, Hollywood took notice and a film version of the book was green lit, financed, and hit screens to respectable box office returns. My career became something I scarcely recognized. But everyone recognized me. Even in Marrakech.

Chapter 7

When I realized that the sound—raw, guttural, ugly—was coming from me, I wasn't surprised. I'd heard it before. And worse. This asshole, my captor, whom I'd nicknamed Hun (as in Attila), wasn't going to get the worst out of me. He wasn't going to break me. I was broken long ago.

My hands were tied behind me to the chair. They didn't do this to keep me from fighting back or escaping, but to stop me from falling over until the beating was done. It was easier for Hun to get in his licks while I was upright.

I'd never been physically beaten before. The sensation was what I imagined being in a car crash would be like. With each landing of Hun's fist, adrenaline made my entire body feel as if it was being sent flying in the opposite direction of the impact. Which was odd because I was attached to that damn chair and going nowhere. But in my mind's eye, I was floating away, with no control over limbs or other body parts. Then, as the power of the blow's force dissipated, the propulsion would too and I'd come to a stop, hovering there, looking down at my body. For a brief second I'd be at peace, weightless, almost euphoric. Then the next hit would meet its mark and I'd slam back into the chair, absorb the pain, and fly off in another direction.

I was acutely, painfully, achingly aware of every inch of my body and every single strike against it. I could sense each individual cell and bursting blood vessel, every nerve ending as it blasted out electric shocks and chemical responses, each bloom of bruise or tear of skin. I could hear my faithful heart, beating as if its rightful place was in my ears instead of my chest.

My vision, at first blurred from the blood pouring into my eyes, became tunneled. Hun's face appeared as if held at bay at the far end of a telescope. I expected to see pure evil, hatred, anger—

whatever it takes to do this to another human being. Instead I saw self-loathing. And pity. For me? For himself? I was astonished to realize that Hun didn't want to do this. For some reason still unknown to me, he was forcing himself—forcing himself to be a monster.

As my eyesight adjusted, so did my other senses, inexplicably amplified. The scent of blood was overpowering.

When blood is moist, the older it is, the sweeter it smells. When dry, it smells musty, even rancid. I was smelling fresh, wet, warm blood. My blood. Sprayed around me as if by a demented abstract artist gone wild with red paint.

One summer, Jenn accidentally dropped a pair of pruning shears on her big toe. It bled with a fervor and flow I'd never seen before. She'd come running into the house, yowling with pain, blood trailing her like a crimson tail. As I set to work on the wound, attempting to stanch the bleeding, I remember noticing a metallic, coppery scent in the air. It has something to do with the proteins in blood plasma transporting copper to bone marrow in order to create new red blood cells. Back then I'd detected only the faintest of whiffs, but now, sitting in that chair, the same scent nearly overwhelmed me, as if I'd just snorted a line of wet iron filings.

Even my taste buds were in on the game. Not just the ones on my bloodied tongue, but thousands more lining my upper esophagus, soft palette, epiglottis, every one detonating like a firework. Sour! Sweet! Savory! And with every proclamation, globs of appropriately flavored saliva sluiced down my throat.

As Hun's fist met my face again and again, the sound of skin against skin was oddly intimate. In the background, I could hear every syllable, every small tic of intonation of the whispered prayer being offered by my tormenter between each ragged draw of breath. The one thing I suddenly couldn't hear, had stopped hearing— blocked out?—was the sound of my own agony.

Only when Hun was finished did I cease to be the superhuman with psychedelically heightened senses. I was just a beaten man, blood dripping off me onto the floor, mixed with sweat and tears.

With great effort I forced my chin up from my chest. Only when I'd completed the painful movement did I urge my eyes open. Only one responded, the other too swollen to comply. Even with that, I could barely manage an abbreviated view.

I was stunned.

Hun stood before me a destroyed man. He was staring at his raw, bloody fists as if they couldn't possibly be his. His chest and shoulders heaved up and then down, like the bow of a ship on troubled waters.

We stayed like that—me on the chair, him standing before me—for a long time.

Finally, Hun opened his mouth. He called for someone, his voice strained.

The second man, young Hun, appeared in the doorway, little more than a blurred shadow to me. They exchanged a stream of words I didn't understand. Young Hun approached me. With a trembling forefinger he lifted my chin, which had begun to slide back toward my chest. I knew what he wanted.

He wanted me to look straight ahead.

Into the camera.

Again.

"He…is…father."

What? The three words had come from young Hun. Stumbling, stilted, nearly unintelligible, barely a whisper—but I heard them. What did they mean? What was young Hun telling me in his broken English? That Hun was actually his father, leaving him powerless to stop what was happening to me? Or was he trying to rationalize the older man's behavior—telling me that Hun was a father, just like me, and that, despite what he was doing to me, he empathized with my pain? Is that why Hun appeared tormented by his own actions? Or had I imagined the whole thing? Was it nothing more than wishful thinking? Desperately, I searched young Hun's face for something more, but he was already pulling away. The moment was over, gone, as if it had never happened. Had it?

Stepping back, the young man held up an iPhone and pointed it at me. Every time it was a different one. I could tell because of the changing case covers. This was the fourth or fifth picture they'd taken of me. Each one using a new phone, probably stolen from an unsuspecting tourist in the *medina*. They'd take my picture, send the file, and toss the phone.

But something was different this time. Something important.

Aside from the day of my arrival, I had never been hurt. The previous pictures had shown me bound, gagged, unshaven, scared, but otherwise okay. This was the first time I'd been beaten. The message they wanted to send to the photograph's recipient—my parents, Jenn, the media?—was clear: meet our demands, or else. The kidnappers were escalating their game.

Chapter 8

Hunger is a strange thing. At first it's pure agony as your body is denied and demands food. Physically, this is excruciating; psychologically, the game is even harder. All you can think about is food: your last meal, how it tasted, the food you'd want to eat if you could have it, your favorite food, food, food, food, FOOD.

Then all of it goes away.

I'd heard of a peculiar phenomenon reported during famines, where starving children will sometimes refuse to eat even when finally offered food. Now I understood. It's as if the body throws up its hands and gives up on ever getting sustenance. Then, as a kind of defense mechanism, it decides it doesn't even want it anymore.

But the absence of hunger pangs doesn't mean the physical effects disappear with them. Ever since I'd been taken from the airport and imprisoned, the sum total of my daily dietary intake consisted of a cup of water and what amounted to less than a slice of bread, twice a day. I began each morning feeling remarkably energized and alert. By midday, a sagging weakness would overtake me. My brain felt dull and my body shook with cold. I would sleep for longer and longer periods. I don't know if it was because I didn't have the energy to stay awake, or if I mentally craved escape from what was happening.

What *was* happening to me?

I had no idea. After being kidnapped, beaten, thrown into this room, forced to defecate and urinate in a hole that was nowhere near deep enough to disguise its purpose, and screamed at in a language I didn't understand, I still had no idea why all of this was happening. What did these men want? And from whom?

Other than Hun—who visited only to yell at me, hurt me, or both—and young Hun, I'd had zero contact with other people. The only improvement to my situation had been having my hands freed and the gag removed. Despite our inability to communicate with words, I clearly understood the threat of what would happen to me if I dared scream for help.

Most days, the only departure from the terrorizing stagnancy of nothing happening was the stealthy hand that slipped my twice-daily dose of bread and water through the door of the cell. A sick part of my brain began to yearn for Hun and young Hun's return, just to have some kind of human interaction, something other than inactivity. Because, I'd found, inside those endless hours of quiet and utter solitude lived something far worse: fear of the unknown. Of what was coming next. And, worst of all, memories of what had led me here.

It was a pitiful, agonizing existence.

Even so, I would come to wish things had stayed exactly as they were.

I thought constantly about the moment, the exact second, when Jenn would know something had gone wrong. How would it have happened? Did the kidnappers contact her directly? Did she hear about it through the media? Some other intermediary? Or had they contacted someone else first? My agent? Publisher? Who broke the news to my parents? What were they thinking this very second? Were they trying to scrape together an impossible sum of money to get me back? Was that why it was taking so long?

Too many days had passed. I couldn't understand a word of what Hun or young Hun said in my presence, but their demeanor told me everything I needed to know. With every visit, I could see their frustration grow. They became increasingly nervous and short-tempered with me and with one another. Something wasn't going according to plan.

The first proof-of-life photographs obviously hadn't done the trick. They needed to step up the threat. That's when the beatings began. The day before yesterday was the second one. Worse than the first. This time Hun didn't stop at the face. He'd pummeled my entire body. When his hands grew sore, he yanked me out of the chair, threw me to the ground, and began kicking me. This time, young Hun stripped me bare before taking the photograph, to better show the growing extent and seriousness of my injuries. My body was a map of their brutality: red and black squiggles for tears in my skin, green blotches for old bruises, blue for new.

Someone was holding out, not giving them what they wanted.

Was it because they couldn't?

Or was it because they didn't want to?

Was Jenn holding all the cards? Was my wife acting out her anger towards me? Was she punishing me for the horrible thing I'd done?

On the worst day of our lives, I came to know something about my wife that I'd never imagined could be true. It rocked me then; it rocked me now. I'd been with this woman for almost twenty years. In that time, we'd had our share of fights. Our fuses burned fast, but not particularly bright. Shouting wasn't our thing, nor was passive aggressiveness. We just got over things. We loved each other. Life was too short to be unhappy. Things were too good the other way.

That night, neither of us was supposed to be home on time.

A few years earlier, we'd scraped together enough money to move from our two-bedroom apartment in downtown Boston to a bigger place in the suburbs—close to schools, a park, public transportation. Normally, when Mikki got home from school at 4:00 p.m., I'd be there. Jenn typically got in by six-thirty, in time for us to eat dinner together. But that day I had a book signing in the city, and Jenn was going out for drinks after work with her friend Katie. Both irregular occurrences, both important. I was feeding a burgeoning career, and Jenn—who rarely managed enough personal time to tie her own shoelaces, never mind have a friend— needed whatever outlets she could find to unwind.

We discussed it and decided that, at thirteen, Mikki was finally old enough to be alone in the house. I promised to be home by seven at the latest, so at most she'd be by herself for three hours.

I'd bring home pizza, so she'd still have dinner with one of us. Jenn would be back by ten.

I screwed up.

Weeks had passed since we'd made the decision. Life had been its regular hectic self in the days leading up to that one. When a colleague who'd stopped by my signing asked me out for a beer, I mindlessly left a phone message at home to tell the girls I'd be late, and accepted.

When I stepped through the front door of the house sometime after ten-thirty that night, Jenn, unusually wan, was right there in my face. Katie's car was in the driveway, so I knew she was somewhere in the house.

"Do you have her?" Jenn asked in a way that immediately put me on alert.

"Who?" I asked, my face already draining of color, my heart thumping.

"Mikki! Is she with you? Why the hell didn't you answer my texts?"

I glanced about wildly, as if that would help. "My phone died...I...didn't you get my phone message from earlier? What are you saying...where's Mikki?" I saw Katie's face peek out from around the corner that led to our front room.

"You don't have her?" Jenn's voice moved to pleading.

"I...I don't..."

"You were supposed to be here!" Now she was screeching.

What the hell is happening? my brain screamed back.

And then she did it. The force of the blow nearly sent me to the floor. My hand rose to meet the burning outline of my wife's hand on my cheek.

"Jenn!" Katie shouted, rushing to her friend's side as if she was the one who'd just been slapped.

"What's going on?" I demanded to know.

Words dripping with acid, eyes blazing through tears, Jenn turned on me with pure hatred and ripped my world apart forever. "Mikki is gone!"

Chapter 9

When he stepped into the room, I knew something bad must have happened. Not that Hun's arrival ever signaled good times.

Today his voice wasn't loud or demanding or harsh. His eyes didn't burn with fever fueled by righteous intent. Instead, they fell on me with something closer to despair. Everything was about to come to an abrupt end.

He said something to me, a lifeless, exacting statement of fact which I was helpless to comprehend.

Our eyes met and held.

He spoke again.

Something in the words told me my ordeal was done, except for one last, unpleasant act about to be played out.

"No," I whispered. "Don't…please, don't."

More words.

He was telling me what happened. About the plan they'd had, about how it had come to a fruitless end. We'd been on a speeding, runaway train, hurtling out of control, about to fly off the tracks unless someone pulled on the brakes. Their bluff had been called. They'd promised to kill me unless they got what they wanted. The look on his defeated face told me that they'd ended up empty-handed. And now their promise would have to be fulfilled.

The kidnapped American had to die.

Young Hun shuffled through the doorway, no doubt in preparation for one last photo shoot. Thanks to the miracle of technology, in a few short seconds young Hun would press a button and broadcast to the world a final image. Jenn would be sitting on our couch, feet tucked up beneath her, laptop perched on her thigh. She'd hear the familiar 'ting' telling her a message had arrived. She'd click on the attachment to access the picture. And then she'd know once and for all: the man who'd failed her was finally dead.

Chapter 10

As horrible as it was, I felt relieved. Relieved to finally know *something*. Mikki had been gone for more than forty-eight hours when the letter appeared in our mailbox. During those long, torturous, sleepless hours, through arguments that morphed into shared agony, interviews and interrogations by police, countless pots of coffee brewed by Katie and other well-meaning friends and family, every horrible thought imaginable had crossed our minds about what might have happened to our little girl. At least now we knew: she was alive.

The note was old-school in every way. It wasn't texted or emailed or even faxed or thrown through our window tied to a rock. It was mailed. The slowest delivery system there is. The kidnappers had cut out letters and words from a variety of sources—newspapers, magazines—and meticulously pasted them onto a blank sheet of paper. The message was short and simple: We have Michelle. We'll trade for $10 million.

That was it. No instructions on what to do next. No warning not to involve the police. No specific threat of harm to come to Mikki if we didn't comply.

Instantly, the authorities we'd been dealing with to this point began to take the situation a whole lot more seriously. Our house was besieged—inside by criminal justice professionals, outside by media. Not only was the kidnapping of a thirteen-year-old girl big news, but when the father of the child is a public figure, suddenly it was circus time.

"Tell me exactly what happened that day," Agent Bukowski asked the question we'd answered about two dozen times since Tuesday, the night Mikki didn't come home. We didn't care. We'd have happily repeated the story two thousand times if we thought it would help.

"Mikki was supposed to come directly home from school, like she did every day," Jenn began.

"Did she usually walk? Get a ride? Would she have been alone?"

"She always walks. Even in winter. Unless the weather is really bad. Her school is only a few blocks away. It's one of the reasons we bought this house."

"Did she walk alone? Did she have friends she might have been with?"

"Mikki has a lot of friends. She's, I guess, what you'd call one of the popular girls at her school."

Jenn's eyes alighted briefly on mine. Our daughter's popularity was one of the things we often joked about when discussing her. Neither of us had been a member of the in-crowd growing up. We'd actually had mild disdain for the kids who were—an attitude we now knew, as adults, was born of petty jealousy. We certainly never imagined a child of ours would be "one of those kids." But there she was, as sweet and as popular as a frozen slushie on a hot day. Usually the topic brought smiles to our faces. Now it hurt like hell.

"She usually walks home with her friend Delores. She lives on the next block. But I talked to Delores' dad and she was sick that day and hadn't been in school."

"So Mikki was alone?"

"Yes," Jenn replied. Then, ever the lawyer, she added, "As far as we know."

"What time was she supposed to be home?"

"Usually no later than four."

"Usually?" Bukowski questioned, his deep-set eyes making a tour of our faces. "Was something different on Tuesday? What time were you expecting her home that day?"

"Same time," Jenn said quickly. "We just don't know...I mean, we didn't expect her...I mean..."

I took over. "What Jenn means to say is that neither of us were going to be here when Mikki got home that day. Usually I was," I hastily added as if I needed to apologize—which I probably did. "That day, both my wife and I had appointments in the city. I was supposed to have been home by seven, but I didn't get here until around ten-thirty. Jenn got home at ten." With every word that came out of my mouth, I kept thinking to myself: *This is bad, this sounds really bad, this sounds fishy even to me.*

"I'm sure it's been covered, but can you confirm that both of you have provided officers with exact details of where you were on Tuesday night? And contact information for the people you were with?"

Bukowski was being straightforward and unapologetic. He was basically saying we needed to prove we didn't do something bad to our own daughter. Fine by me. Do your job and find my kid. I'll tell you anything you want to know.

Our heads bobbed up and down in unison, looking at the investigator like two penitent children caught near an empty cookie jar, and then at each other. Jenn's hatred, which had roared over me like a tsunami on Tuesday night, had since receded. She'd made accusations and stripped me bare and lashed me raw with indictments of guilt. That night, I'd slept on the couch. But eventually her logical lawyer's mind wrested back control from the distraught mother she also was. She knew my mistake had been stupid, but not intentional. We both knew our energies were best spent on solving the problem rather than laying blame.

"When I realized Mikki wasn't with my husband," Jenn said, "that's when we called the police."

"What time was that?"

"Ten thirty-seven, when he came home. I know exactly because I looked at my watch when he opened the front door."

Bukowski referred to his notes, then stated: "Since the last witness to see Mikki observed her leaving school shortly after three-thirty, that means she was missing for a maximum of seven hours before you contacted police."

I swallowed hard. It was a long time. I couldn't bear to think of what my daughter was going through while her mother and I were at separate downtown bars having drinks and laughing it up with friends.

Bukowski was studying the ransom note through a clear plastic evidence bag, deposited there by one of his officers.

"What now?" Jenn wondered aloud. "What do we do now?"

The agent's eyes shifted up to take me in. "Do you have ten million dollars, Mr. Wills?" He'd obviously heard about the book and movie deal.

"No," I told him. "Nowhere near it. This is impossible. I can't raise that kind of money."

He quirked an eyebrow. "Then I guess we negotiate."

"You mean for a smaller amount?"

"No, Mr. Wills. For your daughter's life."

Chapter 11

I was surprised when a third man entered the room. Other than the two Huns, I hadn't seen another human being since I'd been taken. By the look on the new guy's face, he was surprised to see me too.

　　With only a single narrow opening—I'd come to think of it as an air hole—at the top of the room, I'd had no reliable measure of passing time, but I estimated that by this point I'd been in captivity for over a week. In all that time I'd had no way to see my face—no mirror, no reflective surfaces. But I could guess at the vision this newcomer was staring at. A man who'd been severely beaten, bloodied and bruised, covered in cuts and scrapes, hair and clothes in filthy disarray. The water I'd been given was by the cupful. I could use it to clean myself or drink. I drank it. The picture could not have been a pretty one. The look in his eyes confirmed it.

　　The two older men—Hun and the newcomer—began to argue. Young Hun stood back as usual, silent, near the door where he would stay unless called upon. My mind began to wander. I'd been having an increasingly difficult time focusing on anything. I'm not sure whether I was sleeping more or simply losing consciousness with some regularity—often I'd find myself startled awake by some small sound when I hadn't even been aware of falling asleep. The heat, the murkiness, the odious smell of my prison, the wracking pain in most parts of my body—from injuries, from hunger—all once intolerable, now meant little to me.

　　A year ago, I would have claimed that nothing in my privileged life could have prepared me for this. I'd been your typical American who had more than he could ever need, and took most of it for granted. Then Mikki was taken. Lying on this floor, my skin caked with blood and filth, preparing for death, listening to these men argue over how to end my life, was nothing compared to what came after losing my daughter. I'd prayed to every god I could think of for that ordeal to be over. For my daughter to be found and brought safely back to us. Now I prayed for the same thing: I wanted this to be over. But this time, I had no expectations of a safe return home.

As the staccato ping pong of voices played in the background—two strangers determining my fate—all I could think about was how Mikki must have felt when the kidnapper took her. Evidence suggested she'd never even made it home that afternoon—which meant he'd grabbed her off the street, or maybe lured her somewhere. Either way, she would have immediately known something very bad was happening to her. She'd have been frightened from the start. Just the thought of it brought a weight to my chest that threatened my every breath—a feeling once distressingly alien, but now all too familiar. The only difference today was that I simply didn't have enough moisture left in my body for the tears that normally accompanied the attack.

It was a beautiful spring day when we'd splurged on a big party to celebrate Mikki's seventh birthday. She was a fairy princess: beautiful, with hair of woven gold, cheeks perpetually pink, eyes an astoundingly rich cobalt blue, and a smile that could turn barren tundra into a botanical wonderland. The spitting image of her mother. My heart exploded with love each and every time I laid eyes on either one of them.

Having been at school for a year and having already developed her reputation as a social animal, Mikki had many friends and wanted to invite them all. We'd just moved into the new house, complete with a wide open backyard and small above-ground swimming pool. It was the perfect setting in which to create a seven-year-old's dreamland. Jenn went overboard with decorations, attempting to make up for the store-bought cake. We all knew any confection she'd bake would be an unmitigated disaster.

I was in charge of entertainment. I couldn't swing a pony—more my dream than Mikki's, anyway—but instead hired a company specializing in children's birthday parties to provide a magician, a balloon artist, and—the pièce de résistance—a clown named Beeper.

The cake was quickly demolished by hungry little mouths, the gifts ripped open. Forty kids and thirteen parents were seated throughout the yard, finishing off ice cream floats, when Beeper made a noisy entrance in all his multi-colored, polka-dotted, oversized-shoe, red-nosed grandiosity. Mikki—who'd been strategically placed to be the first to greet the surprise guest—took one look, threw back her head, and let loose a blood-curdling scream heard in Fenway Park.

With her princess tiara flying to the ground and fat tears spurting from her eyes, Mikki found me in the crowd and ran toward me as if her life depended on it. I fell to my knees and held open my arms just in time for her to crash into them. Within seconds, my shirt was sodden with baby princess tears. Jenn was leaning over my shoulder saying logical things in a sweet, calming voice, attempting to convince our daughter that the clown was not actually there to eat her. All I did was hold my little girl, one hand gently rubbing her shuddering back, the other cradling her golden head. In that moment, the clown was my enemy too. I would have done anything to protect my child from dangers real or imagined. I pledged to play that role for the rest of my life.

I failed.

I wasn't there to protect my daughter when she needed me most. Instead, I was busy feeding my ego, inviting some sycophant to tell me how great I was, spouting bon mots about my newest writing project as if that was the most important thing in the world. No one was there to rub her back or cradle her head. She'd been alone. Frightened. Confused by what was happening to her and why. Wondering when mommy and daddy would save her. Not yet knowing they never would.

I was ruined that day.

There was no reason to go on.

"Kill me." I calmly said the words aloud.

The two men stopped arguing and stared at me. I prayed they understood. I prayed they'd grant my wish.

Chapter 12

Once again I was tied up and gagged. This time lying contorted on the floor of a van, which was not as bad as you'd expect. Not that I've ever had much call to think about such a thing. If I was an author of thrillers or murder mysteries, maybe then. But I don't write those kinds of books—or even read them much. They don't appeal to me. I write about travel; I write about my observations of people coping with life's normal challenges—often with humorous undertone.

This was not normal.

This was not humorous.

I could think of only one reason for my kidnappers to be moving me: their plan had failed. Whoever was meant to exchange something in return for my freedom had either refused or somehow played their cards wrong. It was time to make good on their threat. It was time to kill me. But, for some reason, they couldn't do it where I was being held.

Based on the fact that the van was packed with several thick rolls of carpet, beside which I was now lying, I began to suspect that the day I'd been abducted from the Marrakech airport, I'd ended up not far from where I'd been planning to go anyway. What better place to stash a hostage than the crowded, famously-bewildering *medina*, where everything and everyone could get lost—and often did? It was a place choked from daybreak to nightfall with merchants, customers, suppliers, tourists, voyeurs, and cadres of enterprising thieves—the air hoarse with the ceaseless chatter of commerce. It was a place where almost nothing would seem out of the ordinary.

Over the past days, I'd frequently heard muffled voices rising through the floorboards from somewhere below me. I'd guessed the voices belonged to my kidnappers. But what if they didn't? What if all this time I was on the second floor of a carpet vendor's shop—one amongst countless others, each a carbon copy of its neighbors, buried deep amidst the endless, crisscrossing streets of the ancient marketplace?

Now the game had changed. It was one thing to keep someone captive in a room above your place of business, another to kill him there.

I was content in the back of the van—comfortable, even. It was nice to finally be out of the cell-like space that had been my jail for the past several days. It smelled immeasurably better, and the fresh air washing over me from a slit of open window felt like cool silk as it brushed my fevered skin.

After interminable stops and starts as the van wove its way out of the *medina* then through busy city traffic, we eventually reached a cruising speed that told me we were on a highway. We'd left Marrakech. Disturbing but not surprising.

Time passed in a foggy blur, the steady hum of the tires lulling me into fits of sleep. There was no use wondering or caring about where I was going, or what would happen when we got there. I already knew.

The agent in charge of Mikki's case told us her abductors likely hadn't taken her far. Maybe somewhere on the outskirts of the city, where they'd be less likely to be spotted by nosy neighbors but still close to the scene of the crime. Maybe not even that far. He was concerned about why they were using the postal system rather than a faster delivery method for their communications with us. The general consensus was that the kidnappers believed that mailing the ransom notes made it easier for them to keep their identities hidden, or—worse from our perspective—they didn't really care how fast this played out.

By the time the second note arrived in our mailbox, Mikki had been gone for five days. Attention from the media had grown exponentially with each passing hour. The resultant frenzy was quickly becoming unbearable to deal with.

Watching Jenn step out of the bathroom that night, my mouth dropped. I was already in bed, under a heavy layer of blankets. Even though we'd been experiencing summer-like temperatures all week, Jenn was always cold. Now I saw why. In only five days, the woman looked as if she'd lost ten pounds. She was wearing a nightshirt I used to love seeing her in. It hugged each curve in the right place, was sexily threadbare, and when she sat down the hem rode up high. But today the garment might have been made for a woman twice her size. It hung off her frame like an oversized bed sheet.

The sight took me by surprise, and I could feel my throat choke up as I jumped out of bed to embrace her. "Oh, Jenn."

I wrapped my arms around her and hoped I could somehow infuse her with my own warmth. She didn't seem surprised or question the sudden show of affection. She was aware of the toll the last few days had taken on her physically. Her head fell into the crook of my neck and I felt pinpricks of ice on my naked back; I realized they were her fingers.

We stood that way for several minutes. Just breathing. Just finding a way to keep on surviving.

"Come on," I finally said, releasing her but holding on to the frozen mitt of her hand. "Get into bed. I'll make you some tea. That'll warm you up."

"No, don't," she quickly said, pulling me under the covers with her. "I've had enough tea to sail a ship. Just stay with me. Talk to me. Tell me everything is going to be…" She stopped, as if frozen, then: "AAAAAAHHHHHHHHHH!" she cried out.

I tightened my hold, hoping the agents sitting downstairs in our living room wouldn't be alarmed and come barging into our bedroom, guns ablaze. But I knew they wouldn't: they were used to this. Used to dealing with people who'd fallen into a hole of utter misery and, struggle as they might, never managed to crawl out, only getting deeper until…

"It's a good thing, you know," I said, swiping a tear from her cheek with my thumb.

"What?" she croaked, a heartbreaking look of hope on her face, as if there could possibly be something positive happening in our lives, some bit of good news that I'd somehow forgotten to share with her.

"The second note," I said. "It means they're ready to make a deal. We can find a way to get Mikki home."

"They want ten million dollars, Jaspar. We don't have that kind of money. We could give them everything we have — this house, my salary, your royalties, whatever we could beg, borrow and steal — and it still wouldn't be enough. God, Jaspar, what's going to happen to our baby when they realize we can't pay?"

"Jenn, you can't think like that. We'll find a way to make this work. These people — whoever they are — they're finally making a move. They've given us a date and a place. It's only two days from now. In two days we'll have Mikki back." I pulled away and patted the area between us, feeling the warmth of the sheets radiate through the palm of my hand. "We're going to put her right here, between us, and we're not going to let her leave this bed until she's thirty-five."

The area around Jenn's mouth, where sexy grins once lived, grew less taut. It was the best she could do. How I longed for her to smile — like she did the first night we met in that campus pub, her pouring shooters down my throat. Or like she did beneath her wedding veil as she floated down the aisle towards me. If only she would smile again — just for a moment, a brief moment. Then maybe my heart could stop clenching, and the agony would go away, just for a moment.

"They want us to go on TV," she said after a minute. "To do one of those things where we plead with the assholes who took her to spare her life and give her back to us."

"I know."

"It's ludicrous. It's not like the kidnappers are going to be sitting around watching TV, see us and suddenly think, hey, you know what, they're right. Let's just call this off and send the little girl back to her mommy and daddy. The media are the only ones who get anything out of that. A perfect photo op of the famous author and his wife bawling their eyes out. Nothing better to sell papers and spike ratings."

"I know."

"I can't do it, Jaspar. I can't go on TV and beg for Mikki's life. I would if I believed for even a second that it would help, but it won't. It never does. These guys want money. Lots of it. They stole a child for Chrissakes! You think they care about what we have to say?"

"I know. You're right. But we have to give them something. I know how the media works, Jenn. If we do nothing, they'll only hound us longer and louder until we do. We need to say something."

"Why? Because you're worried how we'll look if we don't?" She sat up straighter, eyes heating up. I knew the pose. I knew the look. I braced. "If we don't step in front of the cameras and beg those monsters to give our daughter back, then suddenly *we're* the monsters? Suddenly we're suspects in our own daughter's disappearance? Is that it? You're worried about how that will make you look? How it'll ruin the reputation of the oh-so-handsome, ever-so-charming, world-famous Jaspar Wills?" She was a battering ram in desperate need of a door to smash against.

"Jenn, you know I don't give a shit about any of that. I'm only thinking about the right thing to do. I don't know the perfect answer. And neither do you. All I know is that we have to do something."

As quickly as it ignited, her fire extinguished. I got it. We both had unquenchable cauldrons full of hot, boiling anger bubbling up inside of us, with no one to douse—except the kidnappers. But they weren't around. We'd each had mini-explosions over the past few days, usually directed at each other. When it happened, the best the other could do was ride it out, and then move on. Until now we were unaccustomed to fighting with each other like this, using rage and resentment as weapons. We were on the unfamiliar frontlines of a war we didn't start or even understand. But we knew that, unless we had each other's back, we'd never make it out alive.

"What about Katie?" Jenn suddenly said.

"What about Katie?" I asked. She and Jenn had gotten close over the past six months. I didn't really know the woman, but I encouraged the friendship. Jenn was so busy being the perfect mom and lawyer, she forgot about just being Jenn. She was in desperate need of the kind of relationship that involved two women spending time together doing stuff that girlfriends do, spouses not included.

"She's a reporter...or a journalist or something like that," Jenn said. "Out of everyone we know, she'll know what to do. She'll know how to handle the media."

I nodded. Relieved. A problem that actually had a solution. "Sounds good."

Suddenly energized, Jenn hopped out of bed. "I'll call her right now."

"Now?"

"She's up. She's always telling me how she does her best work late at night."

Having arrived at our destination, the back door of the van creaked open. Through a small sliver in the strip of fabric that covered my eyes, I could see it was night. Certain things are best done under the cover of darkness.

Chapter 13

I am alive.

In what circumstances does someone use those three words? I can think of only three. One: in times of personal triumph— successfully scaling Mount Everest; landing a dream job. Two: exclaiming physical exaltation—having sex with a beautiful woman; completing your first full marathon. Three: in moments of survival—when you've escaped, barely, the threat of certain death. Regardless of the circumstance—even if you're struggling for air atop a mountain, admitting to yourself that the woman you just slept with is not your wife, or realizing just how precarious your existence really is—whenever you can say those three words—I AM ALIVE—it feels damn good.

With my blindfold now repositioned so that I couldn't see a thing, two hands dragged me from the back of the van. Being outside had never felt so good. Fresh air. Gentle breeze. Pleasant, earthy smells.

I'd become a bit of a sleuth during my incarceration, specializing in using senses that I normally took for granted to provide me with clues. Changes in the sound the tires made suggested we'd eventually left paved road for gravel and maybe even dirt. Popping in my ears told me our elevation had changed. Given the time it took to reach our destination, my best guess was that we'd ascended into the Atlas Mountains—probably Toubkal, the country's highest peak, in southwestern Morocco, only two hours from Marrakech.

I was alive, but I didn't expect that status to last long. Soon, I suspected, I would be hurtling down the side of that same mountain. The plot, unpleasant as it was for me, made sense. The chance of my bloodied and broken body ever being found in such a desolate area was probably pretty low.

As the men silently led me to my fate, I sucked in fresh drafts of air, deeply, exuberantly, as if they were my last, for surely they were. I began to think of Mikki, and Jenn, and various family and friends. Just as quickly, I pushed them out of my mind. The images simply hurt too much.

The distance between what I'd become and what I was about to be—dead—was not such a lengthy one. Physically, there wasn't much left to save. It was my mind and soul that needed protecting.

In those final moments, as I was being steered toward my end, I suddenly realized something important. Incredible things lived in my mind and soul: memories of loving and being loved, laughing, being cared for and taking care of others, friendships, kindnesses, moments of amazement and awe. There was nothing these men could do to destroy them. They were greater than any of this. They existed in a place I was sadly deficient to describe, a kind of "me" cloud. They would survive beyond whatever happened to me here today.

Whoa. Deep.

Apparently I'd suddenly become a man of spirituality. Of faith. Be it the influence of a guardian angel, or even God, or maybe nothing more than body chemicals run amok in my body doing strange things to my brain—whatever it was, I believed. As much as I'd believed anything in my entire life. I believed in the survival of something greater than my physical being.

I was being propelled forward, my feet tripping across rough, uneven surfaces, the men's fingers clawing my armpits as they urged me along. Just like when I'd been beaten, I felt myself floating above it all. I gazed down on the ghastly scene, the three of us proceeding at death march speed, to the edge of the precipice from which I would be tossed. I felt weightless, free, at peace.

Except I'd written the wrong ending.

There was no precipice. There was no end-over-end tumble down Toubklal mountain.

Instead, I heard a door opening, its bottom edge scraping harshly against hardened earth. The rope binding my hands was loosened. With one final thrust forward, I was set free.

The door closed.

Silence.

Were they gone?

Was I alone?

Unencumbered, my trembling hands rose to the blindfold. Slowly, slowly, I lowered it.

I was ready for anything. Anything but what I saw.

Chapter 14

Hand in hand, Jenn and I approached the dead fountain. Just as the ransom note instructed us to. In my left hand, I carried a briefcase. Inside, astonishingly, was ten million dollars. None of it ours. The money had been supplied by the FBI. On the off chance the kidnappers actually got their hands on it—an eventuality that was nowhere in the plan—each bill was marked and traceable.

We'd had two notes. Both identically prepared with letters and words cut from magazines and newspapers. Both appeared in our post office box with the regular delivery. Both were effectively devoid of clues as to who sent them. The first note told us they had Mikki. The second asked for the money, with instructions on when and where to deliver it.

The investigators were frustrated. Other than through the media—to which there was no guarantee the kidnappers even paid attention—there'd been no opportunity for them to communicate directly with the hostage takers and, consequently, no opportunity for negotiations. "Highly irregular," they called it. Highly effective, as far as I could see. At least so far.

Along with the cash, the briefcase also contained a message. It said everything the officials would have said to the hostage takers, if they could have. Most pointedly that they would never get their hands on the money without proof that Mikki was still alive and well. Although the ten million was in the case, the case itself was constructed of blast-proof titanium, and could only be opened by a complex alphanumeric code entered into a keypad. The agents figured the kidnappers assumed they'd be safe to retrieve the case without interference as long as they still held onto Mikki. Which was true. But the FBI rarely play on the side of any game where the foregone conclusion is their own defeat.

With a visible shake to my hand, I dropped the briefcase into the dried-out bowl of the fountain, which had long ago stopped spewing water. For a moment we stood there, our eyes traveling the circumference of the clearing, hoping beyond reasonable hope that suddenly—miraculously, jubilantly, mercifully—our daughter would appear and rush into our arms.

That did not happen.

Just the typical, casual activity of any urban park on a sunny weekday morning.

"Jaspar, suppose this doesn't work?" Jenn whispered.

I squeezed her hand. It felt cold, clammy, nearly lifeless. We'd placed all of our faith in the expertise of people we'd met only a week ago. Under normal circumstances, such an action would be foolhardy, unwise. But nothing about this was normal or logical.

"It has to work, baby," I said. "There's no other way. Mikki will come back to us. Very soon."

We turned, marched back to our car, and drove away.

Two days later, the case was still in the fountain.

Two days after that, a third note arrived in the mail.

The kidnappers claimed to have spotted police and FBI surveillance teams in the park. They were unhappy about that. In the same bizarre, cut-out-letter fashion, they threatened to give us only one more chance. We were to deliver the money to a different location. If they were allowed to retrieve it unseen, Mikki would appear on our doorstep that same evening. Again, negotiation was not an option.

"We have to do it their way!" Jenn's voice was stern as she addressed the lead FBI agent in our front room, standing as tall and motionless as a slab of granite. "I want my daughter back now!"

I could read the look in the man's eyes. Silently, he was saying: "Do you have ten million dollars to make that happen?" Instead, he said, "If we give them the money without proof that your daughter is still alive, I promise you, Mrs. Wills, the chances of Mikki showing up on your doorstep are less than zero."

"How do you know that? It's not your daughter! It's easy for you to take risks with someone's life when it's not someone you love!"

"Jenn," I reached for her hand. I agreed with everything she was saying, but I knew emotional responses weren't going to help save Mikki. She knew it too. "They want Mikki back as much as we do. They really do. We just have to figure out the best way to make that happen."

"Your husband is right," the agent said. Although there was no visible sign of it, he should have been grateful for my intervention. It may have just saved him a bruised cheek. "I know this isn't easy. I know how horrible this feels. We—all of us here—want what you want."

"No!" She wasn't done yet. "I know you want to get Mikki back. But you want to catch the bad guys too. If you don't, that means you've failed. I don't care about that. I don't care if these people take the money and live happily ever after in Aruba. All I care about is having my baby back. She's only thirteen, for God's sake! She's a child!" Jenn began to sob. I knew her well enough to know she hated how she sounded, hated that she was crying. "Goddammit, you have to help us!"

"We will," he promised.

"How?" I asked, increasing my pressure on Jenn's hand. "You need to tell us exactly what we're going to do next."

Exchanging uneasy glances with his second-in-command, he said, "We do it your way."

"Really?"

Jenn perked up. "We give them the money? No extra demands? No bomb-proof briefcase?"

He hesitated, then added, "With one proviso."

"Tell us," I said.

"We need to be there. Watching. We'll be absolutely invisible this time, but we need to be there."

Jenn began to balk. I squeezed her hand even harder, a silent signal to hold off.

"It's the only insurance you'll have," he continued. "If Mikki isn't sent home as promised, we'll have a next step. Otherwise, it's over. For us. For you. For Mikki."

Slowly, as if her neck were made of metal rods, Jenn nodded her assent.

Two days later, we made the drop.

The briefcase was never picked up. Mikki never came home.

Chapter 15

The enclosure was rectangular, with mud-colored cement walls and a metal grate roof. Having been shoved inside—the door locked, bindings released, blindfold down around my neck—I got the first look at what would become my new home.

My knees buckled. Suddenly I was face-up on the ground, spread-eagled, looking up through the grate at a vista of impenetrable darkness. The ground beneath me was rough but warm from a long day baking in the sun. Its heat began to soak into my skin. The night air was thick with the scent of freshly foraged hay and aged manure. I knew I would not move again until the next day.

It might have been mid-morning by the time the sun rose far enough to breach the top of the enclosure, beaming fingers working their way across my forehead and swollen eyes, urging me awake. The first thing I saw was the pattern of the metal grate that covered the entire structure, as effective at allowing the light in as keeping me from getting out. I wondered how long before the crisscross design would burn itself into my skin.

Having survived the night into a day I had been convinced I'd never see, it occurred to me that, at that very moment—the same moment I began to believe I might live—my loved ones, thirty-five hundred miles away, would begin to believe I was dead.

What else could they think? A gambit had been played. Tit offered for tat. All players had lost. Via photographs and multiple beatings, the Huns had issued their threat and demonstrated their willingness to cause my demise. Whatever they'd asked for, they didn't get. What choice was left?

Instead, I'd been spared. Why? Maybe the threat had always been an empty one. Maybe they'd never really intended to kill me.

Maybe they simply didn't have the guts. So, instead, they dumped me here. Who knew what was coming next. Only one thing was clear: I wasn't dead yet. But for my family, for Jenn, for our friends, the writing on the wall would tell an entirely different story.

Our story came to a bitter end on the third Monday after the second failed attempt to deliver Mikki's ransom money. As had become our habit, we were sitting together on the living room sofa, from where we had an unobstructed view of the front yard. We'd know the precise moment the mailman made his daily delivery.

We were out the front door and at the box before he had time to close the lid. I saw the look of sympathy on his kindly face as he silently moved off, knowing full well what had been happening at this address for the past month. The media attention had been so intense, he'd have to have been living under a rock not to.

I reached in and pulled out the slight pile of mail.

If Jenn's eyes had been hands, they would have been ripping through the collection of letters, flyers, and magazines with lightning speed.

We both knew it at the same time.

The insensitive words of an "abduction specialist" on some late-night talk show echoed in our heads: "…with each day that goes by without hearing from the kidnappers, it's with greater and greater certainty that we, and the police, must presume that Mikki Wills is dead."

Dead.

How could such a small, insignificant-looking word carry such weight? It made me gasp for breath every time I heard it.

"That's it, then," Jenn's hollowed-out voice slipped past pale lips, a final declaration made more to herself than to me.

I knew what she meant. Whether we wanted to or not, we'd unconsciously put a time limit on optimism. A little bit of sand drained from our hourglass of hope each day without the money being picked up, without Mikki coming home—as the FBI and police vacated our house, as calls from media outlets dwindled, as well-meaning relatives and neighbors stopped dropping by. When the looks of caring strangers at the grocery store turned from reassuring to sympathetic. We were no longer parents with a chance at recovering their daughter; we were a lost cause to be pitied. We became angry, bad-tempered, dismissive of others and their useless words of faint comfort—because, deep down, we agreed with them.

"Not yet, Jenn," I implored, reaching out for her. I felt exceptionally exposed, standing out there in our front yard, certain that every eye in the neighborhood, the city, the world, was on us—watching us, wondering what we would do. Would we fall apart? Or would we rally one more time?

Jenn pulled back, staring at me as if I'd just missed the main point of a story she'd been telling. "Yes, Jaspar. It's over. Our daughter is gone. Mikki is gone."

It scared me how calm and dispassionate she sounded. We'd played an unfair game over the past weeks, one that neither of us had a hope of winning. When either of us showed an excessive flash of emotion or passion, whether positive or negative, the other immediately, in an almost Pavlovian fashion, reacted with the opposite sentiment.

I don't think we did it to hurt each other. Instinctively, we must have known it was the only chance we had to keep it together. We were each other's stopgap, personal pressure valves. If one of us became too sad, the other said something happy. If one of us expressed hope, the other played devil's advocate. We knew that if both of us were feeling the same thing, the power of it would be too much. The fall—for we would inevitably fall—from whatever extreme we were experiencing, good or bad, would be catastrophic.

Here and now, in this moment, standing in the front yard next to our mailbox, for Jenn our game had officially been called off. Her statement, announcing her belief that our daughter was gone, dead, finished, was a simple proclamation of fact.

Steady hands reached out for me, cupping my face. Her head moved up, then down, up, then down, as if to punctuate her certainty and influence my own.

The mail fluttered to the ground.

"No," I whispered.

She continued to nod, her beautiful eyes pulling me close, comforting me, caressing me with love, as they so often had in our marriage.

"No." I tried again, knowing deep down that I was only fooling myself, hoping to prolong my time in a world where I believed my daughter still lived.

How ironic, I thought, as I lay unmoving on the ground of my rectangle, blazing sun beating down on me. How ironic that it was in this place—this miserable, awful place—that I would find what I'd needed so badly on that black day by the mailbox. I found hope. Hope for Mikki. Hope that my baby had not just disappeared from our lives, never to be seen again. Hope born of the belief that, since I had been spared, she might have been too.

For the first time since I'd been taken, my cracked, bruised lips spread into a painful smile.

Chapter 16

At that time of year, temperatures in the Atlas Mountains can regularly reach the low nineties—higher when magnified within the confines of my sun-soaked prison. Only a small portion of the area, beneath a lean-to type of construction—maybe one-sixth of the rectangle—was shaded from the brutal intensity of the Moroccan sun. It was there that I spent most of my daylight hours. I only dared venture out to drink water from the dribbling spigot of a pump at the opposite end of the enclosure, or to collect the plate of bread and sometimes olives that was shoved through the door twice a day by a faceless entity—man, woman, Hun, camel, goat; I didn't know.

In the center of the space, rising seven feet off the ground, was a stone pedestal, the approximate length and width of a double bed. I had no way to know what it might have once been used for, but my distressed mind imagined it as some sort of sacrificial altar. For some inexplicable reason, I was unusually drawn to it. On the third night I found myself attempting to hoist my pitifully weakened body atop it. It wasn't until the eighth night that I succeeded.

The top surface was unlike the rest of the rough-hewn plinth. Here the stone was worn smooth, and felt surprisingly cool against the skin. At its center was a slight but noticeable indentation, as if some great weight had lain there for centuries, wearing down the rock face, by happenstance molding it perfectly to fit my body. I didn't know when I awoke the next morning, comfortably nestled into the depression, that I would sleep there every night thereafter, even when it rained. I didn't know that I'd found the center of my existence, the one place in hell that I would love.

There were many things to recommend my spot atop the pedestal. First, it was the rectangle's highest point. Every king, ruler, lord of every land seeks high ground—preferable for defense and safety from all manner of foe, be it mankind or animal, natural or unnatural. Second, because of its height and nearness to the sky, it gave me the sensation of *almost* being outside the box. The grate, securely fastened to the top of the structure, ensured the impossibility of freedom, but even being a few feet closer to it was exhilarating. Finally, and most importantly, it was in this magical, mystical spot that, every night, I visited with my daughter.

Lowering my body into the soft embrace of the welcoming stone, I would close my eyes and Mikki would be there, cuddling up next to me as she often had as a small child. Jenn believed, for everyone's good, that children should stay out of their parents' bed. I understood and agreed. I also believed that some rules are meant to be broken when only one of the parents is around.

On those nights, our routine was unvarying. Mikki would ask what I had written about that day. It was her way of requesting story time. Clever girl. And as it just so happens, telling stories is my specialty. We had our staple favorites that I'd recite if I was tired or not feeling particularly creative, but often I'd just start talking, making things up as I went along. Some of these tall tales were markedly better than others. But her favorite kind, and mine, was when I'd hit on a particularly outrageous, outlandish saga, and just keep chugging along like a stubborn locomotive, any hope of a coherent storyline or rational ending fading further with every passing word. We'd hold out as long as we could, pretending to follow the plot, until one of us could stand it no longer and broke, both of us descending into fits of uncontrollable laughter at the ridiculousness of what had come out of my mouth. None of this helped with adhering to bedtime schedules, but these moments with my daughter are among my most cherished.

And so, night after night, as the sun fell below the roofline of my rectangle and heat began to seep from the day, I would strain fading muscles to hoist my deteriorated body into my spot. I would close my eyes and await my daughter's arrival. When she appeared, settling in next to me, I would retell those old stories as I remembered them. Her petite, delicate body would relax in my arms, where she felt safe and protected. I was comforted by the gentle up and down of her shoulders and chest as she breathed easily, without a care in the world. I delighted in the sniggers that burbled up in her whenever I said something especially silly, usually for that express purpose. I smelled the fresh fragrance of berry-scented shampoo in her flaxen hair. I ran my hand over exuberant curls, held back from her face by her favorite pink barrettes.

Those fucking barrettes.

Chapter 17

I couldn't decide if these things were what I wanted, needed, or simply missed. But as the days of my captivity multiplied, their overwhelming desirability grew and took root inside my brain, refusing to budge. Clean clothing. A close shave. Red licorice. Wine. The smell of Jenn's perfume. Just about anything on a computer screen. The sound of voices. The sound of someone laughing at something I said or wrote. Traffic. Reading. Someone touching me. Hot water. Coffee. A ringing cell phone. A mirror. Happiness.

By any standards, the conditions of my habitation were deplorable. I relieved myself through a hole in a wooden bench. There might have been an access point outside the rectangle through which someone could clean out the refuse, but to my knowledge that never happened. After my first full week, I stopped noticing the permanent stench permeating the area. My hair grew; my face itched from an unruly beard. Growing a beard was something I'd never done in real life. I was vaguely curious to see what I looked like—until I remembered that no reflection in any mirror could show Jaspar Wills. He was gone. My teeth felt spongy from weeks of going unbrushed; my nails grew long and unkempt, my skin tight and dry. I was in dire need of a change in wardrobe. Not only were my clothes—the same jeans and shirt I'd set off in from Boston—filthy and torn, but the pants only stayed around my shrinking waist if I held them there. My kingdom for a belt.

With patience, and sustained up and down motion, the water pump would provide enough trickles of water to keep me reasonably hydrated and clean. But without so much as a pail or basin, the process was often painstaking—and on bad days, of which there were many, exhaustion easily won out over a full bath.

I worried about my health. As a tourist in Morocco, I would never drink water from a tap. As a prisoner, I was forced to. In the early days I constantly experienced diarrhea, which contributed to my already feeble state, but not so much any longer. I don't know if my system eventually adjusted, or if there was just too little of anything left in reserve for my body to expel.

Prolonged near-starvation is never a good thing. I could tell from my decreasing levels of energy and my sustained lethargy that its frightening effects were overtaking me. Although generally a person who enjoyed robust health, in the real world I reinforced it with a daily intake of vitamins, various supplements, and medication to control a genetically-induced cholesterol problem. Without those pills, who knew what was happening to my body. Wouldn't that be a farce? If, despite everything else, I ended up being taken out by a coronary attack caused by unchecked low-density lipoproteins.

The only aspect of my situation that could be judged as improving was the state of the injuries I'd suffered at the hands of Hun. Despite the conditions I was forced to endure, with no beatings to perpetuate or aggravate my legion of cuts and bruises, they were slowly beginning to heal.

Physically, I was holding on. My greatest concern was for my mental health. In the real world, I was bombarded by mental stimuli. If I wasn't writing, I was researching. If I wasn't interviewing someone, I was planning a book tour or outlining a new idea or communicating with readers, booksellers, agents. I enjoyed challenging conversations and the odd feisty squabble with my wife. I watched movies and TV, read books and magazines, listened to news radio and a wide variety of music. I thrived on travel. Sure, on occasion I enjoyed a rainy Sunday afternoon catnap or a mindless walk in the park, but generally I was the kind of guy in a perpetual dance with the world around me—the more stimulation, the better.

Now my dance partner was monotony. The same rectangle. The same shitter. The same begrudging water pump. The same stone pedestal. The same metal grate. The same dry bread. I spent every day huddled in my lean-to, hiding from the harsh rays and blistering heat of an unrelenting sun, and every night on top of a rock, curled into a fetal position, reciting stories to a ghost, tortured by my own mind.

Why didn't Mikki's captors pick up the money?

It was a question asked millions of times. By me. By Jenn. People who knew us asked the question. People who only knew us by our story asked the question. The unspoken answer haunted all of us. Only one seemed likely: somehow, Mikki had died. Perhaps from injuries sustained during the initial abduction; perhaps by accident during her incarceration; even, perhaps, by her own hand. With nothing left to trade, the kidnappers had disappeared. Gone to find another payday with another victim.

Now, I knew better. For reasons I'd probably never know, the kidnappers had decided that picking up the money was too risky. They were right. They'd spotted the police and FBI on the first attempt, and maybe the second. They knew that they would have been caught, eventually. Maybe this had been their first time. Kidnappers have to start somewhere, and no library or bookstore I know of stocks a copy of *Kidnapping for Dummies*. They realized they were on the losing side of the game and needed to cut their losses and run.

No one could be so monstrous as to kill Mikki, an innocent thirteen-year-old girl. Who could have so dark a heart? Even the Huns hadn't been able to kill me. Mikki's abductors would not have hurt her either. No. They would have broken camp and run, taking Mikki with them, eventually stashing her someplace. Just as I'd been stashed in a rectangle in the Atlas Mountains.

Where was she?

Finally, something worthwhile to think about.

Chapter 18

After three days with no bread being delivered through the doorway, I knew the plan.

With only water left to sustain me, the Huns—or whoever was on the other side of the locked door—were waiting for me to starve to death. It was perfect, really. And who could blame them? All they'd wanted was to make some quick cash by kidnapping a rich, spoiled American, and instead they had ended up with a lifelong dependent. Not a good deal for them. They didn't have it in them to outright murder me. But to let nature take its course once food was out of the picture? I guess, after weeks of thinking about it, they'd decided their consciences could live with that.

I didn't really mind anymore. What had been happening in the rectangle wasn't life. It was merely inadvertent survival, one breath following another. Still, I'd kept on drinking the water and eating the bread, feeling grotesquely euphoric when it arrived accompanied by olives, the flavor exploding in my mouth with near-hallucinogenic vividness.

At most there were three of them. The first one, a perfect, salty-meaty-oily orb, would disappear down my gullet before my eyes had time to register its existence. The second soon after. By the third, I'd attempt to exert self-control.

With the olive soaking in its bed of succulent juices and the shorn crust of bread carefully arranged on a cracked ceramic plate, I'd scurry to the shaded comfort beneath my slanted roof. Once settled, I'd pick up the slippery drupe and admire its dark color and the sensual texture of its skin, glistening with translucent oil, pungent and spicy. My trembling fingers would hold it out in front of me, as if it were the world's last remaining Fabergé egg. I would extend my tongue and wait for the intoxicating impact of taste buds against olive, savoring the sensation for as long as I could.

Eventually I would rub the olive against my teeth, as if testing a pearl. Finally, sinking it into the fleshy nest of my mouth, I would suck away the olive's oily residue from my fingers, then bite down and consume the tantalizing fruit. Immediately after, I would toss a morsel of bread into my mouth. I'd let it sit there, absorbing whatever essence remained of the olive and its flavors. Although nowhere near the heavenly sensation of the olive itself, the subtle replica had its own gifts to share in prolonging the experience.

I don't even like olives.

Ordinary and commonplace become extraordinary when commonplace is gone. And in the extraordinary are moments of joyous escape.

Could a man who got so excited over olives be prepared to die?

My most fervent hope was that whoever had Mikki would give her an olive. Just one. Or, better yet, *Reese's Pieces* ice cream. It was her all-time favorite.

I had grown used to waking up every morning, high atop my stone perch, with Mikki gone. We had a routine. Every night she came to me, and as she lay cradled in my arms I would tell her my stories. Then, sometime after I'd fallen asleep, she would silently slip away. So when I awoke on the fourth day since the bread deliveries had ended, I was stunned to see her staring down at me.

It was true. I was right. They hadn't killed Mikki after all. She'd been alive all this time. Kept from us, but alive. And now here she was. With me. Everything was going to be alright.

At first all I could manage was a stupid, crooked smile. My body had grown very weak. I'd barely been awake for more than a few hours the previous day. I didn't feel hungry, but I was still aware enough to know that my body must be.

Mikki smiled back. I felt the soft, warm palm of her hand rest against my forehead, then move slowly down my left cheek.

"Mikki." For some reason, the best I could manage was a hoarse whisper.

"Isaque ihla wawal?" The words flowed smoothly from her mouth. I couldn't quite make them out, but it sounded as if she was asking me if I was okay. Typical Mikki, always thinking about someone besides herself. She was the one who'd been imprisoned and kept from her family for months and months. Me? I was a relative newbie at this. Besides, I was her father. I should be looking after her. I should be the one asking if she was okay. But somehow I couldn't quite get the words to work in my mouth.

I struggled to sit up. The best I could do was to pull myself up far enough to rest on my elbows, the bone aching and skin burning where they rested against the stone. I stared at my lost daughter, delirious with happiness. It was back. Happiness was back. God, how I missed it. God, how I missed her.

At thirteen, Mikki was tall, almost the height of her mother. But on our nights atop the pedestal, she was still a child— sometimes nothing more than a wriggly baby, sometimes her six-year-old size. This worked well, making it easier for the two of us to fit within the stone's indentation. Not to mention that the thirteen-year-old version I knew from back home was no longer keen to cuddle with her old dad.

Beholding my daughter through a feverish haze, I idly wondered how and why she came to be here this morning, taller than ever, towering over me, gazing down at me with the eyes of a Madonna. With some effort, I turned and craned my head to see over the edge of the pedestal. I saw that she'd dragged over a collection of old crates and piled them against the stone platform in order to climb to the top. I also noticed that not only was she bigger and older than she'd been last night, or any night, but her face... it was different.

More words I couldn't understand burbled through her lips.

Suddenly I was concerned. "Mikki, what's wrong with you? What's happened to you?" *My God, what did they do to her?*

She responded, her voice calm, loving.

Alarm bells began to clang. I tried to sit up, and again failed. Something was wrong. This was not my daughter! "Where's Mikki?"

My brain began to clear. The soupy gobbledygook that now resided there most of the time disappeared into the recesses like murky dishwater down a garburator. I studied the face, so close to mine. How had I ever mistaken this person for Mikki? This woman's hair was dark and shiny, like wet coal. Her eyes were those of someone twice Mikki's age. Her satin-like skin was the color of weak tea. She wore a colorless shawl of delicate material — silk, maybe — that felt pleasingly cool whenever it brushed against my skin.

I fell back and stared up at my grate roof, bitterly disappointed. I wasn't so far gone as to be unaware that, at times, I'd been falling into periods of lack of focus — delusion? — thanks to the combination of starvation, extremities of heat, mental anguish, and boredom. But I was okay with that. At times like these, delusion can be a dear friend.

I closed my eyes and counted to ten.

She was still there.

It was clear that this woman did not speak my language. Nor could I speak hers.

My eyes followed as she placed a small hand against her chest, skin glistening as if oiled, nails smooth and short. She said one word. She was telling me her name.

"Asmae?" I repeated the word to confirm.

"Naâm," she responded, her voice so beseechingly sweet and kind that it nearly made me weep. She then spoke at length, hurriedly, until her words stumbled, and then she looked away as if embarrassed to have gone on for so long.

I had no idea what she was talking about, but given the circumstances and my condition, I made an educated guess: "I suppose you thought I was dead?"

She shrugged and said something more, slower, as if that would help.

We weren't getting very far. Wincing with the effort, I positioned my hand on my chest, as she had done, and croaked my name: "Jaspar."

She smiled and did her best to repeat it. I did my best to smile back, feeling self-conscious about my teeth, my breath, me in general. It hurt to smile. The skin of my lips had grown permanently chapped and cracked from too much sun—not to mention unaccustomed to the act.

Asmae made a motion as if using a spoon, and then pointed down. She wanted me to come off the pedestal to eat. I was happy to think bread might be back on the menu. Maybe even olives? I nodded feebly, but barely moved.

She pulled back. I watched as she took full note of the state I was in. When she was done, her eyes reaching out for mine, she silently took my dirty, rough hand in her tiny, tender one, and squeezed—lightly, but enough for me to know that she was doing it. Then, very carefully, she lowered herself off the pedestal and was gone.

For long moments after, I could still feel her touch on my forehead, my cheek, my hand. Touch. Such a small thing. It had been so long since anyone had touched me without intending to cause pain.

I knew how powerful small things could be. For Jenn and me, it had been nothing more than a plastic, pink barrette. That one small thing that gave us something we wanted, and then took everything else away.

Chapter 19

One of the great joys of being self-employed is never having to wake up to an alarm clock. Even so, six days a week an alarm did ring in our bedroom, at exactly 6:00 a.m. Jenn was a light sleeper and a disciplined riser, so it rarely managed more than a peep before her hand shot out from beneath the covers to silence it. I usually didn't remember it. I'd wake on my own about an hour later, get Mikki to school or wherever she had to be that day, and eventually end up behind my computer.

In the two months since that awful morning in our front yard, standing beside a mailbox that had yet again failed to deliver a letter from our daughter's kidnapper, we'd created a new version of our lives. While Jenn returned to work with a vengeance, working longer, harder hours, I'd taken to sleeping in, later and later every day. What did I have to wake up for? The emptiness and resounding silence of an abruptly-childless house was nearly unbearable. The laughing, the petty squabbles, the occasional tears, the distinct scent of a teenage girl's perfume—always something flowery and named after a singer I'd never heard of—the mysterious phone calls ripe with gossip and secrets about boys, the constant texting and selfie-taking. The assorted accoutrement of someone enslaved to fashion and pop culture—scattered magazines, smears of makeup on the bathroom sink, megalithic piles of disposed Kleenex, bottles and vials and jars of haircare and skincare product. Shoes, shoes, shoes.

All gone.

GONE.

Most of the stuff was still in Mikki's room, but no matter how I tried to preserve it—even going so far as to spritz the air with her perfume—the essence of my daughter was slowly, inexorably, agonizingly disappearing.

Unlike Jenn, who'd taken on more responsibility at work, some days staying at the office until the wee hours of the morning, my own work repelled me. It wasn't that I had writer's block, because I could almost understand that. No, this was something deeper. I felt as if I might never *want* to write again. Ever.

The pressure was on. *In The Middle*, as big as it had been, for as long as it had been, was becoming old news. Everyone who was ever going to had bought the book, seen the movie, raved about it, or torn it apart. It was so yesterday. My agent, my publisher, my accountant, my fans, were all asking the same question: what's next?

The money wasn't running out—yet. But it would. Jenn was making a decent salary, but we had a large monthly nut to crack, and we were young. There was still a lot of life left to pay for. And I needed to work. Not just for the money, but for me.

The day after our bitter realization by the mailbox, Jenn woke up, woke me, announced she was going back to work, and did it. She never looked back. At first I couldn't understand how she could do it. Secretly, I began to judge her for the apparent ease with which she did. But slowly I figured it out. She was reaching out for something to hold on to. During the relentless storm of what had happened to us—what was still happening to us—she'd wisely grabbed an anchor. I, however, opted for floating aimlessly about. I was jealous of her.

The police assured us that they were still on the case, still actively searching for Mikki. Words can lie. The looks on their faces told the truth. Clues and leads had all but dried up. The damn TV expert was right. The longer Mikki was missing, the less probable it was that she would ever be found. And if she was—well, it wasn't likely to be a happy ending to the story.

Jenn and I did our best to support each other. In spite of her declarations that she didn't blame me for not coming home early on the night of Mikki's disappearance, deep down I doubted her. And I doubted myself. I told myself I wasn't to blame; our therapist did the same. But guilt is an intrusive, nasty thing, nearly impossible to eradicate entirely.

I needed to write. Something—anything—to run interference with my mind. I needed the distraction. I needed Jaspar Wills back.

As unexpected and unsolicited as it had been, the fame and attention that had attached itself to *In The Middle* was nothing short of extraordinary. The media circus, the TV and radio talk shows, the speaking engagements, the travel opportunities, the glitzy parties at clubs and mansions, the invitations to be everything from a guest of honor at literary conventions to a judge at beauty contests, the adulation of millions—all of it was heady, exciting, addictive stuff. I wasn't the first—nor would I be the last—author to experience this, but I'd ridden the wave for significantly longer than many of my peers who'd had similar runaway hits. It helped that I was keen to do it, that I was young and had plenty of energy. The subsequent movie adaptation was like exchanging a match with a firecracker. Suddenly the book had a whole new life, a new rash of fans, people discovering my writing for the first time—followed by a fresh round of interviews and events, this time on a scale even bigger and ritzier than before.

Then, it was over. Suddenly, instead of people holding out copies of the book for my autograph—eyes wide with admiration, words dripping with praise—they stood before me empty-handed. Asking to be filled up, to be given something more—and quickly, because if I didn't comply they'd forget about me and move on to the next literary superstar holding the magic keys to the zeitgeist. Maybe it would be a teenage lesbian werewolf with an especially kind heart, or a cooking guru with recipes for heart-healthy fast foods made in a deep fryer, or an alien who arrives on earth from outer space dispensing relationship advice with the clichéd lesson that we all have the same problems no matter where in the universe we're from.

I wanted to do it. Badly. I wanted to give them exactly what they wanted. I knew I could do it. I had it in me, ideas for a hundred more *In The Middle*s. Once the whirlwind of traveling and promotional activities and—let's be honest—fete-feasts was over,

I'd have the time to allow my creativity to unleash the next something special. I *would* do it.

Then, my daughter was taken and my life imploded.

I'd lost confidence that I would ever get my old life back—or anything resembling it. I lived only for sleep. Deep, mindless, soulless, blinding, undemanding sleep.

So when the alarm startled me awake, its jarring blasts insisting that a bomb was about to detonate next to my head, it took me a moment to figure out what to do. Eventually, I rolled over to Jenn's side of the bed and took a poorly-aimed swipe at the damn thing. Nothing. The bleating continued—persistent, ear-splitting. I opened one eye and locked a hate-filled gaze on the ugly clock face. Where the hell was the doohickey that shut this thing up?

When several more slaphappy attempts went unrewarded, I pulled myself up on one elbow, grabbed the clock, forced my second eye open, and stared uncomprehendingly at the contraption, the shut-off procedure not particularly intuitive at six o'clock in the fucking morning.

That's when it struck me.

It was 6:00 a.m. Where was my wife? Why wasn't she here to shut off the alarm like she always did?

I studied the tangle of bed sheets as if that would help. No water glass on the nightstand. Jenn always brought a glass of water to bed with her and never took the empty one back to the kitchen in the morning, leaving that chore for me. I searched my sleep-fogged memory for clues.

At least once in the course of every night of our marriage, even if it was just for a few minutes, we would unconsciously slip into the spooning position. As far as I could recall, that hadn't happened last night. *Why not?*

The alarm ringing in my head began to rival the mechanical one next to it.

Suddenly another bell joined the clamor.

What the hell is happening?

The phone.

I grabbed it and shouted into the defenseless receiver. "Hold on!"

Who's calling the house at six in the morning?

With unnecessary might, I pulled the alarm clock's cord out of the wall.

The bleating continued. Damn battery backup.

Fuck redundancy systems!

I turned the device upside down, looking for the battery compartment; instead I found a switch labeled "Alarm On/Off" and gratefully moved it to the desired position.

Blessed silence restored, I returned to the phone. "Hello?"

"Jaspar? Is that you?"

It was Jenn's friend, Katie. "Yeah, Katie, I…"

"Jaspar, Jenn's in jail."

"What?" Nothing about this morning was making sense. "Why?"

"She's been arrested. For attempted murder."

Chapter 20

The police precinct's waiting room was as cheerless and uninviting as the fittingly overcast Wednesday morning. Katie Edwards, newly minted toast-of-the-town newsy—thanks to her friendship with my wife and resultant primetime access to the goulash our lives had become—was as camera-ready as you'd expect a reporter-on-the-rise to be. I found her multitasking between iPhone and iPad when I walked in. She was laughably well put-together for so early in the morning, especially compared to my barely-conscious, unshaven, uncaffeinated, distraught self.

There were half a dozen others spread throughout the room, none talking to each other. Katie waved me over and I settled into the seat next to hers. She handed me a paper cup of coffee.

"I thought you'd need this," she said, assessing me with her inquisitive journalist's eyes.

"What's going on, Katie?" I needed to know, mindlessly sipping the lukewarm drink. It might have been machine-quality, but it tasted great. "Thanks for this, by the way."

"A lawyer called me. Someone from Jenn's firm, I think."

"Jenn has a lawyer?"

"Yeah…" She consulted a notebook. "Shelley Brown. You know her?"

I shrugged. I had probably met the woman at an office Christmas party or something. "Why did this lawyer call you and not me?" Another even more disconcerting thought stuck its tongue out at me: *Why did Jenn call a lawyer and not me?*

Katie must have read my mind. "It's attempted murder, Jaspar, not a parking ticket. This is serious. Jenn would have known she needed someone to represent her. I'm guessing she told the lawyer to call me so you'd hear it from a friend and not a stranger."

I stared at her. Katie and I were not friends. Actually, we barely knew each other. She and Jenn had hit it off earlier that year, when Katie had come to Jenn's firm with a legal problem. Something about a deadbeat boyfriend. I hadn't paid much attention. I was just glad that Jenn had found someone to socialize with other than the single-minded, legal eagle, type As she worked with. Socializing with other lawyers is just like being at the office, except with drinks and pretzels and no one taking notes. It wasn't until the night Mikki disappeared that I thought of Katie as anything other than the friend who dropped Jenn off after a girl's night out.

Ever since Mikki's disappearance, Katie had become a much bigger part of our lives. She held Jenn's hand, lent an extra shoulder to cry on, made tea, poured wine, provided whatever Jenn needed whenever I couldn't. When asked to deal with the outrageous media frenzy that had erupted once news of the kidnapping got out, she'd seamlessly jumped to the helm of our rocky boat and taken over, giving us one less thing to worry about. Sure, it was great for her career—something she readily acknowledged—but if someone could benefit from this hell and keep us out of it at the same time, I was all for it. As I looked at her that morning, I realized I might have been wrong about Katie Edwards. Maybe, sometime during the maelstrom of shit we'd suffered through together, she'd become my friend too.

"What happened, Katie? What the hell is going on? You're kidding about the murder thing, right? I mean, who on earth would Jenn ever want to murder?"

The answer was a drop kick to my stomach.

Chapter 21

By some great power, or the celestial movement of stars and moon unknown to me, I had entered a new phase of my incarceration in the rectangle. Each day was an invitation to something new, a gentle, slow progression into a different reality—all thanks to the benevolent graces of Asmae.

When I'd finally managed to crawl down from my nighttime perch on her first visit, I found the meal she'd brought me wasn't the usual dry crust of bread. There wasn't even a single wondrous olive. Instead, on a platter laid out on a crate that doubled as a table, was a veritable smorgasbord of delights. Along with double my typical bread allotment was a ramekin of oil, another of honey, a small *tagine* containing a mixture of moist cooked lamb, apricot and vegetables, and a dollop of couscous. It was more food than I'd consumed all month. Although my desiccated salivary glands were telling me to do one thing, my stomach demanded another, performing its own version of a dry heave.

That day, over several hours, I only managed to swallow a miniscule portion of the couscous, along with small pieces of bread dipped in honey and oil. When Asmae appeared again just before sunset, bearing a second platter, I apologized, trying to explain my predicament with hand signals—not easy to do—and then spent the rest of my gesticulations thanking her in every way I could think of. With just that diminutive improvement in my diet, I could already feel my writer's brain—once bursting with exposition and clever turns of phrase—if not exactly come back to life, then at least peep its intention to do so...but only if I continued to provide nutrients for my body, despite how it currently repelled them. Asmae nodded often, smiled widely, said little, and stayed only a few moments.

Somehow, my new caregiver/warden must have comprehended my speechless performance. Over the next several days, thrice-daily platters were prepared for the constitution of someone unaccustomed to eating actual meals. Every day the rations were adjusted for what had transpired the day before. If I ate one spoonful of couscous on day one, day two brought a spoonful and a half. If I didn't touch any meat, fish was attempted the following meal. If I vomited or experienced diarrhea, the menu item that caused the reaction was immediately discontinued.

Sometimes the platter appeared at the opening of the door as before, slid through on the ground and left there for me to retrieve. Other times, Asmae would bring the fare in herself, arranging it on the crate-table, all the while cooing something that I concluded was either her describing the meal's contents or asking after my well-being.

Oftentimes she'd find me prone in the lean-to's shade, asleep and difficult to wake. I knew I'd grown dangerously thin and, by all other measures, dreadful and likely repulsive in appearance, so I understood the concern I regularly saw in her eyes.

I'd never been an exceedingly vain man, but I'd come to know—especially during the heady years following the release of *In The Middle*—the value of looking a certain way, of putting forward the best possible you. People react positively, and sometimes unreasonably exuberantly, to someone who is—by nothing more than cut of jaw, placement of cheek, color of eye, fit of clothes—defined by society as more attractive than others. More books were sold. Everyone benefited—publisher, agent, booksellers, me. My looks were something I'd been given, and had spit and polished as required. But, like everything else, they too had been taken from me. My current state was by far the least of my losses, but it was a loss nonetheless.

It was a blistering hot afternoon like countless ones before it, the sun pounding the rectangle with bolts of neon. As usual, I'd taken to the small haven of shade provided by the lean-to, and fallen asleep on the bamboo mat I used as a daybed. I'd been feeling poorly for days, which was nothing new, and running a fever. I could only guess at why. Perhaps I was fighting an infection—or perhaps my body was simply complaining, yet again, about its stunning fall from grace.

The sensation of a cool cloth pressed against my steaming forehead, perfumed with a delicate floral scent I'd come to associate with Asmae, was nothing short of miraculous. I didn't open my eyes. It might have been because of my weakened state—or it might have been because of a desire to perpetuate the joy of what I admitted might be nothing but another hallucination.

Taking great care, Asmae unfastened the two remaining functional buttons of my shirt. She gently ran the cloth across my chest, and then down into the deep hollow of my belly. With a refreshed towel, she next ministered to my arms, paying special attention to my ruined hands. I loved every second, each pass across my starving skin bringing me closer to feeling once more like a human being...and I simultaneously hated every second, for fear it would be the last.

Maintaining an almost reverential silence, by which she asked permission to continue and I acquiesced, Asmae again dipped the cloth into a basin of water and wrung it out, setting off a flutter of aromas, and then laid it aside. With a touch so light it might have been the work of an angel, she rolled up the hem of each pant leg. She laid the cool, fragrant towel across the bridge of my right foot, then moved it up the leg, down the backside, and tenderly around the rough, chapped bottom of the foot, repeating the same route on the left.

Laying a buttery-soft hand against my forehead, she checked my fever. Whether my temperature told the story or not, I felt as revived and well as if she'd just given me an entire body transplant.

This is how it can be.

Our lives had been stolen and gutted, Mikki's and mine, and that was a horrible thing. But empathy, compassion, and kindness are powerful salves. Through Asmae and what she was doing for me, I suddenly knew what was possible. For me. For my daughter. Peacefulness filled me and took me to sleep.

When next I woke, the sun was dipping below my cement horizon, delivering a merciful abatement from the day's heat. Tempered shadows of dusk revealed hints of color in an otherwise sun-bleached world. For long moments I lay there, enjoying the return of fresh night air, breathing in the perfume of a dinner platter that must have arrived during my slumber. I felt rejuvenated by the thought of someone like Asmae helping Mikki. I tried to recall the lessons we'd taught our daughter in the short years we'd had her. Would she know the difference between a person like Asmae, who came into your life to save it...and someone like Scott Walker, who came to destroy it?

Chapter 22

It's shocking, the first time you embrace the love of your life and feel them almost-imperceptibly pull away. There is always a message in such a withdrawal. But, instead of focusing on what it might be, I pushed all negative thoughts away. After all, these were not the best of times. We were in the windowless, shabby back room of a police precinct, my wife having been arrested for attempting to murder our neighbor, Scott Walker.

I can't remember ever looking at Jenn and thinking she was anything but outrageously gorgeous. But that morning, when I stepped into the room they were keeping her in, she appeared as grey and dull and dispirited as the space itself. As soon as our perfunctory embrace was done, the subtle disconnection overlooked, she fell into a folding chair. She introduced her new lawyer, Muriel Cope, who'd stepped in to replace Shelley Brown. Something about Jenn's law firm being unable or unwilling to represent one of their own partners.

After a brisk handshake and a tense sideways glance at her client, Cope announced, "I'll leave you two to talk."

I stopped her. "Wait. What's this about? What's going to happen next?"

She and Jenn exchanged another look, then: "Why don't you and Jenn talk first? Then we can deal with what's ahead of us." Briefcase and iPhone in hand, she left the room.

I sat in the chair opposite Jenn and reached across the table. Pretending to ignore the gesture, she quickly pulled her hands away, burying them in her lap. Her eyes were anywhere but on mine. I was already worried and confused, but now an air raid siren was blowing my head apart, warning me of impending disaster. "Jenn," I pleaded, "I need you to tell me what's going on. Is it true? Did you try to kill Scott?"

Tear-blurred eyes fell on me, and my heart lurched.

"Yes."

With that one, simple word, I realized our lives were about to be turned upside down. Again. In the nearly two decades I'd known my wife, no one could have ever convinced me she would be capable of harming another person—or even giving it a try. Yet, for reasons that eluded me, as I sat there looking at the stranger's face she wore that morning I didn't doubt her confession for a second. "Why?" I asked. "Why would you do something like that? Why Scott?"

Scott Walker was the father of Mikki's best friend, Delores, and a neighbor. They lived on the next block over from ours. A few years earlier, based on the strength of our daughters' friendship, we'd attempted socializing with Scott and his girlfriend Anna, who was not Delores' mother. It wasn't a disaster, but the pairing didn't click, and we'd seen little of the couple since.

"Muriel thinks the charges will be dropped soon."

My heart leapt, a thrill ran through my chest and, unaccountably, a nervous chuckle erupted from my mouth. "Jenn, oh God, that's great news!" I enthused, a flicker of hope ignited. "So this *is* some sort of crazy mistake. You can't imagine all the stuff that's been going through my head." I so wanted to touch her, to pull her into my arms, but her body language continued to tell me that any sort of physical intimacy remained unwelcome.

"There's been no mistake, Jaspar."

I was becoming exasperated. For someone who relied on fact, logic, and clarity to do her job, Jenn was being stingy with all three.

"I did try to… I did attack Scott," she said, her voice flat.

I sucked in as much air as I could manage, held it, counted to five, and then expelled it. "Jenn, you have to help me out here. What did you do? Why?"

"I found…" Squeezing her eyes tight, fat tears slipped down her cheeks, leaving damp hoary scars. "I found her pink barrette, Jaspar. Mikki's pink barrette."

I shook my head, more confused than ever. "What are you talking about?"

"You know how before…right before she was gone, how she'd been on a kick, always wearing those pink barrettes? They were her latest fashion statement. I think she was trying to see if she could turn something only little girls were expected to wear into a teenage fad."

I nodded. I did recall hearing something along those lines. But, truth be told, I'd paid little attention, as befits most fads—especially those indulged in by thirteen-year-old girls and their friends.

"I found one," she repeated. "I knew it was hers because she'd initialed them on the back with a Sharpie. It was her distinctive mark, the right side of the 'M' for Mikki becoming the left side of the 'W' for Wills."

Again I nodded. This was something I'd seen her do on her school books, or whenever she left us a message on the notepad in the kitchen. "So you found one of her pink barrettes. I don't get why that means anything."

"Think, Jaspar. Think about when we talked to the police that night. Do you remember when they asked us to…"

Suddenly I made the connection. I finished the sentence: "…describe what she was wearing the last time we saw her."

"Yes."

"That morning, when she left for school, she was wearing her pink barrettes."

"Yes."

"My God, Jenn, you found one? Where?"

She looked away. The tears had stopped. She busied herself looking for a Kleenex to blow her nose.

"Where, Jenn? Where did you find the barrette? And what does this have to do with Scott Walker?" Was she telling one story to divert me from another she didn't want to tell?

Our eyes caught and held. She said nothing, as if silently willing me to come up with the answer on my own. For a full moment we sat like that, in that grimy room, staring at each other.

Then as dreadful realization dawned in my eyes, fear bloomed in hers.

"D-did Scott find it?" I finally uttered, desperate for an alternative to the inconceivable scenario slowly forming in my mind.

"No," she whispered. "I found it."

"Where?"

"In Scott's house."

I could feel blood racing through every vein, triple time, to match the beating of my heart. "Where?"

"In his bedroom." As she began to recite the facts I had every right to know, her voice grew leaden, her eyes dead. "In the bed. It was wedged between the mattress and the headboard."

I thought I might be sick. "Mikki was in Scott Walker's bed?"

She nodded.

I pulled in a ragged, tortured breath, and begged my stomach not to betray me. A starburst of pain radiated outwards from the base of my skull. My head began to pound. My mouth grew impossibly dry. "With Scott?"

Her shoulders moved in an indeterminate way. I didn't know if she was saying, "Of course, you idiot, how else would the barrette get there?" or, "I don't know."

And as if these thoughts weren't disturbing enough, ugly enough, heartbreaking enough, one more came crashing through my brain like a runaway train flying off a bridge into a depthless, dark ravine: "Jenn, how did *you* find the barrette in Scott Walker's bed?"

Chapter 23

"Jaspar, I'm sorry."

I'm sorry. Two words that, put together, convey so much...or pitifully little. They can be all you'll ever need to hear, or hopelessly insufficient.

It was Jenn's turn to reach across the table, her trembling, red-splotched hands searching for mine. It was my turn to withhold. The situation was one of those idiotic scenarios where she knows I know, I know she knows I know, and I think I know what I know, but I need her to say it. Otherwise, I simply could never believe it.

I waited.

She took a few moments to stare into space, sniff back a few more tears—of sadness? regret?—and, like a lawyer preparing for opening statements, choose her words carefully.

"I'd been stopping by the house—the Walker house—to see Delores," she started out. "I...I don't exactly know why. I guess it made me feel better, you know? To talk to Mikki's best friend. They were so close. It made me feel close to her again. I know it sounds crazy now that I say it out loud, but it's how I felt." A quick sigh, then: "One day, Delores showed me a picture of them together, one I'd never seen before. I thought I was going to fall apart when I saw it, Jaspar. The pictures we have, the ones we've looked at a million times since that night, they feel like...memories, something that's long gone, Mikki in the past, Mikki *before*. But this picture, the one Delores showed me, it wasn't a memory. It was something new. It was like I was sharing a new experience with Mikki, seeing her in a way I hadn't before, with her doing something new, being in a new place. I...I just so needed that. Being with Delores gave me that."

"I get it, Jenn." I did. But she was stalling. Focusing on the innocent act, delaying the guilty. "Then what happened?"

"Sometimes, Scott would be there."

My breathing grew shallow. My gut constricted, growing taut in anticipation of a blow.

"We would talk. He and Anna…do you remember her? She was the girlfriend we met. Well, anyway, they broke up a while ago."

I wanted to yell out how very much I couldn't give a fucking, flying rat's ass about that. Instead I held my tongue, staring at the woman sitting across from me, watching my wife slowly disappear and someone unfamiliar take her place.

"He could see how much I was getting out of spending time with Delores. He told me I could drop by anytime."

I'm sure he did.

"You can figure out the rest."

Oh, no you don't. I wasn't about to let her get off so easily, sloughing off the dirty details as if they meant nothing. I was broiling in hell and wanted her in the fire with me. "Tell me."

The lawyer in her rose to the surface. She faced me dead on and unequivocally stated, "We slept together."

The torture I would eventually suffer at the hands of Hun was nothing compared to this.

"I don't even know why I did it," she said matter-of-factly. "I didn't feel anything. He didn't give me anything I was looking for, or needed. But I just kept doing it."

The knife plunged deeper.

"Last night, he left the bed to go to the bathroom…"

I could see it in my head. A moment so simple, a moment any couple can relate to. Having just made love, the man gets up, naked, pads his way to the bathroom…*Stop it!* Self-flagellation had never been my style.

Jenn kept on. "My hand happened to move into the crack between the headboard and the mattress. That's when I found it. I thought I was going crazy, seeing something that wasn't really there because I was so desperate to see or touch anything that belonged to her.

"I'd dreamt about those barrettes so many times since we lost her, and now I had one in my hand. Once I knew it was real, I couldn't believe it. I was so confused. I turned it over and over, I saw her initials...and that was it...I didn't think about it anymore. I knew...I knew how it got there. I knew what must have happened in that bed. I made up my mind and I did what I had to do, Jaspar."

"What did you do?"

"I found a pair of scissors in the bedside table." Her eyes were growing unfocused as she recalled the sequence of events. "I walked to the bathroom. He was washing up. He must have heard me behind him. I caught his eye in the mirror. I could see him smile at me. I stabbed him in the back. Then again and again and again."

Jenn had recited her actions in an even, emotionless tone. Despite what was happening to us, I still knew my wife. Or thought I did. She was keeping her outside calm, to get through what she needed to get through—but inside, her guts were being ripped into bloody shreds.

A merciless part of me was glad.

"At first he was stunned, of course," she kept on. "Then he tried to stop me. He kept yelling: 'What's wrong with you? Stop it! Stop it! Stop it!' The sound of his voice, pleading like he didn't deserve to die for what he'd done, just made me angrier. I screamed at him. I wanted him to admit what he'd done to Mikki. I wanted him to tell me where she is. He acted like he had no idea what I was talking about."

She hesitated, chewed her bottom lip, and then said, "I remember arms flailing. His. Mine. And blood. Everywhere. Mostly his. I kept hacking at him. The tap was still running and the sink was overflowing. He staggered. Fell against the wall. Slid down. Towards the floor. Into the pink water."

"Fuck," I whispered.

"Then more screams. But they weren't mine. Or his."

What? "Who...?"

"Delores. In all the panic and craziness, I totally forgot she was in the house. I lowered the scissors. Scott was quiet now. So was I. But, oh Christ, Jaspar, she never stopped. I can still hear her. 'Kill him! Kill him! Kill him!'"

Chapter 24

Aside from our parents, who can we indisputably claim has changed our life? Parents do it by first giving us life, and then molding and influencing it through lessons taught and examples set. They provide the basics: food, shelter, protection from harm. They lead us to spirituality, or away from it. They educate us. Teach us who to respect, who to fear, who to emulate, who to love, who to hate. They teach kindness, rudeness, empathy, carelessness. Then they send us on our way, setting us free to explore and open ourselves up to new influences.

When first breaching adulthood, we tend to resist the impact of others, more interested in self-discovery and being our own person. The smartest of us strike a balance between learning from others and finding ourselves. We stand on our own two feet, but know the graciousness and courage of seeking and accepting help when it's needed.

Throughout life, friends, spouses, teachers, mentors, employers, even children, affect our lives, affect decisions, turn a moral compass—sometimes profoundly. Occasionally, when these influencers present themselves, we ignore them, or actively push them away. From fear, uncertainty, cowardice. Sometimes, opportunities arise in places so foreign, situations so unfamiliar, from sources so unlikely, for reasons so obscure, that we risk missing them all together.

Asmae's presence in my rectangle grew with each passing day, although not in a physical way. She rarely stayed longer than a few minutes, if at all. Days would sometimes pass without my seeing her face.

In the beginning, I suspect she feared for my life and kind-heartedly took it upon herself to heal me, should I be healable.

Within three weeks of her first visit, I was returning to the man I'd once been. Not the pre-Mikki man, but certainly the pre-Morocco man. Although still thin and unable to eat more than a pittance, I was once again beginning to experience a desire for food, and hunger when it didn't appear when I expected it to. Bouts of fever and stomach ailments and blinding headaches troubled me less and less often. My mind grew clearer. I was able to focus on my surroundings and my situation, as meager and hopeless as they were.

Asmae did not come to this unexpected arrangement as someone experienced in caring for a prisoner. But she was watchful and thoughtful and must have spent significant amounts of time considering my needs, although I asked for nothing. Every so often, along with my meal, something more would appear with the tray of food. Towels for cleaning myself. A hairbrush. Nail clippers. A mirror. A clean shirt. A collection of small ceramic bottles containing oils and lotions. If I left one untouched, Asmae knew it was because I was uncertain about its use. The very next day she would find a way to instruct me. A lock of her own hair, tied with a silk ribbon and laid next to one vessel, told me it held shampoo. A slight impression of her hand left in the dirt floor next to another told me that the contents were meant as a lotion for my hands and body. The most cherished of my new possessions were a shabby notebook, a nub of pencil, and a small blade with which to sharpen it.

Of the many things my body and mind ached for, the ability to express myself in writing was near the top of the list. It was something I'd done nearly all my life. Not unlike eating and breathing, without it I would eventually perish.

The day I received the magnificent gift of pencil and paper was a day of rebirth. I finally had a purpose. I could finally tell my story. Silent and hiding in the deepest coves of my mind was a faint hope—a wish, a dream, a nugget of optimism—that one day my daughter would read my words. She'd know I had lived her pain, shared her loneliness, understood the feelings of betrayal and abandonment, and knew how the fear of death could turn into unspeakable attraction. I was coming to believe that in my struggles to persevere—and by way of an inexplicable, mystical connection between a guilt-ridden, self-loathing, piteous father and his lost daughter—I would somehow reach her, touch her, pull her along with me...so that someday, somehow, we might be reunited. And she would forgive me.

By night, I still lay atop my stone pedestal, my version of Mikki nestled next to me. But in all other ways, my days in the rectangle had changed. Mornings, and early evenings after the sun fell below the berm of my enclosure, were set aside for my new cleaning rituals. Now, with a dented tin basin, argan soaps and body lotions, a toothbrush and comb, and a collection of rags—little more than scraps of old clothing—I was able to maintain a reasonable grooming regime. After breakfast, I would retreat to the shade of the lean-to. But instead of falling into my usual somnambulistic state, I used the time to write in my new notebook, words interspersed with rudimentary sketches of the things I'd written about, or things I'd seen or dreamed of since being held captive.

After lunch, the temperature would soar. Even in the lean-to, it was too hot for any activity other than sipping water from the cracked jug Asmae had brought me. During these hours I did a lot of thinking. I thought about Mikki—wondering where she might be at that very moment, wondering if hers was a similar environment to mine. I thought about the stories I would tell her that night—some of them newly made up, perhaps taken from the notes I'd written that morning or to be written the following day. I thought about food. I thought about Asmae. I thought a lot about Asmae.

Who was she? Who was this woman who'd suddenly appeared in my life, and saved it? Was she a wife? A daughter? A mother? Did the Huns know what she was doing? Had they left me here to die—but she, having discovered me, covertly decided to do what needed to be done to keep me alive? Was that why all the gifts she brought me were used or slightly damaged? Was she bringing me things that others had thrown out, and therefore would never notice missing?

I made a guessing game of predicting Asmae's daily routine, if there was such a thing. On the days I forecast a visit, I would wait by the door of the rectangle in anticipation of her arrival. The worst were the days when the door would inch open, but instead of Asmae only a platter of food would arrive.

I was tortured by the question of why she came inside the rectangle on some days but not others. Were some days more dangerous, the risk of discovery too great?

I missed Asmae when she didn't visit. I missed her smell, how her eyes crinkled at the corners when she smiled, how unintelligible words—strange coming from anyone else's mouth—spilled forth from hers sounding like a summer day's sonnet. I attempted to sketch her once, so I'd have something to look at on the days when she didn't come to me. I quickly learned that drawing the human face is one of the most difficult things to do, the results of my efforts childish and cartoonish.

Each day when the sun disappeared from sight, and prior to my evening grooming and the arrival of supper, I would exercise. Now that I was being fed regularly and my health was slowly returning, I decided a light daily workout would benefit me. In my previous life I'd been a staunch believer in "strong body, strong mind." If I was going to get through this—if I was going to do what needed to be done—I'd need both.

Like Asmae, I had assessed the situation and identified what needed to be done. For her, whatever the risk, whatever the danger, she'd found a way to save my life. I, on the other hand, whatever the risk, whatever the danger, would have to find a way to end hers.

Chapter 25

Day after day, side by side, we sat in that courtroom in silence, witnessing the judicial system do its best to bring Scott Walker to justice. Each night we returned to our quiet, dark house, prepared a simple meal, sat on the sofa in silence, and watched the talking heads on TV spout their opinions on the day's proceedings. We found that sitting side by side, wherever we were—at home, in the courtroom, in the back of a cab—was the best positioning for us. It provided the illusion of intimacy without ever having to actually look at each other. To face each other, or have any sort of discussion beyond a word or two, was simply too difficult. Too many realities threatened to attack our well-being, our relationship, our sanity— each already dangerously precarious—and derail our ability to get up the next day and do it all over again.

The facts, sensationalized by the media, went like this: our neighbor, Scott Walker, had kidnapped Mikki. Walker, described by everyone who knew him as friendly and nonviolent—as many psychopaths are—was also being accused, by his own similarly-aged daughter, of abuse. My wife, unaware of any of this, had committed adultery with Walker. As for Mikki, she was most likely dead. Her body would be discovered one day: a Jane Doe skeleton in an unmarked grave.

Our lawyers were assiduously attempting to convince a hastily convened jury to conclude beyond a reasonable doubt that Scott Walker had done all of these heinous things: kidnap, abuse, adultery, murder. All we could do was sit back and watch. In silence. Side by side.

We were surprised when Anna Martens, Walker's former girlfriend, was called to the stand as a witness for the defense.

"Good morning," the lawyer began. "My name is Allen Krenshaw. For the court, would you please state your full name and occupation?"

"Dr. Anna Martens. I'm a surgical resident at Boston Children's Hospital."

"Dr. Martens, do you recognize the defendant?"

"Yes. Scott Walker."

"What is your relationship with Mr. Walker?"

"Now? None. We have no relationship other than as acquaintances. But we did have a relationship in the past. For just under three years."

"A sexual relationship?"

She raised an eyebrow at the description. "A romantic relationship. And yes, our romantic relationship included a sexual component."

"Very good. Thank you." He cleared his throat, then: "During the course of your *romantic* relationship with Mr. Walker, did you have opportunity to become acquainted with his daughter, Delores?"

"Of course. Because of where I worked, where he lived, and the demands of my career, Scott and I never chose to live together. But I spent a great deal of time at his home. As a single father, he was the sole caregiver for Delores, which meant she was often included in our time together. I cared…care…a great deal for her."

"Last year your relationship with Mr. Walker came to an end?"

"That's correct. It was a mutually agreed upon, natural end."

"I see. What age was Delores Walker at that time?"

"She'd just turned twelve."

"Objection, your Honor," our side spoke up. "I've held my tongue longer than I should have. Mr. Walker's daughter and her relationship with her father's former lover is neither relevant nor of interest to these proceedings."

"Your Honor, I must strongly disagree with Ms. Cope," Krenshaw shot back. "It was the prosecution who first brought up the allegations, by Delores Walker, of ritual abuse. Allegations which, I must remind the jury, have not been proven in any court of law. Certainly we have the right to explore and present witnesses to refute these claims. Ms. Martens had an intimate relationship with both Scott Walker and his daughter throughout the period in question. As such, she is singularly—"

"Yes, yes, yes, I get your point," the judge interjected. "Overruled. You may continue, Mr. Krenshaw. But I'm only giving you an inch, so don't take a mile, or I might change my mind."

I knew what was at stake here. Jenn claimed that when Delores walked in on the horrific scene of her slashing away at Scott Walker, instead of begging her to stop, she'd pleaded for her to kill him. Later, Delores professed to police that her father repeatedly abused her—not sexually, but by regularly losing his temper, at one point slapping her across the face. According to our lawyers, the jury had the right to know about this and Delores was put on the stand. The jurors were then expertly led to conclude that it wasn't a big leap from physically hurting your daughter to rationalizing the abduction of someone else's, so that you could do to another young girl what you wanted, deep down, to do to your own child. The jury needed to believe that Scott Walker was a very sick and twisted individual.

Cool and collected, Krenshaw turned his back on Cope and refocused on Anna. "You stated that Delores was twelve at the time your relationship with her father ended, is that correct?"

"Correct."

"Did your relationship with the defendant end on good terms?"

Anna's smile was lopsided as she shot a glance in Walker's direction. Even from where I sat, I could tell that, although they were no longer a couple, there was little if any malice between them. "I wouldn't say that," she responded. "As I said, it was mutual. But that doesn't mean it was easy. With time we got over it."

Anna was an excellent witness. She was logical, likeable, relatable. I could see the jury empathizing with her. On the other hand, I could see our team getting antsy. They'd opened the door, and now there was little they could do but sit on their hands and hope they wouldn't regret it.

"How would you describe Mr. Walker's parenting skills?"

Anna Martens answered, "I think it's important to know that Scott was not the kind of guy who ever pictured himself raising a child alone, never mind a soon-to-be teenage girl. The unexpected death of his wife foisted him into that position. They'd just moved to a new city. There were no grandparents or siblings, and few friends in a position to help. Scott had to figure it out by himself. By the time I came around, he'd done it. From what I saw, although he was strict and maybe at times a little inflexible, he was doing a good job. I witnessed him being affectionate with his daughter, protective, and," she looked at the jury with a small smile, "as probably any parent can relate to, I suspected he was in a constant, low-grade state of terror as to what was coming next."

More than a couple of the jurors smiled knowingly.

"So you would say Scott Walker was a good parent?"

"Yes."

"During your three-year experience as part of the Walker family, Dr. Martens, did you witness any instances of abuse similar in nature to what was earlier described to this court by Delores Walker?"

Anna spent a few seconds studying the face of her former boyfriend. Then, in slow, evenly paced words, she said, "I did not. In my opinion, Delores Walker is a typical, rebellious teenager. She's a daughter upset with a father who isn't giving her the freedoms she believes she is entitled to. I believe Delores is too young to understand the importance and permanence of what is happening in this courtroom. I believe Delores doesn't know the danger she has put her father in. I believe Delores will come to regret everything she has said about her father. I believe Delores Walker is lying."

Anna Martens' final words caused a mini uproar in the courtroom, particularly from the team of lawyers on the prosecutorial side of the room. While everyone was busy yelling at everyone else, I watched the faces of Anna and Scott. Hers, sympathetic; his, heart-wrenchingly sad, and earnestly grateful.

I could feel Jenn trembling next to me. Both of us could feel the same thing: the tide had begun to turn. The problem all along had been the amount of circumstantial evidence being packaged into a cannonball meant to blast Scott Walker into jail for a very long time. Everything the prosecution had presented before resting their case had been persuasive. But where was the irrefutable proof?

When it was revealed that Mikki *had* been in the Walker house the day she disappeared, that, for me, was the final nail in Scott Walker's coffin. Until then, we had all believed that Mikki had left school and was walking home alone when she'd been taken. Normally she would have been with Delores, but she'd stayed home sick that day. In court, Delores revealed that Mikki had stopped at the Walker house to bring her homework. Walker, who worked in construction, had stayed home that day to care for his daughter.

The revelation was meant to be damning, but the defense team had done a respectable job of rendering it almost benign. Delores admitted that she never saw Mikki and her father interact during the time Mikki was in the house, and that it was possible he hadn't even been aware of her presence. The prosecution accepted the admission with little resistance, instead biding their time before delivering the second and more powerful half of what was meant to be a devastating one-two punch.

Chapter 26

"He raped a girl."

Asmae didn't understand. As far as she knew, I could have been whispering sweet nothings into her ear, sharing a recipe for crumb cake, or telling her my life story. As always, though, she listened intently, as if to pay respect to my words and communicate her hopeless, yet nonetheless sincere, desire to comprehend.

The first few times we lay together atop the pedestal in my rectangle, nothing happened. She'd slip into the spot next to me as if she'd always been there, and together we'd stare at the star-spangled sky without saying a word. It was as if we'd effortlessly shifted from one level of a predetermined recovery program to the next. She wouldn't stay long—twenty or thirty minutes at most. Only when it would have become mentally intolerable and physically impossible for me to continue down our chaste path would she leave.

Until the night she didn't.

Instead of moving away, she moved into me. I almost burst into tears at the invitation, my body so desperately yearning for intimacy that it ached. Lying against me as she was, her back to my front, our eyes did not meet, but the message was clear. I buried my face in her neck. Her hair smelled spicy, her smooth skin sweet and warm in the dying hours of a sweltering day. I could tell, by the puffing out of her cheeks, that she was smiling. Jenn might have let out a teasing laugh; Asmae never would.

Her clothes fell away as if they'd been nothing more than a temporary covering for a body meant to be naked. I ran my hands over every inch of the freshly exposed skin—first her arms and thighs, belly and back, and then moving, tentatively, to explore more intimate areas.

Still in our spooning position, I somehow managed to pull off my shirt, and then my pants. When I was undressed, I was surprised when she pushed against me with a fierce resolve, short, quick breaths escaping her scarlet-tinged lips. Unable to stand it any longer, I maneuvered her body until we were face to face, chest to chest, our skin glistening and wet, aglow in the moonlight. A battle of emotions raged in her deep, brown eyes: uncertainty, lust, fear, desire. She murmured something in her strange tongue—to me, forevermore, the language of love.

Only a careless man, an insensitive man, relies solely on the verbal tells of the woman he is with. Even in a debate of which kind of "no" means "no" and which means "yes," nonverbal cues always provide the most vital information. Asmae and I didn't need to understand each other's words to understand each other. As almost any man in my circumstance would be, I was nearly overcome with desire to enter Asmae as quickly as possible. The language of her body, her eyes, her breathing, however, told me to wait, to tease, to make an attempt and then withdraw. The more I did this, the more I fueled her willingness and wantonness. Her body grew slick with sweat, allowing my hands to glide easily across it as I caressed—at first gently, then insistently, and then gently once more.

When she was ready, I knew it.

Every day after that one, she came to me and we made love. Afterwards, we'd talk. Both of us. We'd tell stories the other could never understand. Perhaps that was why they were so easily told. Secrets shared that would never be betrayed.

"He said it happened when both he and the girl were eighteen," I continued my tale of Scott Walker's past. "With his girlfriend. He claimed she accused him of rape because he broke up with her—a spurned teenager's revenge. He was charged, but never convicted."

I stopped there to let her take a turn. Although I was beginning to recognize the sound of certain words she used regularly, none of them meant anything to me. Still, as she spoke, I listened with patience, and wondered if she was sharing the same kind of confidences and admissions with me as I was with her. I stored the mysterious tales in a hidden pocket deep within my brain, for a day in the future when I might retrieve them, to be translated by a much wiser me.

Ultimately, Scott Walker went free. I got the feeling—undoubtedly the wishful thinking of a grieving father—that the jury really did want to find him guilty. But they'd taken their responsibility seriously. They found themselves unable to convict beyond a reasonable doubt on the evidence provided to them. Soon after, Walker and his daughter left our neighborhood—left Boston—for who knows where, never to be heard from again. Just like Mikki.

The generous, rational side of me hoped, for Delores' sake, that the man Anna Martens described in the courtroom was the real Scott Walker. That, as Delores grew and matured, she would become sorry for how she had almost destroyed her father's life with a lie. That Scott continued to be a good father and protect his daughter from harm.

The other side of me—the inconsolable father with a hole so big in his heart that it shouldn't have been beating—wanted to hunt Scott Walker down, torture him until he admitted what he'd done and where to find our daughter, and then see him rot in jail for the rest of his life.

I don't make these comments lightly. I am not a violent man—nor a vengeful one. I've never had fantasies of ramming my car into the guy who cut me off in traffic, or beating up a former classmate who bullied me in school. I like peace. I respect the rule of law. But then again, I'd never imagined a world where I would be a father who had lost his child. In the blink of an eye. Here today, gone tomorrow. No explanation, aside from a couple of sick ransom notes that really told us nothing. If, by the cruel quirk of some miserable fate, my child *had* to leave my life, even one last torturous goodbye would have been immeasurably better than this hell. Or so I imagined.

"Who are you?" I asked the woman in my arms one night: a woman who'd gone from stranger to caregiver to lover.

Asmae looked at me, her eyes quizzical. She knew I was asking her something. What she didn't know was that she had made a grave mistake.

By making me strong again, Asmae had awakened in me the desire, the pull, the insatiable need, to return to my old life—ruined as it was. Now that I was able, now that an opportunity had presented itself when for so long I'd believed there to be none, the question I kept asking myself was: *What am I willing to do to regain my freedom?*

Was I willing to risk my life? I had no idea what was outside the cement walls of my rectangle. It might be some kind of insurmountable physical barrier, or a line of armed guards ready to mow me down if I so much as stuck a toe outside the door.

If the answer was yes, an even more difficult question arose: was I willing to commit an act of barbarism to have that chance?

It was clear that Asmae was my way out of the rectangle. My *only* way. What was unclear was whether she would help me or hinder me. What if she was disinclined to let me go? What would I do? What *could* I do?

I gazed down at her kind, caring face, watching flickering bursts of starlight dance merrily in her eyes. Languidly, I ran a finger across her cheek, something I knew she drew pleasure from. Then, in an act of pitiful cowardice, I leaned down and kissed her. Did she—this sweet, benevolent, angel—know that the silent language of lovers can easily camouflage brutal betrayal...and an irony so horrible that I could barely admit it in my own mind?

Did she know that, by the act of saving my life, she had risked her own?

Chapter 27

"Will you leave me?"

It was all over. Everything. The trial. Our time as Mikki's parents. Our marriage?

Any couples counsellor will tell you that the key to a strong relationship is communication. Sometimes that's bullshit.

Particularly throughout the trial, talking to each other—rehashing, arguing, pointing fingers, building suspicions, tearing them down, second guessing—would have destroyed us. As it was, we had more than enough communication coming at us from other sources: lawyers, friends, family, workmates, neighbors, media, media, media. The quiet world we shared when we were finally home alone at night was a refuge, a silent bubble where we could convalesce.

It wasn't as if we were completely ignoring each other. We spoke enough to make life happen. "What do you want for dinner?" "Red or white?" "I'll pick up the dry-cleaning." "You shower first." We weren't sexually intimate, but we sat next to each other on the couch when we watched TV, we slept in the same bed, we walked into court hand in hand. Ironically, we were probably kinder to each other the deeper we got into the house of horrors. We'd do small things for each other, like holding open a car door, fetching the other one a sweater if it was chilly, preparing a favorite dessert after a particularly brutal day, running interference with phone calls from well-meaning but nosy relatives.

Somehow, we made it through.

Then, when it was finished, a new struggle began.

The respite of silence was over.

"Do you *want* me to leave?" I replied to Jenn's question.

We were together in our living room—we used to call it the family room. Jenn was on the couch, laptop on thigh, glass of wine at the ready. I was in the adjoining chair, attempting to read a book—the same one I had been trying to read for six months but had never made it past the first chapter. It was Friday night; another weekend loomed. They were the worst. Without the structure of a workday, endless hours yawned before us like a chasm. Inevitably, Jenn would head into the office anyway, and I'd sit in front of my computer accomplishing nothing.

"God, no, Jaspar. I love you. I'm just afraid that after all of this, after…what I did…that you don't love me anymore."

As usual, we'd allowed the room to grow much too dim as afternoon slid into evening, the only light coming from a fish tank— home to Mikki's favorite pet goldfish, who seemed intent on outliving all of us. Normally I'd get up and switch on a few lamps, but not this time. This time I preferred the indistinct, blurred figures we'd become. For this conversation, low visibility was preferable.

"I love you, Jenn," I told her with certainty. "I'm just not sure how to forgive you."

Her breath caught. A lone tear, reflecting the fish tank's somber light, slid down her gaunt face like a silver bullet. "I know," she whispered.

"It's just going to take some time, you know? If I could pull myself away from the emotions of it, if I could pretend I'm the writer and you're my heroine, I can almost figure it out, draw you as an empathetic character. But sitting here, as your husband, as Mikki's dad, I just can't. Not yet. You have to understand that."

A single nod. "I do."

"But if we can get past this somehow, Jenn, if I can get past it, there's nothing I want more than to get back to us."

"Jaspar," her tone was contrite, her voice a raspy wisp, "I don't think that can ever happen. There is no us anymore. What we were—you, me, Mikki—it's gone, dead, there's no going back. And we can't go back to the two of us before Mikki. We have to figure out if we can be the two of us after her. That's going to be really hard to do."

She was right. That was going to be fucking hard to do. Maybe impossible.

In the end, it was easier to pretend to stay together than to actually pull apart.

A month later, I was packing for Morocco.

Chapter 28

After what one or both must have decided was a respectful period of time following the trial, my agent and publisher invited me to an expensive downtown lunch under the guise of "just wanting to know how you and Jenn are doing." In reality, it was a pitch meeting. They were impatient for me to deliver a follow-up to *In The Middle*. I was being encouraged to "put my pain on paper." Aside from my agent and publisher being shit-eating, money-grubbing, insensitive assholes, it wasn't such a bad idea.

I couldn't blame them for bringing it up. Their jobs were to advise me, to look after my best interests, to make me money so that they could make money. I balked at the idea and told them to forget it. I lied and promised I was working on something else that was going to blow their socks off. I went home and began writing the story they wanted.

Almost immediately, I knew it wasn't going to work. There were too many gaping holes. Mikki was never found; the man we believed kidnapped her had escaped prosecution and left town; our lives were in shambles; the end. I'm not a writer who necessarily believes every story has to have a happy ending, but this one had *no* ending. It was an impossible book to write.

In the end, I concluded that I would simply do what I had promised to do: I'd write something that was going to blow everyone's socks off.

Suddenly I was the Amazing Fucking Kreskin. Once again, a very clear message came to me. I could not do it.

I finally had to admit it: I'd lost it. I'd lost the passion to write. Words flowed, but when I read them back, I was stunned to find them less than mediocre, exceedingly melodramatic, and ultimately good for only one thing: a shredder. A generous reviewer had once cleverly anointed me the Rumpelstiltskin of literature, claiming my prose to be "as captivating and alluring as spun gold." But now, every word I wrote immediately tarnished like tacky brass.

I needed inspiration. I needed escape—from Boston, from my life, and although I'd never say the words out loud, from Jenn. In the past, travel had always proven itself a reliable antidote for whatever ailed me, and ultimately drove me to excel. I began to research possibilities—privately at first. When I was ready, I brought the idea up with Jenn. Before I knew it, tickets were booked, bags were packed, and I was gone. Then, in a quirk of fate, so was my life. Everyone outside of the rectangle believed I was dead.

Only one person knew the truth. Asmae.

On the day of my great escape, I waited patiently for her. Unlike countless times before—when I'd hover by the door anticipating her arrival like a lovesick puppy, anxious for her company—I was now a predator, and she my unsuspecting prey. I planned as best I could. I'd been stockpiling non-perishable foodstuffs, a few days' supply of bread, and a canteen of water. I'd packed my meagre collection of personal belongings—toothbrush, soap—and a treasured souvenir: a chip off the stone pedestal on top of which I'd spent countless hours with Mikki, and then Asmae.

For several days I argued with myself about whether to make my big move during her morning visit or evening. Evening offered the protection of darkness as I made my getaway. If there were guards watching the rectangle, they were less likely to be vigilant late at night.

A morning escape had the potential advantage of giving me a greater head start. A young Berber woman living in the Atlas Mountains likely lived with family—maybe even a husband—or friends who looked after her wellbeing. If Asmae was to disappear, the alarm would be raised—but not until her routine was broken. Since she'd been staying with me, sometimes far into the night, to make love, anyone Asmae had in her life was used to her evening absences.

I could reasonably assume that Asmae's accepted daily schedule typically kept her from home until late. It wouldn't be until she failed to come home to sleep that someone would eventually notice.

I had no idea who Asmae really was. Although we'd become intimate and I'd grown fond of her, without the benefit of exchanging words we could only get so far in getting to know one another. For all I knew, Asmae could be Mrs. Hun, in on the whole thing. I hadn't seen either Hun since they'd dropped me off here. But that didn't mean they weren't out there somewhere, still pulling the strings that ran my life and ensured my imprisonment.

On the other hand, Asmae could be an innocent village girl who had inadvertently discovered me abandoned in my rectangle prison and decided to save me.

The truth was something I'd likely never know.

Like pretty much every one before it, the day I chose to liberate myself was stiflingly hot, the sky searing blue, the air as still as pond water. The sole access point into or out of the rectangle was the door through which Asmae arrived and departed. It locked on the outside. The only time the door was left unlocked was when Asmae was with me. During one of our first sexual encounters, I'd found the key hidden in a pocket, deep in the folds of her colorful kaftan, and stored the information away for later use.

I'd settled on an evening escape. I was counting on there being no one on the other side of the door. The way I figured it, why would it be locked if there was? If I was wrong, it didn't really matter. They'd kill me just as easily, day or night.

Hearing the telltale sounds of Asmae's approach, I quickly hid the rucksack I'd fashioned from old towels, and stood by the door in greeting, as I often did.

She smiled warmly when she entered. It nearly broke my heart to know I would soon break hers.

We wandered into the lean-to, where she laid out my meal—tonight a fish *tagine* with potatoes, tomatoes and green peppers, and a honey cake for dessert. After preparations were complete, Asmae's habit was to either leave immediately or she would sit. If she sat, which she now did more often than not, it was a sign that she intended to stay, and the evening would eventually lead to her joining me atop the pedestal.

I breathed a sigh of relief when she lowered herself to the ground. If she hadn't, I'd have had to make my move instantly, swiftly, and with greater force than I hoped would be necessary.

My plan was to gain my freedom that night with the least possible cost to Asmae. Only if she surprised me—with a show of resistance or a heretofore concealed weapon—would I be driven to commit the unthinkable. I had considered this for many anguished hours. How far was I willing to go to win back my liberty? If she stood in my way, would I turn to brutality? Would I murder the hand that had literally fed me?

My decisions that evening will haunt me for the rest of my days. Should I have done what I did? The way I did it? Should I have accepted the generosity of her provision in eating that last supper, the generosity of her heart in accepting her love? As we lay entwined one last time atop the stone pedestal, a mellow bath of moonlight melting over our naked bodies and drawing out hues of umber and cayenne from her skin, I found myself resisting the next step. I put off the inevitable by kissing the top of her head, her cheeks, her breasts, her soft shoulders. I watched, breath bated, as she found the spot where I'd chipped out a chunk of the rock as a keepsake, her tiny fingers questioning the imperfection in an otherwise smooth surface. A small frown passed fleetingly across her face, but she said nothing.

I questioned my resolve.

But there was no other way.

If I could have made her understand the words, "Will you come with me?" would I have spoken them?

I'll never know for sure.

Instead, as she closed her eyes for a brief rest, I pulled the key from the fabric of her dress, which we'd used to soften our nest. With one last, urgent kiss, like Prince Charming's awakening gift to Sleeping Beauty, I made my dastardly intentions known.

She opened her eyes.

I held the key aloft, its gold metallic edge catching the light.

Her reaction was startling, immediately plain and clear, and wholly probable and true to her noble, selfless spirit.
Slowly, with great assurance and wordless bounty, Asmae nodded her assent.

Perhaps she'd been waiting for me to do this exact thing all along. Perhaps she'd even told me to do it in words I didn't understand...or didn't want to understand. Perhaps this was the secret she had been trying to share with me all this time: Jaspar, you are set free.

PART II

Chapter 29

Sitting outside the modest but charming brownstone in suburban Boston, Katie Edwards was torn. The move she was about to make was a no-brainer. She had to do it. No question about it. But it wasn't going to be easy—not after all they'd been through together over the past months. She knew friendship and career were uneasy bedfellows; sooner or later, one had to crawl on top of the other.

The weather was bitingly cold. She adjusted the heater in her little car to its highest setting. Along with post-Christmas, mid-winter blues, January had brought with it spitefully low temperatures and almost daily snowfall. Katie blew warmth into the icy cocoon of her hands as she eyed up the house, unobtrusively perched in its peaceful neighborhood. You'd never know that less than six months ago the same lawn had been crawling with cameras, lights, reporters, and gawkers, the surrounding streets clogged for blocks by news vans and police vehicles. You'd never know that this was the home of arguably the most famous—and infamous—couple in all of Boston right now. The celebrated author and his lawyer wife (and Katie's friend) had been thrust into the glare of ceaseless media attention, thanks to the unthinkable abduction of their thirteen-year-old daughter, followed by an attempted murder shocker and a sizzling, scandal-a-minute trial. Every second of it with Katie Edwards as its public face.

And now this. It was unbelievable, really.

She had to go in there. But how? As friend? Reporter? Both?

Switching off the engine, she tightened the scarf around her neck and straightened the beret on her head. Grabbing her purse, Katie exited the car. She dashed up the familiar walkway and rang the bell.

Jennifer Wills looked awful. Her face was a pale, blotchy mess, her ordinarily smartly-styled blond hair struggling to stay in a topknot. She wore makeup, but today it looked as if it had been applied by a visually-impaired chimpanzee.

Like a marionette let loose from its strings, as soon as she saw Katie, Jenn crumpled into her arms and erupted into tears. Katie gently urged her friend inside, closing the door and bad weather behind them.

"I wasn't sure if you'd heard yet." Katie's voice was muffled by Jenn's heavy sweater. It smelled of her friend's favorite perfume and the warm mustiness that comes with being worn over and over again and, quite possibly, slept in more than once. "I came as soon as it started showing up on the news services."

Jenn pulled back and searched her friend's face. "What do you know? What *is* happening? The cops—or somebody—called, but they said they couldn't tell me much."

"Come on, let's sit down," Katie urged, drawing the other woman into the dim front room. A TV was flashing images of the breaking story, recounted by a young female reporter Katie recognized. Sinking to the couch, hands clasped together, the women listened.

"A local man being held captive in the North African country of Morocco has been identified as thirty-six-year-old Jaspar Wills. Wills is the author of the bestselling novel In The Middle, *which inspired the critically acclaimed movie of the same name.*

"Earlier today, Maghreb Arab Press, Morocco's official news agency, and the English language online newspaper, Morocco Newsline, were simultaneously contacted by someone claiming to represent Wills' kidnappers. Senator Richard Crawley's office has confirmed that the senator was informed of the abduction by the FBI.

"The kidnappers are demanding the release of Qasim Al-Harthi. Al-Harthi was sentenced to life in prison following a 2012 Marrakech bombing in which thirteen people were killed, including two Americans. Well known Islamist militant organization, Al Qaeda in the Islamic Maghreb, also known as AQIM, were widely blamed for the bombing. Al Qaeda denied responsibility for the blast, and allegations of Al-Harthi's connections to the organization were never proven.

"Tonight a U.S. State Department representative is calling the kidnapping a "very grave matter" and says "we are keeping Mr. Wills' family informed of any developments and taking every appropriate step."

"What does that mean?" Jenn cried, frustration seeping through every word. "They haven't informed me of anything. What appropriate steps are they talking about?"

"It's difficult to say," Katie responded, knowing that the first thing that leapt to mind was not what Jenn needed to hear: the United States government did not negotiate with terrorists. "It probably means they're trying to contact the kidnappers to figure out how to end this."

"We all know how well that goes!" Jenn spit out, her bitterness as sharp as claws. "Look at what 'trying to figure it out' did for Mikki. We lost her! And now I'm going to lose Jaspar too. Christ, Katie, why is this happening to us?"

Jenn buried her head in her hands. She hated the sound of her own voice. She was a lawyer, for God's sake. She was used to being the calm, collected one in times of high stress and tension. She was usually the one laser-focused on facts, logical next steps, resolution techniques. Now, instead, she was being weak, a blubbering mess, withering under pressure at a time when she most needed her wits about her.

"Jenn," Katie murmured, "we'll get through this."

Once again the two women embraced. It was far from an unusual stance for them. Since September, when Mikki was taken, Katie often found herself in the role of comforter—at first alongside Jaspar, and then in lieu of him during the fiercest days of the trial.

Glancing about the shadowy, sullen home, dread and grief pulsating from its walls, Katie thought about how many pots of tea she had brewed here, how many bottles of wine she'd brought over, and pizzas, and tub after tub of ice cream—whatever it took to calm the frayed nerves and anesthetize the anxiety of its inhabitants.

After a few minutes, Katie gently repositioned Jenn so that she was lying back against a pillow. Getting up, she retrieved a blanket from the back of the sofa and covered her friend, who was shaking as if she'd been left outside in an arctic storm. "I'll make some tea. And where's the thermostat? It's freezing in here," she lied.

"Why would they take him?" Jenn was not yet ready for warmth. "Why Jaspar, of all people? First our daughter is kidnapped, and now him? Is this some kind of crazy cosmic joke?"

Katie shrugged. "Why not him? He was in the wrong place at the right time. Traveling alone. American. Whoever the kidnappers are, they don't care about Jaspar, or you, or what the two of you have been through. They just care about getting what they want."

"What do they want? Why take an American? This man the kidnappers want released, he's Moroccan, in a Moroccan prison. What does that have to do with us? The U.S. can't do anything about it."

"Obviously they think we can. Pressure from the American government speaks loudly anywhere in the world. Maybe they're looking for vengeance, fame, political attention paid to their cause. By involving the U.S., they're guaranteed exposure. Who knows what they really want? It could be anything."

"They're not going to get it, though, are they?"

Their eyes held. The truth was unspeakable.

After a moment, Katie whispered, "I don't know." She watched as the other woman disappeared into a ball, knees braced against her chest, face buried in the quivering folds of her arms. "Do you still love him?"

Jenn looked up, her face puffy and patterned with the weave of her sweater. "Of course I do. Why would you ask that?"

"I just thought…with him leaving so suddenly…I thought maybe you two were…"

"Separating? Getting a divorce?"

Katie looked away. She knew it wasn't the best time for this conversation. But she was a reporter. Good reporters never shy away from asking tough questions in difficult situations, even when extenuating circumstances sometimes dictate they should. Like maybe now. Jenn was in pain. She needed Katie the friend, not Katie the reporter. But, damn it, she and Jenn never tiptoed around each other. It was probably one of the reasons they got along so well.

In the end, Jenn made the decision of whether or not to keep going down this road for both of them. "Because of what I did?" Jenn made it sound like a challenge. "You think Jaspar went to Morocco because I slept with Scott Walker?"

"I don't think anything." Katie made a move for the kitchen. "I'm going to get that tea."

"Wait, Katie. You need to know that I love Jaspar. With all my heart. I have since the first day I laid eyes on him. That's not the problem. The problem is…I'm afraid…I'm afraid he may stop loving me. He says he understands what happened between me and Scott." She attempted to hide a nervous laugh by swiping at her nose with a raggedy Kleenex. "But I don't know how he can. I don't even know what the hell I was doing, or why. I just…I just went a bit crazy for a while."

"A lot was going on." Katie abandoned the kitchen run, but remained standing, looking down at her friend.

"A lot was going on for him too," Jenn said, "but he didn't go out and have sex with a neighbor."

"It sounds like he forgave you."

Jenn's head moved back and forth, eyes blindly pinned to the TV screen. "No. He didn't. But he was trying to. He just needed to get away from all of this. That's why he went to Morocco. To clear his head, get back to writing. That's all he was trying to do. And look where it got him."

A shrill ring ripped through the room, an unwelcome intruder demanding attention.

"It's them," Jenn said, staring at the telephone, her voice deadened. "I can tell. It's like before. They'll never stop calling."

Katie knew "them" also included her. The media had caught wind of the news. It had been months since Mikki's disappearance and the sensational trial that followed it. Everything about the child's kidnapping had been meaty and juicy, like a plump, well-marinated tenderloin, spitting and hissing atop a piping hot grill. Eventually, as with any story, the smorgasbord had come to an end. Newshounds directed their attentions elsewhere, looking for something fresher and tastier. But now, what a twist: Abducted girl's famous father kidnapped! Impossible to resist.

"Do you want me handle it?" Katie asked.

Jenn nodded, massaging her throbbing temples as another talking head on TV breathlessly described to a rapt audience the developing details in what was sure to become a major news bonanza.

As Katie reached for the telephone, mentally preparing to take on the familiar role of family spokesperson, her eyes were drawn to the screen. Audiovisual experts had already pulled up an impressive array of stock photography and video—Jaspar being interviewed following Mikki's kidnapping, Jaspar's most recent book jacket head shot, Jaspar on a national talk show—the story all the more enthralling because it involved a celebrity, one who was young, handsome, and tragic. Katie knew what sold in the world of TV. This was going to be pure gold.

Chapter 30

Six months later

"In a shocking turn to the story that has captivated the nation since September of last year, when his thirteen-year-old daughter was kidnapped and held for ransom, bestselling author Jaspar Wills surprised the world late last week when he surfaced at a police station in Marrakech, after having been presumed dead following his own abduction by terrorists in Morocco five-and-a-half months ago." Inwardly, Katie scowled at whoever had written the run-on sentence she'd just recited off the teleprompter. At the same time, she gave the camera a nuanced look, one she'd perfected over the past months: a look that compelled viewers to listen to her, trust her, feel deeply about what she was telling them.

"It's a complex, heart-wrenching story that tore a family apart. A story that finally has..." she paused here, looking off camera for barely a millisecond, then, "...if not an entirely happy ending, at least the beginnings of a silver lining around a very stormy cloud. Jaspar Wills and his wife, Jennifer, have joined us here today, in their first public interview since Jaspar's return home this past weekend. Jaspar, Jenn, welcome."

The camera panned wider to show the couple next to Katie, sitting in separate chairs positioned close together. Katie reached for Jaspar, who was nearest, and squeezed his hand. The audience would not be surprised at this show of intimacy between interviewer and subject—they expected it. Katie Edwards, since the early days of Mikki Wills' kidnapping, had been their eyes, ears, and heart when it came to anything to do with the Wills. In the beginning, she'd been relatively unknown on the Boston news scene—unless you happened to be one of the handful of people who read her chatty articles published in a fledgling weekly, or caught her late-night weather reports on a local, non-network, basement-budget, ratings-challenged TV station. But that was then. This was now.

A lot had changed for Katie Edwards in the past ten months. To some, it appeared as if she'd been thrust into the limelight with the same urgent, uncontrollable ferocity as the Wills had been—all by virtue of her pre-existing relationship with the couple.

In the not-so-dark corners of bars frequented by reporters, news writers, and all manner of newshounds, the grumblings could easily be overheard about Edwards' dumb luck at being in the right place at the right time with the right friends, propelling the inexperienced newcomer to dizzying heights of success far exceeding her abilities. The same snarks begrudgingly agreed the rookie had that "something special" that viewers fell for, but there was no excusing the fact that she'd leapfrogged over way too many hurdles way too fast. Hurdles that novice journalists were meant to scratch and claw their way over, as a kind of boot camp, necessary to earn your stripes in the world of serious journalism—and the respect of your contemporaries.

According to these colleagues, Katie Edwards had neglected to pay her dues. She'd become famous overnight only because of her insider access to the city's hottest story, a story that refused to die. A story that, even in its death throes, had suddenly reinvented itself and grabbed the world's attention all over again.

Katie did not entirely disagree with her detractors. She knew it was delusional to contend that she'd gone from a nearly bankrupt, nobody freelancer, to a popular beat reporter for a local news channel, to an on-air personality for a major network affiliate, all in under a year, just because of how good she was. Yes, she'd hopped over the velvet rope. Yes, it was because of her close relationship with the players in the juiciest story around. Sure, she'd grasped the gold ring under somewhat fluky circumstances. But, goddammit, she didn't still have a firm hold on it for the same reasons. She was smart. She was talented. People loved her.

Creating her own opportunities was nothing new for Katie. Ever since she'd single-handedly turned her pitiful high school newspaper into must-read material, Katie knew she had a knack for identifying the stories people *really* wanted to be told and *how* to tell them.

"I know this is going to be difficult for you," Katie told the couple, soothing and sympathetic, "having to re-live everything you've been through for our audience. I want to thank you for agreeing to do so. I know our viewers appreciate it too."

Jaspar cleared his throat and responded, "We know people are interested in our story. We're grateful for the support they've shown us, all the messages and prayers. But Katie, we want to be clear: this will be the last time we speak about this publicly."

"All we want is to go back to our normal lives," Jenn added. "Now that Jaspar is home, we want to try as best we can to move on."

Katie's gaze slid into the camera. "Sadly, Jaspar and Jenn will be moving on without their beautiful daughter, Mikki, at their side. For those of you just joining us, or unfamiliar with their story, I'm here with Jaspar and Jennifer Wills. Last September, while walking home from school on a sunny, tree-lined street in the safe, upper middle-class suburban Boston neighborhood where she lived with her parents, thirteen-year-old Mikki Wills was abducted." Katie knew that behind her and on TV screens across the country, a cornucopia of visual gems was being displayed. Images of a beautiful, golden-haired princess: Mikki Wills. Gone. Vanished. Only the hardest hearts would be left unaffected.

"Ten months later, Mikki is still missing. During the course of negotiations, communication with Mikki's kidnappers was suddenly and inexplicably cut off. Jaspar and Jenn never heard from Mikki or her abductors again." She waited a beat to allow the devastating facts to soak in. "In January, Mikki's father traveled to Morocco, where another unthinkable tragedy awaited. But first,

Jaspar, can you tell us about the purpose of your trip—and why Morocco?"

Jaspar responded with his carefully prepared statement. "Of course. I made the trip to Morocco for work, to research a new book I was planning to write."

Katie nodded, giving the camera a few seconds of silence to feast on the author's wan, hollowed-out face. Once again the experts behind the scenes knew just what to do. They'd moved to a split screen, one half showing the ravaged man currently sitting next to Katie, the other showing a slideshow of images—at first playing up the handsome, hardy, famous author everyone knew from ten months earlier. Then, as the story progressed and grew grisly and disturbing, so too would the images of Jaspar Wills. They would show the series of pictures released by his kidnappers in an effort to convince the U.S. government to do their bidding. Pictures of a sad and frightened man, a man bound and bloody and beaten to within an inch of his life. The metamorphosis was nothing short of shocking.

"Can you tell us what happened when you first arrived in Marrakech?"

"I'd arranged for a car to take me to my hotel. When it didn't arrive, I hired a taxi."

Glancing at the camera, Katie reported: "In the taxi, Jaspar eventually began to realize he wasn't being taken to his hotel." Doing little to disguise a shiver, she added, "I know for anyone who's ever traveled to a foreign country, this is their worst nightmare. You expect things to work the way they do here in the United States. You expect a cab driver to take you where you ask them...*pay them*...to. You expect to be safe. Jaspar, tell us what happened next."

"I'd never been to Marrakech before, so I was unfamiliar with the city and where we were going. But eventually I started to wonder if something was wrong."

"What was it that made you suspicious?"

"The trip was taking too long. We were heading into a part of the city where it didn't seem likely a hotel would be."

"What were you feeling at that moment—the moment you knew something wasn't right?"

"Well, at first I was irritated. I thought, this guy is taking me on a joyride to up the fare. I asked him where we were going. But he wouldn't answer me. It was hot. I was exhausted from the long trip. I thought maybe I was being paranoid. But as time passed, I became increasingly concerned and…"

"Were you frightened?"

"Yes."

"What then?"

"Again, I confronted the driver. I asked him where he was taking me. When he wouldn't answer, I demanded to be let out of the car. Which, as it turns out, was a mistake."

"Why was that?"

"He had a gun. He hit me on the head…I think with the gun. I must have been knocked out cold, because the next thing I knew I was waking up in a dark room."

"Were you in pain? Had you been beaten?"

"Yes…no. I mean yes, I was in pain, from the wound on my head where he'd hit me. But the real beatings didn't start until later, for the proof-of-life photographs…"

Katie interrupted. "For our viewers who may not be familiar with proof-of-life photographs, what can happen in these situations—when someone is kidnapped and demands are made as conditions of release—a common first step is for negotiators to establish that the kidnap victim is still alive. The abductors are asked to prove this, often by means of what is known as a proof-of-life photograph. Somewhere in the photograph will be a dated document, like a newspaper, to prove the victim is alive as of that date." Behind Katie the scroll showed Jaspar, worsening in condition with each passing photograph, holding up a newspaper. "In Jaspar's case, the kidnappers were demanding the release of a young man named Qasim Al-Harthi.

"Back in 2012, a bomb exploded in a popular café in Marrakech, the same city where Jaspar Wills was abducted," Katie announced, now in full reporter mode. "The blast killed thirteen people, including two Americans." On screen, images pulled from archives followed the narrative. "Soon after the bombing, six suspects were apprehended near the café and charged with the murders. Among them was twenty-three-year-old Al-Harthi, who was later tried and sentenced to death.

"Al-Harthi's family and supporters, however, believe the young man was convicted based on eyewitness reports manufactured by the police. They claimed that none of the witnesses brought forth by the defense were allowed to testify. They suggested the Moroccan government was only interested in a speedy conviction in order to mollify the United States and other home countries of victims killed or injured in the explosion. To this day, they contend that the real criminals were never apprehended." Katie's attention shifted back to Jaspar. "Were you aware of any of this while you were being held?"

"No. During my initial incarceration, the only people I was in contact with were my captors: two men, neither of whom spoke English. I had no idea what was going on. When they took the first proof-of-life photograph, I guessed there had to be some kind of ransom involved. But I had no way of knowing what they were asking for, from whom, or why."

Katie's eyes hinted to the audience that what was coming next wasn't good. "As frustrating as that must have been for you, things were about to become considerably worse, weren't they?"

"Yes. To say the least. Throughout the ordeal, I was in a constant state of uncertainty. I feared what might happen next. It was like knowing you're going to fall, but not when or how far."

"Horrible."

"Yes, it was. Sometimes I wouldn't see the two men for a day or more. Sometimes their visits were only hours apart. But each time, I could tell by their faces and voices that something was going wrong. Of course I couldn't understand them, but it was obvious to me that they weren't getting what they wanted. That was when the beatings began."

"Until then, had they treated you well?"

Jaspar shrugged. "I wouldn't go that far. I had very little food or water. It was extremely hot in the room. I often felt as if I was about to faint. And I probably did. I can't be sure, because after a while time became a blur. Especially once the beatings began. There was no time to recover between attacks, so the pain and my wounds just got worse and worse. Each time they beat me was more violent than the last. They wanted blood and gore; they wanted whoever was seeing those pictures to know they meant business."

Perfectly timed, the final proof-of-life picture America ever saw of Jaspar Wills filled viewers' screens. Although many of the people in the studio that day had seen the image before, an inaudible shockwave reverberated through the room, followed by a gasp, and then pulsating silence.

Immediately prior to the broadcast, the network had issued a warning declaring certain content about to be aired to be graphic and not suitable for all viewers. The bloodied, bloated, bruised face before them now was why.

Oddly enough, the image was less familiar to its subject than to most of the rest of the country. Jaspar studied the larger than life face staring out at him from the screen behind Katie, and tried to remember wearing that mask. But nothing came. Perhaps if he'd seen himself in a mirror at the time—that horrifying image, the wasted face and dead eyes—the memory might have been stronger. Instead, for him, the day that photograph had been taken had been just another in a string of days that, by then, he was convinced were leading to his death. This was a picture of a man who was dying. His mind, heart, soul—everything that had once been Jaspar Wills— was entirely disengaged, exorcised from the crumbling physical shell. This was a man prepared to face whatever came after life.

Hearing a stifled sob next to him, Jaspar dragged his attention away from the thing on the screen and comforted his wife as best he could.

Katie, eyes glistening, lips tight, swung back toward the camera dedicated solely to her. "The final, public statement by the American government on this matter came as a shock to everyone— especially Jaspar's wife, Jenn. It read as follows: '…while the United

States, along with Moroccan government officials, have cooperated fully in talks with the hostage takers in order to secure the release of American citizen Jaspar Wills, communications have been abruptly cut off and all further attempts to resuscitate them have failed. Exhaustive investigations by the U.S. military and intelligence communities, while still ongoing, indicate that Mr. Wills is *irretrievable*." Katie visibly winced as she looked at her two guests. "Irretrievable," she gravely repeated. "Jenn, that must be one of the most devastating words to hear about your missing husband. Can you tell us about that?"

Jenn nodded. "I can't even begin to explain how it felt. Basically they were telling me that my husband was dead, they had no idea where he was, his body was lost, never to be found, and there was nothing they could do about it."

Katie turned to Jaspar. "Your wife and family are at home, believing you are dead, planning your funeral. Jaspar, can you tell us what really happened next?"

Jaspar fixed Katie with a direct gaze, and stated: "I died."

Chapter 31

The screen went black.

"Jaspar?" Jenn shifted in her regular spot on the sofa to look at her husband. Sitting on the coffee table in front of them was a half-empty bottle of red wine and a pizza, homemade by Katie, uneaten and nearly cold. "Why did you turn it off?"

"Some of the best stuff is coming up," Katie pressed. She was sitting in an armchair, re-positioned next to the couch for better viewing of the television. "The story about the Berber woman who saved your life, and then how you hitchhiked into Marrakech and turned up at the police station. It's terrific stuff, Jaspar, really good."

"I don't want to see it," he responded, leaning over to refill his wine glass. "I meant it when I said that interview was the last of it. It's over. We need to forget about all of this. We have to start letting it go."

Jenn's response was a guffaw weighed down by heavy doubt. "I think we'll be waiting a while before that happens. Unless we completely stop watching TV, using our iPhones, listening to radio, reading newspapers. After Katie's broadcast tonight, it's all people will be talking about for weeks."

"I know," Jaspar relented. "And I know we had to do it. But the beast will only get bigger if we feed it. Otherwise it eventually starves and goes away. Isn't that right, Katie? You know how it works."

Katie's look was noncommittal. "Eventually," she allowed. "I totally get what you're saying, Jaspar. After a year of this shit, and everything you've been through physically and mentally, you *need* to let this go." She picked up a limp piece of pizza, then immediately put it back. "I want you two to know how grateful I am that you trusted me to tell your story. Besides, the more people who associate me with the story instead of you, the better it is, right?"

"You should have some before it gets stone cold," Jenn indicated the pizza. "After all, you made it. You should get to eat some."

Jaspar rose and switched on an overhead light to brighten the dreariness that had settled over the room. "I'll get more wine." He headed for the kitchen.

Katie waited until he was gone before asking, "Do you think he's doing okay?"

Jenn shrugged. "Hard to tell. He just got back. This is all happening so fast. Too fast. But he's the one who wanted it done this way. You know I wanted to wait before doing the interview. But he wanted it over and done with." She took a thoughtful sip of wine. "Still, he's not talking much. And then of course there's the elephant in the room."

Katie was mildly surprised at this admission of the elephant's existence. She thought she was the only one who could feel its trunk tightening around the house, squeezing out every last bit of air, making it almost impossible to breathe. "You mean whether or not he's going to stay? Here? With you?"

Jenn nodded. "I guess it's a good sign that when he came back, he came back *here*. But really, where else does he have to go? Is he here because he wants to be, or because he has to be? Right now, I don't think I want to know the answer. So until he's stronger, I don't want to push things."

Katie had sensed the push and pull between the couple— two people whose love for one another had always been abundantly obvious to anyone who spent time with them. But now, after months of tragedy upon betrayal upon physical separation, it was a miracle they were able to hold things together as well as they were. "Maybe he wants to be pushed," she tried. "Maybe it's like the interview. Maybe he needs to deal with all this shit right now. Get it over with, then get over it. Maybe you both need that. Push him, Jenn. It's time."

Jenn stared at her friend, surprised at the comment, caught off guard by the idea. Katie had come to her a year-and-a-half ago as a new client, fresh from a bad break-up with a long-term boyfriend who'd left her high and dry. He'd taken everything, even their cat. She didn't care about the "stuff," she'd said, but she really wanted that cat back. Unfortunately, with Massachusetts not recognizing common law relationships, there was little Jenn could do for her. From that frail beginning, their short-lived professional relationship had somehow morphed into friendship. During that time, Jenn had come to suspect that Katie had a dark, wounded side when it came to men—and here was another sign of it.

Jaspar was back, topping up glasses. No one was touching the food.

"Jaspar," Katie began, "this might not be the right time to bring this up...or maybe it's the perfect time, I dunno."

Jenn nearly choked on her freshly-poured wine as she listened to the words spilling out of Katie's mouth. She'd thought they'd been talking in abstractions, possibilities for an uncertain time in the future—not *right now.*

Katie kept on. "It kind of goes along with what you said about wanting to wash your hands of all this. It mainly concerns you, Jaspar, but I wanted to bring it up with both of you here."

Jenn, a questioning eye searching the other woman, held on to a sigh of relief until she was certain it was deserved.

"First, you should know the idea wasn't mine. I was approached by someone."

"What's this about?" Jaspar, as confused as Jenn, asked while settling into his seat.

"Of course I immediately thought you'd be the best person to do it, not me. But now, well, maybe that's not the case."

"What idea are you talking about?" Jenn asked, swallowing more red wine than she probably needed.

"A book." Katie let the two words sit in the room for a second or two, using the time to gauge reactions. If there was one thing she was good at, it was measuring the mood of her audience. Jenn was perplexed, Jaspar uncomfortable.

"What are you talking about?" Jaspar's voice was uncharacteristically harsh. "What book?"

"Your book," Katie said. "Yours and Jenn's. And Mikki's. Your story."

"Somebody asked you what exactly?"

"If I'd write it."

"What?" Jenn knew she sounded incredulous, but didn't care. "You?"

"I know," Katie quickly countered. "Crazy, right? Jaspar's the famous author. He should do it. Of course he should do it. That's what I told them."

"My publisher already asked me," Jaspar said, downing a healthy swig. "Not recently, of course, but after the trial. They wanted the story even back then, before the rest of this crap happened. I told them no. Then I tried to write it anyway."

"You did?" Jenn asked, still not sure what was happening. She wondered if maybe she'd had too much to drink.

"I tried. I couldn't do it then. I can't do it now."

"That's what I'm thinking," Katie chattered on. "Not that you can't, but that you shouldn't. Not if you want to get away from all of this. But you know how it works, Jaspar—they're not going to let it go. It's too good a story. For a book. Even a movie. If you don't do it, someone else will." Katie hesitated, counted to five, then: "Maybe… maybe it *should* be me. With your help, of course. I'd need your input." She turned to Jenn for support. "And yours too. We'd only put out there what you want out there. It's the perfect way to end this, once and for all. On your terms, but without having to relive it all over again."

In an instant, the atmosphere in the room changed. The air sparked with electricity, like a storm about to hit—fed by Jaspar, but sensed by all. Katie grew wary, Jenn bewildered.

"Get the fuck out of here!" Jaspar was on his feet, roaring. "Get out!"

Jenn's body pressed back against the sofa, aghast at her husband's sudden ferocity. Katie leaned in, ears perked, attracted to the outburst, but at the same time thinking: *Where the hell is this coming from?*

"Now! Out!" Jaspar menaced, inching closer to Katie as if he was about to physically pick her up and throw her through the front window if she didn't move. "I want you out of this house. You're nothing but a soul-sucking user, and I want you gone."

"Jaspar!" Jenn cried out as she leapt from the couch, only partially recuperated from her initial shock. "What is wrong with you? Why are you being like this?"

Katie rose too—slowly, like an attacked animal, instinctively knowing she needed to be on even ground to stand any chance of survival. "Jaspar, exactly what is the problem here?"

"You know damn well what the problem is, Katie Edwards, star of network news. Haven't you paved your road with enough of our blood and tears? Isn't your career big enough yet? Or do you need something else horrible to happen to us?"

Rows of silent consternation furrowed Katie's brow. She felt for these people, she really did. She knew Jaspar had been to hell and back and somehow lived to tell about it. But none of that gave him the right to treat her like some kind of predatory bottom feeder. She got enough of that at work and from social media.

"Ever since Mikki was taken, you've done nothing but use us," Jaspar rallied on. "You've built your entire fucking livelihood out of our misery. And now you want to keep on doing it by writing a book about us. Not only do you want to take advantage of my dead daughter and my dead marriage, now you want to take over my dead career too!"

"Jaspar!" Jenn screamed, tears streaming down burning cheeks.

Katie was silent, listening carefully.

"Well, you're never going to have it. There is no way I'm going to allow you to have any more of this story—for TV, for some fucking book, or in your fucking goddamned dreams—do you understand me? It's over!"

Katie understood all too well. She'd have to change the book she'd already started. But that was an easy fix. All she had to do was add one word to the title: unauthorized.

Chapter 32

When the phone rang, Katie debated letting it go to message. She'd just gotten in. Spread-eagled on the bed and soaked to the bone with sweat, she wanted nothing more than rest—and hotel air conditioning. It had been a good day. She'd talked to scores of people throughout the *medina*, leaving them flyers with Jaspar's picture and her contact information should anyone want to…*Shit!* She jumped out of bed and grabbed the phone. Her first lead could be calling right now!

"Hello? Kate Edwards here."

"Kate," the voice on the other end growled. "What the fuck is going on? Did you know about this?"

It was Carl Daum, her agent. Unlike her employer, he'd fully supported her taking an unscheduled, five-day absence from her on-air responsibilities to fly to Morocco to research the book. She was using up vacation days, so it wasn't like the station was paying for her absenteeism. Still, they weren't pleased to have their popular new "face of the evening news" suddenly out of the picture. In conciliation, she'd promised them big things—the least of which was major buzz when their star anchor published a book brimming with first-hand, never-before-revealed details about the biggest story to hit Boston—hell, the whole state; maybe even the country—in a decade.

People were desperate for juicy, behind-the-scenes secrets. And everyone knew that Kate Edwards was just the person to deliver them. She'd been in the know and on the front lines from the harrowing first hours of Mikki Wills' disappearance right up to the final hours of Jaspar Wills' escape from his own kidnapping drama in Morocco. The story had everything. A missing child. International intrigue. Mystery. Celebrity. Violence. Sex.

Heartbreak. Betrayal. Could any book be better positioned for the top of every bestseller list in the country? Katie didn't think so.

There was only one problem: *getting* the first-hand, never-before-revealed details. Since that horrible night, when Jaspar made it abundantly clear that he would not be cooperating with her on the book, Katie knew she was on her own. She had to get something new, something flashy, something big. To guarantee the book's place on every must-read list, she had to dig up intimate facts about Jaspar's time in Marrakech—something no other blog, current affairs program, or clever reporter had yet uncovered.

She had one thing going for her: big story or not, times were tough. No one was willing to foot the bill to send a news team to Africa on an exploratory mission. No one, that is, but Kate Edwards.

This was her next best chance to climb another rung up the ladder of success. Each one had been successively more difficult to reach than the last, but so what? Nothing worthwhile was easy to get. Katie was ready for a big move. No more local hoo-ha. No more network affiliate. It was time to reach for the stars. She wanted permanent national exposure. If her take on the Jaspar Wills story worked out the way she planned, she'd be on her way—perhaps even eclipsing the fame of her subject. She didn't need Jaspar to make this happen. It would have been easier, she had to admit—but, like everything else she'd accomplished in life so far, she could, and would, do it on her own.

Five days wasn't a lot of time. Katie knew she had to go hard. She'd need to shake bushes, dig in dirt, employ feminine wiles or even bribery—whatever worked to achieve her goal. Five days was the longest she could stay away from work, and most definitely the longest she could put off her responsibilities at home. In five days she had to catch a big fish and reel it in. Nothing less than a whopper would be acceptable. She was feeling the stress—and so, apparently, was her agent.

"Carl, I don't know what you're talking about. I'm on another continent, for Pete's sake. So why don't you calm down and tell me what's up?"

"What's up? What's up? Check your messages, why don't you? Then you'll know what's up."

Katie scrambled for her iPhone. "I've been out all day, I haven't…" She stopped short when she saw the unusually long roster of messages on the screen. Publisher. Publisher. Agent. Publisher. TV station. Publisher. TV station. Publisher. Agent. Agent…A cold tremor of worry slithered up her spine. "What is this? What's going on? Just tell me."

"You know the highly-anticipated, behind-the-scenes, tell-all book you're over there researching?"

"Carl, if you don't fucking spit it out right now, I swear…"

"You got it, sweetheart. That book you're writing? That book we promised to deliver to the publisher in return for big bucks…of which I get ten percent? That book you're missing valuable on-air time for? Well, that book is coming out in hardcover next month."

For a moment, Katie was too stunned to speak. "Wh-what? Did…how can that be? I don't even have a first draft finished. How can they publish what I haven't even written yet? A month isn't enough time. I've never written a full-length book before. You have to negotiate."

"Don't worry about it, sweetheart," he reassured, his tone anything but soothing. "Because somebody else is writing it for you."

"What?" Katie pulled the phone away from her ear, looking at it as if Carl had suddenly begun to spout gibberish. After a long, hot day of dealing with people, most of whom she could barely understand, her patience was wearing dangerously thin. She took a deep breath, swiped a hand across her slick forehead, and then said, "I don't think I heard you right. What did you say? Exactly who is doing what?"

"Jaspar Wills, that's who. Jaspar Wills is writing the book, that book, your book. Now it's his book."

Wedging the hotel phone into the crook between her shoulder and her neck, Katie frantically began punching buttons on her iPhone. "That can't be," she argued. "He swore to me he wasn't going to write about this. That's the only reason I agreed to do it.

That's why the publishers agreed. That's why I'm in this fucking sweat lodge of a country being jostled about by unwashed hordes and eating couscous and lamb *tagine* until I puke!"

She stopped dead when she saw it. Amazon. The online retailer was already listing Jaspar Wills' upcoming book, *Set Free*, available for pre-order. "Oh. God." The two words came out as a tortured whisper.

"I hope you were wearing protection, honey," Daum said mercilessly. "Because it looks like your best friend and confidant just screwed you royally. And, worst of all, me too. I suggest you forget about your research and the fuckin' couscous, and catch a plane back here so you can prepare yourself for what you're *really* going to do next."

Katie fell back on the bed, eyes closed tight. "What's that?"

"What you do best, sweetheart: a live, prime time, network interview with Jaspar Wills to talk about *his* newest bestseller."

Katie blanched at the words, simultaneously replaying the vivid memory of being verbally and nearly physically assaulted by Jaspar, right before he kicked her out of his house. And now they were supposed to appear on live TV together? How was that going to work? A few times since the altercation, Jenn had lamely attempted to broker peace between the two, but Jaspar wouldn't budge. In the weeks that had passed, he'd steadfastly refused to see her or talk to her about the book or anything else. Now she knew why. He was planning to betray her all along.

"Screw that," she bawled into the phone. "I'm staying right here and getting my story. There's something good here, I know it."

"Yeah, there is," Carl agreed. "And Jaspar Wills has a first-person account of it. He was in the front seat of this thing, Kate, not you. How can you possibly do better than that?" he reasoned.

"I don't know, Carl. I just feel it. There's something here. I just have to dig deeper. I know you took a chance on making this deal with the publisher. I'm not going to disappoint you. I'll be back next Monday like I planned. I'm going to bring back a big story and everyone is going to go crazy over it. Maybe I can't write and publish a book in a month's time, but I've got millions of people sitting in their living rooms, just waiting to hear what I have to say. If I put this thing together right, if I sell it right, every publisher is going to be shitting their pants wanting to cash in on it."

She could hear the big man breathing heavily. She could picture him sitting behind his desk, belly protruding over his lap more than ever since he'd quit smoking cold turkey. He'd given up cigarettes, but not the heavy glass ashtray on his desk—which he was probably caressing right now, a pathetic replacement habit. "Yeah, well," he grumbled, "you better dig real deep and get something real good, real fast. I'll get on the horn with the publisher and make nice. I'm sure they're about as happy as a blind mouse in a cat house right now."

Katie smiled. "Thank you, Carl."

She hung up just as another call came in.

"Hello?"

"This is the journalist, Kate Edwards?" Heavy French accent.

"Yes, it is."

"I am Mehdi Ahmadi. I know about your friend."

"My friend?"

At first Katie worried she'd lost the connection, but then: "Jaspar Wills. I find him."

After the news she'd just had, she hadn't thought she'd be capable of it for a very long time, but Katie was definitely smiling as she mouthed the word: bingo.

Chapter 33

Jemaa el Fna, *hammam*-level steamy even well past dusk, was a dizzying carnival of food vendors, storytellers, snake charmers, acrobats, musicians, entertainers, and petty criminals. Katie struggled through the crowds to one end of the massive market square. She knew *calèches* congregated there, waiting for someone like her—someone who had no idea how to get to where they were going, and willing to pay a premium to do so.

The man on the phone, Mehdi Ahmadi, had asked to meet her in the *medina*. When Katie had first arrived in Marrakech, confident in her typically superb navigational skills, she'd made the newcomer's mistake of attempting to locate an address within the old city's writhing mess of narrow streets, twisting lanes, and goat paths. She'd gotten hopelessly lost and struggled to find her way out for hours. Today she didn't have the luxury of wasting time. Even if the place ended up being only a short distance away, she now understood that traversing a block in the famed *medina* of Marrakech is not even remotely the same thing as traversing a block in pretty much any other city in the world.

Particularly during peak periods, drivers of the horse-drawn cabs were notorious for turning down short-haul fares in the hope of securing something longer, like the *medina* wall tours that tourists were suckers for. Money was the only key to getting what you wanted. Katie marched up to the first man in line and immediately handed over one hundred and twenty *dirham*—about twelve dollars—no bargaining attempted. Along with the money, she gave him a sheet of paper indicating the address she was looking for. He shrugged, barked something at the next guy in line, and then helped her into the cab.

As the sorry-looking pair of horses skillfully maneuvered the chaos of other carriages, speeding motorbikes and scooters, donkey-led delivery wagons, jostling locals, and overwhelmed tourists who weren't looking where they were going, Katie sat back and pulled in a deep, calming breath, the first of the day.

In the failing light of early evening, the *calèche* appeared deceptively cheery. Its brightly-painted exterior was festooned with beaded streamers and clusters of plastic flowers, the interior made cozy by patchwork throws tacked to the walls and strewn across bench seats. The telltale light of day would reveal the artifice. The carriage was rickety and in poor repair, the inside torn and faded and filthy from scores of dusty journeys through the city's sun-soaked streets. Still, there was something magical about the experience. A ride in the *calèche* was like floating inside a bubble. From within its unruffled, relaxing parallel universe, one could idly observe the pandemonium and tumult of the massive market square outside, all of it whizzing by as if in double time.

The driver was no slouch. With generous fare already in hand, it behooved him to deliver Katie to her destination as fast as possible. The sooner he dumped her, the sooner he could return to the *medina* and the possibility of flossing another silly American tourist. Instead of driving through the colorful circus, the *calèche* operator immediately directed his horses out of Jemaa el Fna and down the quieter perimeter road encircling the orange-red clay ramparts of the old city, only zipping back inside when nearing their destination. Within fifteen minutes the carriage shuddered to a stop.

"Is this it?" They were halfway down a narrow, poorly-lit street. Katie was not at all certain she should get out.

The driver pointed to a door in the nearest building and grunted something she couldn't make out. Only half-turning in his seat, he returned the paper with the address on it, swiveled back, and yanked up the hood of his *djellaba*. Quite clearly their time together was over. Gathering her courage, Katie stepped out of the cab into the street. Only as the horses and carriage moved off did she wonder: *How the hell am I going to get back to the hotel*?

She'd have to think about that later. For now, she had plenty of other things to worry about.

Despite lights and reasonable foot traffic at either end, the street itself was dark and eerily noiseless. The door the driver had pointed out bore no distinguishing markings or numbers matching the address Ahmadi had given her. With no obvious alternative, Katie knocked on it—timidly at first, and then stronger.

What do I do if no one answers? Where do I go for help? She checked her phone. No bars. *Shit.*

Trying to ignore the mistake of not having done so a wee bit earlier, Katie reviewed her predicament. Was all of this pure idiocy—agreeing to meet a stranger, in a strange place, at night, without telling a soul where she was going? It wasn't like her to allow herself to spin so far out of control. It was, she realized, a sign of how desperate she'd become. She needed to find something, anything, to make her trip to Marrakech worthwhile—to redeem herself in a plot gone bad.

When there was no response after a full minute, she tried the doorknob. It turned. She pushed and found herself entering a miniscule alcove with barely enough lighting to see her hand in front of her. To the left was an opening with improved illumination. Gentle, rhythmic drumming, and fragrant wafts of something delicious being cooked nearby, beckoned her.

She stepped forward, placing each foot carefully in front of the other. As the space revealed itself, Katie came to realize she was in some kind of restaurant. She stopped at what might be a hostess station, and waited. Seated on a low stool nearby was an elderly man, gnarled fingers dancing across the top of a small, round drum. He was accompanied by a second, younger man, strumming a strange-looking stringed instrument. Katie's mouth watered as the symphony of spicy aromas grew stronger.

The greeting came first in Arabic, then in French, and finally in broken English.

"I was told I'd find Mehdi Ahmadi here?" Katie responded.

Not knowing what else to do, she thrust the paper with the address on it toward the young man who'd approached her. Briefly studying it, he looked up, his smile dazzling in the dim surroundings. "This address is for the back door. I show you."

That wasn't the back door?

Katie's head swirled with unhappy thoughts as she followed the man outside and down an alley she hadn't noticed before. It was barely wide enough to pass through without turning sideways. Once again, Katie began questioning the wisdom of what she was doing.

Trust your gut, she advised herself. *Trust your gut.*

In a quivering voice that did little to instill confidence, her gut responded: *Keep going.*

Eventually the man came to a halt. With a shove of his shoulder, he forced open a door that, from Katie's perspective, hadn't been there a second ago. He shouted something to whoever was inside, then, with another of his beguiling smiles, was gone.

"Salam?" a man appeared in the doorway. By his smocked getup, Katie guessed he was a restaurant employee—probably a dishwasher or cook.

"Mehdi Ahmadi?"

He nodded. He was quite young, just out of his teens at most, very thin, and suffered from a bad case of acne. "You are she?" he asked.

"I'm Kate Edwards. You called me on the phone. You said you knew something about Jaspar Wills?"

More nodding. He shot a glance over his shoulder, as if to check whether anyone could overhear their conversation. He moved into the alley, closing in on Katie, but saying nothing. Large eyes dug into hers, as if trying to communicate telepathically.

"What is it?" Katie asked after an uncomfortable silence. "What do you know about my friend?"

He cast about nervously, then: "You have money?"

Now she understood. It was bribe time. Katie had nothing against bribery. She respected both sides of the equation. It was simple market economics. One side was looking for valuable information; the other had it to sell. But here was the rub. She had no idea what she was there to buy. Her boss, her agent, her publisher—they were all right. What story could she hope to uncover in Marrakech that Jaspar himself, the man who'd personally lived the nightmare, didn't already have to tell?

Sure, Jaspar could share whatever transcendent, spiritual, or emotional journey he decided to create for his fans. But Katie might just have something better: cold hard facts. Sometimes left buried deep beneath softer, prettier surfaces, facts were the real glittering gold for an investigative journalist. Digging up the truth had always been Katie's specialty. Packaged the right way, facts can sell just as well, if not better. Jaspar could recount how he'd been taken from the Marrakech airport—but who took him? Why? What was going on in their world to drive them to make such a drastic, reckless move? Where did the kidnappers take him? Where did they hold him? Where did they transport him after the kidnapping was rendered a failure? Who saw something? Who knew something? Were the kidnappers scared? Crazy? Righteous? Were they zealots, greedy, or just plain stupid? All she needed was something real, something factual, something solid, and she'd be on her way to hitting a home run.

"No," she told him, forcing her voice to sound authoritative. She couldn't let this guy get even a whiff of the fear she felt—never mind the nagging doubt. "I have nothing to give you—until I know what you have to give me. Then we can talk about money."

She watched his nose quiver, his eyes continue their nervous dance.

Sensing he needed more goading, she pressed on. "On the phone, you said something about *finding* Jaspar Wills?" Obviously this couldn't be true. Jaspar Wills was safe and sound and at home in Boston, about to scoop her with his own version of *her* story.

She watched the young man's right hand drop to his side and dig into a pocket hidden behind his smock.

"Do you have something for me?" she demanded to know.

He said nothing.

"Something worth money?"

She had to be careful here. The pocket could just as easily hold a gun or some other weapon.

It was neither.

With a barely suppressed gasp, Katie's eyes grew wide as she beheld what young Mehdi Ahmadi had brought her.

Chapter 34

"Be calm," Katie urged herself, as she struggled to stay within the boundaries of a stingy slice of shade. It was the only shade to be found near the café at the southern edge of Jemaa el Fna.

Le Grand Balcon du Café Glacier was a natural place to meet. Right next to Hotel CTM, its second floor balcony was well known by tourists for providing arguably the best view of the marketplace and nearby Koutoubia Mosque. Ahmadi would know that, unlike many other places within the *medina*, Katie would have no trouble finding it.

Last night, she'd given her young informant four hundred dirhams—about forty bucks. An outlandish price, but this wasn't just any driver's license he'd pulled from his pocket. It belonged to Jaspar Wills. She had promised him another six hundred if he met her the next day. She wanted the rest of Jaspar's belongings, which he claimed to have, and for him to show her exactly where he'd found them. If he actually came through, she thought, the bounty would be worth immeasurably more than that. When their negotiations were complete, Ahmadi had found her a cab and she had gratefully returned to the hotel.

Katie was excited that she'd actually found something important, something Jaspar Wills didn't have—at least not anymore. She'd spent a restless night considering how best to use the license to her benefit, and a restless morning nervous about this meeting. Would Ahmadi show up? Did he really have more to sell her? Should she have offered a greater sum?

Through a blur of crisscrossing traffic that included beasts of burden, racing motorbikes, and scooters, Katie was relieved when she caught sight of the young Moroccan. He was standing next to a vendor stall hawking fresh orange juice and dates. Gone was his restaurant worker attire, replaced by a white hooded kaftan and a pair of woven leather sandals. Despite the heat, Katie shivered as she felt his dark eyes boring into her. Was the look predatory? Sexual? Threatening? How long had he been standing there, watching her?

He wasn't making a move, so, collecting her gumption and regretfully abandoning the shade, she carefully navigated her way through the melee of people and animals and speeding machines.

"Mehdi, hello. Did you bring more of Jaspar's things?" she asked when they were face to face.

"You don't tell people, yes?" he stuttered, his eyes hard brown marbles in quaking bowls of vanilla pudding.

"Tell who what?" Katie was confused.

"About me. You don't tell people about me."

"Of course not," she lied. But it wasn't a big lie. She would eventually tell the whole world about him, along with everything else she'd discovered in Marrakech. Certainly, if she believed he was in danger from being publicly exposed, she'd change his name to "protect the innocent." But as of right now, she was far from convinced that Mehdi Ahmadi was any kind of innocent. Especially since he had yet to tell her exactly how it was that he had come to be in possession of Jaspar Wills' personal effects. For all she knew, he was the kidnapper. Her heart thrilled at the thought. *How great would that be?*

"Follow," was all he said before suddenly scampering away.

"Oh shit," she muttered.

As Katie feared, the young Arab was heading into the no-man's land of the *souks*. Fast. She needed to half-run just to keep up, all the while frantically searching for signs or anything at all that would help maintain her bearings. The likelihood was high that she'd need to find her own way back. As quickly as they passed, she recited the markers in her head: *Souk Roseaux. Rue Des Banques. Chez Chegrouni on the right. Left at Mosque Karbouch. Olive stalls. Right at Souk Smarine. Left into another alley. Left again. Right and left again. Squeezing between two cement walls. Another frickin' nameless narrow alleyway. Really bad smell. Bunch of places selling fabric and stuff. Right at place selling something that looks like animal heads in steaming bowls…*

Oh, who the hell am I kidding? I'm done for. In under two minutes she was hopelessly lost.

Much to Katie's relief, Ahmadi stopped just shy of her point of no return. He looked at her expectantly. Wiping perspiration from her eyes, she was glad for her choice of lightweight cotton clothing and running shoes. She returned the stare.

"It's here," he said.

"What's here?"

Ahmadi dug into his pockets and pulled out a wallet, a set of keys, and a pair of sunglasses. He handed them to her like they were hot potatoes.

Searching the wallet, she asked, "Did all of these things belong to Jaspar?" She didn't need his answer. The wallet, although without a single dollar bill or credit card, contained several pieces of identification. The keys and sunglasses could have been anyone's, but the wallet—or at least its contents—definitely belonged to Jaspar Wills. Every piece represented a precious visual aid for her upcoming breaking news story. "How did you get these?"

"It's here," he repeated.

Katie studied the area. Then she understood. She approached a dumpster shoved up against a corrugated metal wall. "You found these things here? In the garbage?"

He nodded. "In the suitcase."

"Suitcase? You found these in a suitcase? Jaspar's suitcase? Where is it?"

His reply was two nods and a shrug.

"How big was this suitcase?"

With his hands, Ahmadi made a shape of about twenty-four inches wide by eighteen inches tall. Katie nodded her understanding. Jaspar's carry-on bag had been tossed into this dumpster. According to his story, the kidnapper, pretending to be a taxi driver, had abducted him right from the airport. He'd still have had all of his luggage with him. Ahmadi had found the carry-on, but where was the rest?

"Was there a bigger suitcase too?" Katie asked.

Ahmadi's narrow shoulders bounced up and down and he looked away, watching a passing family bickering about whatever it is that Moroccan families bicker about. He was a rotten liar. Katie figured he probably wouldn't cop to having found anything he'd already used or sold, like Jaspar's clothing and whatever other valuables he may have found in either piece of luggage. She couldn't fault the guy. He was merely trying to capitalize on an unexpected payday as best he could.

Slowly tracing a circle around the immediate area with a reporter's eye, Katie took in every bit of detail. They were in a passageway that was probably used solely as back alley access for various *souk* stalls and stores, and maybe as a shortcut for locals with an impeccable sense of direction. Although not yet 10:00 a.m., the temperature was already hovering in the eighties. At either end of the alley, Katie could see buyers, sellers, and innumerable varieties of con men, all of them zipping back and forth in hard pursuit of commerce, getting as much done as possible before the even more punishing heat of afternoon.

"More money now." Ahmadi was getting jittery again, hopping from foot to foot as if standing on a bed of burning coals.

Katie mindlessly pulled out the promised sum. Even the bills were limp and damp. As she handed them to the young man, her mind was elsewhere, busily trying to imagine what must have transpired in this exact spot on the day of the kidnapping. Jaspar had said that when he finally figured out something was fishy, he was already in the car. When he confronted the driver, he'd been hit and fell unconscious, still in the car. Which meant he had no way of knowing what happened next.

No. Way.

Katie felt a physical jolt. Exhilaration. Everything she was seeing now, everything Ahmadi was showing her and telling her—this entire part of the story—was hers, only hers.

Although much of the *souk* area was off limits to large motorized vehicles, she'd seen delivery trucks and even a small minibus squeeze down nearby streets. The fake taxi could have made it to this spot, or at least close by. The kidnappers would have wanted to drive Jaspar as near to where they planned to stash him as possible. Then what?

Jaspar had told her, and everyone who'd watched them on TV, that when he woke up he'd already been moved to the room where he was initially imprisoned. Since Jaspar was not moving under his own power, it meant the taxi driver/kidnapper would have had to carry him. Could he have managed that on his own, or did he have an accomplice waiting here to help him? Either way, he wouldn't have wanted the extra burden of a suitcase and carry-on. He would have disposed of them. In this dumpster.

Voices in Katie's head began to shriek. It wasn't definite…but there was a very good chance that Jaspar had been held somewhere near here!

"Ahmadi," she asked, not bothering to disguise her excitement, "which of these businesses use this dumpster?"

But she was too late. The young man had taken his money and run.

Chapter 35

Exploring the *souks* of Marrakech is like a tumble backwards in time. In hidden *fondouks* and courtyards, traditional craft makers and trades thrive in ways that have barely changed since Andalusian refugees first introduced them over a thousand years ago. Within the ramparts of the *medina*, peddlers and purchasers haggle over everything from hand-knotted, vegetable-dyed carpets and rugs, to exotic edibles, spices, nuts, herbs, olives and local sweets. Endless varieties of argan oil products compete with leather goods, ranging from satchels and belts to the distinctive pointed-toe *babouche* slippers worn by most men, and jewelry made of silver and semi-precious stones. There's marquetry of cedar, thuya, oak, and earthenware ceramics, from the gaudy and touristy to the extravagant pieces created at pottery centers in Safi, Fez, Meknes and Salé. Casks of perfume smelling of musk, orange flower, patchouli, and amber sit alongside precious—and not-so-precious— works of art. The bounty is endless. But as Katie Edwards trudged through the constricted passageways, the ground worn smooth by millions before her, her body broiling and growing sluggish, feet ablaze with blisters, shirt soaked through with sweat, her focus was on the one item proving almost impossible to find: information.

After young Ahmadi had abandoned her, Katie was left with only two options. The first was to find the restaurant where she'd first met him and drag him back to the *medina* to help her. But that, she knew, was a fool's errand, only for those who had time to waste getting hopelessly lost. Even if she did happen to locate the restaurant, she couldn't count on Ahmadi being there.

The second option, no less difficult but with some potential for success—slight as it might be—was to canvass the businesses nearest the dumpster where Jaspar Wells' personal belongings had been found. With any luck, she'd find someone who saw or knew something.

So far, option two was proving fruitless.

Exhausted and hot and growing increasingly irritable and dejected, Katie found a store that sold bottled water—she'd run out an hour earlier—made her purchase, and squeezed into the shade of a nearby alcove. She hoped that hydration and a few minutes of rest would revive her before she tackled the next parade of stores.

After downing several gulps of water in the ersatz coolness, Katie was surprised to realize that she was enjoying herself. The sights and sounds and smells of the bustling marketplace were nothing short of intoxicating. For the first time since arriving in the African city, she was allowing its charms to wash over her instead of actively resisting them.

This place, at first blush, was aggressive, frantic, perilous, overwhelming, moving at hysterical speed. If you allowed it to, it would crush you down and grind you into powder, like a stone pestle against a dry, brittle, hot pepper. But Katie was beginning to see that there was undeniable beauty here, too. Placid, tawny shades harmonizing with effervescent hues. Ancient tranquility awash in modern vitality. Bins overflowing with spices. Carts laden down with heavy bolts of woven fabric. Tapestries hanging from wires strung twenty feet overhead. Riotously colored scarves, tunics, and headpieces. Aggressive aromas of something old mixed with something zesty, piquant, sickly sweet. The swirl of languages, arguments and haggling, laughter and harassment and persistence, was heady, sometimes gruff, sometimes humorous, always intense. But, my God, Katie thought to herself, spending time in the *souks* of Marrakech, one couldn't help but feel alive-with-an-exclamation-point.

With her mind let loose, like a flower floating aimlessly down a fragrant rosewater river, now a part of her environment instead of battling against it, Katie suddenly found her eureka. She knew what to do next.

Like the peddlers around her, each an expert in the wares they sold and how to put them into the hands of others, journalists

were also professional tradespeople. They collected information—
reams and reams of it. Most of it left unused. The best bits were
repackaged for public consumption, hung out with a big For Sale
sign. But smart reporters, like Katie, didn't forget about the stuff
that never got used. Because every so often—like right now—that
was the stuff that put you on the right path, the perfect yellow brick
road leading straight to Oz.

Pulling her iPhone from her pants pocket, Katie was grateful
to see that her heavenly slice of shade was also a free Wi-Fi spot.
She connected and accessed her iCloud account, where she'd stored
all her files relating to Jaspar, Jenn, and Mikki Wills. Sweaty fingers
and the small screen hindered her search, but soon enough she
found what she was looking for: background information on Qasim
Al-Harthi. The young man imprisoned for his role in the Marrakech
café bombing. The man whose release Jaspar's kidnappers had
demanded in return for setting him free.

Her heart beating double time, Katie scrolled through the
digital article looking for the exact trinket of information she hoped
she was remembering correctly.

Finally, there it was. A stray strand among the facts that had
been patch worked together in an effort to identify Al-Harthi's
closest friends, known associates, and relatives. Details were sparse,
which was probably why she and the news station—and the police,
for that matter—hadn't focused on this data when investigating the
kidnapping. But one name on the list had stuck in Katie's mind.
Until now, it had meant nothing to her. For all anyone knew, it
could have referred to anyone or anything.

Katie's face lit up as she read the name on the screen.

Heat and fatigue long forgotten, excitement bubbled up in
Katie. Quite possibly, she was the only person in the world to figure
this out. There'd be no stopping her now.

Chapter 36

Maps and GPS were useless in the *souks*. It took Katie forty-five minutes to find the place she was looking for, ostensibly just around the corner. Not bad, really—yesterday it probably would have taken her twice as long. Katie was beginning to get a feel for how the *medina* worked, and how best to navigate its senseless grid of lanes and alleyways. She still got lost—but, when she did, she had a much better sense of just how lost she was and the best way to get un-lost.

Mattar was the name of a store. She'd been in it. One of dozens since being left at the dumpster by Ahmadi. As she stepped to the front of the building, she couldn't quite remember who she'd talked to there—only that they'd said what everyone else did when she showed them the picture of Jaspar Wills: "I've never seen this man."

The store specialized in men's clothing, and was considerably more substantial than others in this section of the *medina*. Instead of having their entire inventory crammed into an eight-by-twenty stall, Mattar operated out of an actual two-story building, complete with functioning door and roof. If she remembered correctly—and she sure hoped she did—the business was one of the few that made an attempt at providing an air-conditioned environment for their customers.

When she opened the door, a late-middle-aged man and woman, sitting shoulder to shoulder behind a counter at the far end of the store, looked up from where they were eating lunch from ceramic containers. What happened next occurred in triple time. The woman spoke harshly to the man; the man retorted, jumped up from his meal, threw down his utensils and napkin, rounded the counter, sped down the narrow space toward Katie, placed his hands on her shoulders, and pushed.

The next thing Katie knew, she'd been unceremoniously shoved out of the store and into the street, nearly landing on her ass, suffering the stares of surprised passersby.

"What the fuck?" she cried out, immediately hoping that none of the passersby understood English.

Without thinking about what she was doing, Katie raced back to the door, which had been forcefully slammed shut following her expulsion. Intending to burst back in, she grabbed the knob and pushed. The door didn't budge. She'd been locked out.

Anyone else would have been pissed off. Katie Edwards, however, was infused with exhilaration. There was only one reason the couple would have acted as they had. She was right—these people knew something about Jaspar Wills. And soon, she would know it too.

Wearing a sleeveless mauve silk blouse and a floor-length skirt with oversized floral print, her hair pulled back into a Grace Kelly bun, Katie knew she looked good. But looks could be deceiving. Beneath the chic outfit, she was a wet rag. She'd spent over six hours in the *souks*, waiting for the owners of Mattar Menswear to finally decide she was gone and reopen for business. After all, how long could they afford to leave their doors shuttered just to keep out one pesky American journalist?

As it turned out, longer than she could last in the sweltering, congested, gritty street, with nothing to sustain her except her fledgling belief that whoever was behind the locked door knew something that would blow the lid off this story.

When it was obvious that they'd either snuck out the back or simply refused to open the doors if there was even a hint of her within spitting distance, Katie gave up for the night. It was a tough call—she only had two days left before she was on a plane back to Boston, a flight she could *not* miss. But it was a smart one. She'd try again tomorrow, refreshed—and with a full supply of necessities for a long-term vigil, if required.

She battled her way out of Jemaa el Fna, past Koutoubia Mosque, down Avenue Houman El Fetouaki, and risked life and limb to cross Bab Jedid roundabout, finally reaching the relatively quiet neighborhood of Hivernage, where Hotel Es Saadi was located. Feeling entirely wrung out, the twenty minute walk had taken her nearly twice as long as it should have.

Twenty acres of luscious gardens surrounded the resort. By the time Katie reached the blessedly cool grand lobby, she felt surprisingly resuscitated. A quick dip in the hotel pool, followed by a brisk shower, gave heft to a second wind. She put on her best going-out outfit, the one she'd packed "just in case"—as any smart traveler does—and headed out to find alcohol and dinner, in that order.

As she made her way to the complex's main building, down gently-curving pathways lined with palm trees, orange trees, bougainvillea, and Marrakech roses, all delicately lit by ground-level lanterns, Katie knew she wouldn't be leaving the hotel grounds. The setting was simply too wonderful.

The Egyptian Bar was in the Palace building. With its thickly upholstered chairs, wood-paneled walls and ceiling, elegant background music courtesy of a tuxedoed piano player, and languorous paintings by the likes of Sir Arthur Alma Thadema, Edwin Long, and Alexandre Cabanel, it was the perfect place to sit back, have a strong drink, and leisurely consider which of the property's several restaurants to choose for dinner.

The lounge was half full, with a few groups of four or six, several couples, and even a spattering of singles like herself. Finding a good corner spot, Katie could observe the room's goings on while maintaining her privacy. After being served an unstinting dirty martini, Katie settled in with her iPad. She intended to rehash her progress, make notes on what she'd learned today, and strategize for tomorrow.

Katie was unsure of how much time had passed when her server returned, offering a refreshed drink and a small plate of appetizers. Enjoying the pleasant environment, Katie accepted the appetizers—thinking she'd forgo dinner and order something more substantial from room service later on if need be—and requested a half-bottle of Laurent Perrier Brut champagne. Scant minutes later, she was surprised when, instead of the half bottle, a full one arrived.

"I'm sorry, but before you open that," she interrupted the waiter as he prepared to do just that, "I don't think that's the bottle I ordered."

"You are correct, madam," he answered with a discrete smile and a nod toward the bar. "The bottle is compliments of the gentleman. He's asked for permission to speak with you."

Katie's eyes moved to the dimly-lit, dark-paneled bar, behind which two white-coated bartenders busied themselves. Only one man sat there, half-turned on his stool in order to gauge her reaction to his gift and request. Impossible to be sure given the distance, Katie judged the man, an Arabian, to be about her age. He was sharply-dressed in a smart blue suit, Arctic-white shirt, no tie. His dress shoes were shiny and black, as was his hair—worn just long enough to curl over the top of his collar. She'd always found dark-featured men attractive; this one was exceptionally so.

Katie performed a hasty self-evaluation. Had her day in the scorching sun—and her generous martini—dulled her senses and impaired her decision-making abilities? How bad of an idea was this, anyway? Could she afford the distraction? Perhaps a distraction was exactly the thing she needed to get her through another day in Marrakech.

She nodded to the server.

Although he surely must have seen the approval, the man gallantly waited until the waiter returned with verbal confirmation before making his way over.

Standing over her, his smile a row of pearls glittering in the bar's dusky light, he inquired: "English or French?"

Without skipping a beat, Katie replied, "Arabic."

He stepped back, surprised.

"Okay," she quickly relented with a laugh, "you got me. I'm American. I only speak English. Is it that obvious?"

"Not obvious," he said, in a deep, softly-accented voice. "It's simply that I cannot imagine a world where a beautiful woman such as yourself would have knowledge of more than one language."

Katie gave him an "oh, really?" kind of look. "Why exactly do you think a beautiful woman couldn't learn more than one language?"

"She would have no time. All of it would surely be spent fighting off fools such as myself."

They both grinned. He indicated the seat next to her; she confirmed it was okay for him to sit in it.

"My name is Tarek. Yours?"

"Katie. Katie Edwards."

Katie liked meeting men when she was away from home. Somehow it freed her to act in whatever way happened to suit her that night: silly, serious, mysterious, sensual. As Tarek poured the champagne left behind by the waiter, she pretended to search for something in her handbag, all the while surreptitiously admiring the man. His strong, steady hands, lightly dusted with dark hair. The long legs and narrow waist. His cologne: a thick, musky scent she'd come to learn most Arabian men favored.

They toasted and drank.

After a tick of silence, he began: "May I ask what brings you to Marrakech?"

"I'm a writer."

"I see. So you're writing about Marrakech, then? Or perhaps all of Morocco?"

"Yes." It seemed as good a story as any, seeing as the truth was not an option.

"You do this alone?"

Katie smirked. What he really wanted to know was if she was single—or at least here by herself.

"Yes. Do you find that strange?"

"I find it...unusual."

They smiled more at each other. Drank more. Made more small talk. Time passed pleasurably.

After a while, accepting her second—or was it third?—refill, Katie asked, "What do you do, Tarek?"

He cocked an eyebrow—a move she found resplendently attractive—and made a rumbling noise beneath his breath. "Well, the answer to your question is somewhat...complex."

"I'm an intelligent woman; give it a try."

Katie was beginning to think about hinting that they move their conversation to a more private and comfortable location. Why not? They were both adults, obviously attracted to one another, and with just the right amount of champagne glow to make their status as strangers less important.

"I assist people with problems," he told her with an enigmatic smile.

"Really? How interesting. Are you working on anyone's problem right now?" She could hear flirtation in her voice. She hoped he did too.

His smile faltered. "As a matter of fact, I am."

Alcohol may have dimmed her reporter's sensitivities, but Katie knew enough to ask the follow-up question. "What is it?"

"The problem," he responded, face grown grim, "is you."

Katie felt her face flush and the mood change.

"So, Ms. Edwards," Tarek murmured, "I will ask you this one more time. What are you doing in Marrakech?"

Chapter 37

"I already told you." Katie was pissed off to hear the tremor in her voice. "I'm a writer."

Tarek leaned back, evaluating his companion with cold eyes. "And yet, somehow, I do not believe you."

She'd had enough. "Listen, just because you've paid for a few glasses of champagne, doesn't mean I have to sit here and be talked to that way." She made a move to collect her things.

"I think you do."

There was something about how he said the benign words that caused Katie to stop what she was doing and stare at the man. His face was as handsome and pleasant as ever. Her eyes moved lower. Tarek had opened his jacket, revealing a trio of small knives suspended against the silk lining.

"Who are you?" she blurted out angrily. Mostly she was mad at herself. It was true that she'd never been an investigative journalist courageously reporting nail-biting stories from war-torn, third-world hellholes—a fact many of her colleagues regularly pointed out. But who cared what they thought? Katie knew that, given the opportunity, she could be just as accomplished, just as sharp, just as brave as Christiane Amanpour or Diane Sawyer. Yet here she was, covering her first international story from a foreign post, face-to-face with a potentially dangerous source, and already she could feel cold sweat pooling under her arms and at her lower back, probably staining her silk blouse.

"I've told you who I am," he calmly replied. "I've been honest with you, Katie. Why won't you return the favor?"

"You're a man who 'solves other people's problems' and threatens innocent women in public places with sharp knives. Yeah, that sounds like a real honest guy to me."

"I'm sorry your opinion of me cannot be higher. I assure you, my intent is to bring you no harm. My only wish is to convince you to tell me the truth. So, let's begin again. Why were you in the *souks* today? Why do you insist on harassing my friends?"

Katie's ears perked up. Damn. She *was* good. She'd rattled a few bushes and now it was raining acorns. Fear and doubt fell away, replaced by burgeoning confidence. "That's what this is about? The couple from the store? Mr. and Mrs. Mattar, or whatever their names are?"

He nodded matter-of-factly. "Yes, Katie, that is what this is about. Why are you bothering the Mattars?"

"I wasn't *bothering* them. I only wanted to talk to them. But before I could, they threw me out of their store like I was some kind of thief. As far as I'm concerned, they harassed me—not the other way around."

Tarek pursed his lips and studied his opponent. As he did so, Katie noted something she hadn't fully realized before: when a bad man reveals his true nature, handsomeness seamlessly mutates into repulsiveness. She used the silent moment to assess her surroundings and identify the nearest source of help, should she need it to get away from this jackass.

For now, she felt relatively safe. If anything, the lounge was busier than before. No one was paying them particular attention, but getting it would not be a problem. Tarek's knives were menacing and she was uneasy, but Katie was proud to realize that she hadn't been reduced to a quivering mound of jelly.

"You were at their shop earlier today," Tarek stated.

"Yes."

"Why?"

"I wanted to show them a picture of my friend, a man named Jaspar Wills. About a year ago, he was kidnapped. His captors held him somewhere in the *medina*." She stopped there for a brief moment, her mind spinning with prospects. She decided on a tack. "I know it was the Mattars' shop. On the second floor."

"How do you know this?"

Katie froze her face, hoping to disguise the lie. "What does that matter? I just know."

"Are you with the American police?"

"No. Believe it or not, I was honest with you, Tarek. I *am* a writer. But I'm not writing about Marrakech. I'm writing a book about the kidnapping."

"I see."

More silence. Katie resisted taking another swig of champagne. But, goddamn, she needed it.

"What is your interest in the Mattars?"

"Like I told you, I'm not the police. I'm not here to accuse anyone of anything—including the Mattars. I just want information. Inside information. For my story. I want to talk to your friends about what they know. What they saw."

"This will be impossible."

Katie felt her stomach drop. Great. Now what? Should she push her luck and threaten the knife-happy louse with going to the police? If she did, would she survive the night? What would Christiane do?

Tarek relieved her of having to make a decision. "I have a proposal for you, Kate Edwards."

"What kind of proposal?"

"Your friend was not held at the Mattars' store for long."

Katie thrilled at the admission. She'd taken a chance and proven her instincts right. Her eyes narrowed as she considered her next move. "Yes, that's true," Katie agreed. "He was moved. To somewhere in the Atlas Mountains."

"I will take you there."

A kaleidoscope of butterflies invaded Katie's belly.

Tarek leaned across the table, his lips nearly grazing her cheek. He whispered into her ear: "But only if you promise to leave the Mattars alone."

If Katie knew one thing for sure, it was that any good story must have momentum to survive. Once a story stopped moving forward, try as you might to drum up interest, it was pretty much dead. Tarek's offer not only kept her story alive, but took it in a whole new, exciting direction.

Was it wise to team up with a blade-wielding stranger who'd plied her with liquor for the sole purpose of manipulating her? Probably not. But Katie knew she had only two days left. She needed to up the ante. The scariest ride at any amusement park is usually the fastest one, but it's also the most satisfying, the one everyone talks about for weeks afterwards. It was time, Katie decided, to get on that ride, close her eyes, and prepare to scream.

Chapter 38

All was perfect. Bright lights cast everything in their path into unnaturally stark relief, sharper and more vivid than real life. Cameras were positioned around the space like a posse of mechanical aliens, glaring eyes demanding attention, challenging their subjects to entertain, inform, educate, titillate. Katie Edwards was suffused with that warm feeling you get when you know you're well prepared to deliver all of that and more. She was glad to be home, glad to be back in front of an audience—her people; people who trusted her to bring them unfiltered, unfettered truth.

She had smiled warmly when Jaspar and Jennifer Wills were escorted into the studio. She was already in her spot, reviewing her notes, when they'd arrived. She stood, flattening imaginary creases in her tight, steel-blue skirt. They shook hands. Techs seated the couple and outfitted them with microphones, while makeup people touched up their pale faces and straightened their hair. Katie remembered the long, bordering-on-groveling phone call it took to convince the Wills to appear on her show.

She'd begun with an apology. It covered the wide gamut of issues—all apparently her fault—that had driven the wedge into their friendship. She told them about abandoning her book the instant she'd heard that Jaspar had changed his mind and was releasing his own. Then, after skillfully taking the two on a trip down memory lane, reminding them of all they'd been through together, Katie suggested one last public appearance as a trio. The same trio the public had pretty much come to see as a family unit. It would be a reunion. One that would be a distinct and definite closure to the saga that had played out for the past year. Closure for them, the people of Boston, the entire country.

Set Free was Jaspar Wills' true-life account of the whole thing, beginning with the day his daughter disappeared and ending on the day he returned to Boston following his own kidnapping. The book had debuted at number one on the New York Times bestseller list, and had remained there ever since.

Although the interview had been publicized as a promotion piece for Wills and his new book, everyone knew the truth. This was going to be reality TV at its best—which was why the network had committed to sixty minutes live in prime time. No book, no matter how popular, could command the same. This was all about show business, about media darling Kate Edwards doing what she did best: taking viewers by the hand and leading them into a private world. Once there, award-winning author Jaspar Wills and his beautiful wife would bare their souls for all to see.

In *Set Free*, Jaspar revealed intimate details never discussed in the interviews following his stunning return. He recounted the severity of the beatings he'd endured, his serious contemplation of suicide, and meticulously described his frequent escapes into what he termed "dreamscape reality"—a place where he spent great swaths of time in the company of his daughter. He talked about an eventual "soul-refreshing" salvation at the hands of a woman whose real identity he'd never know, and—the most provocative revelation of all—his fleeting sexual relationship with her.

Fans were dying to hear more. They were desperate to see the reaction of Jennifer Wills as her husband publicly admitted his infidelity—all on the heels of her own shocking affair with the man accused of kidnapping their daughter. This was prime time soap opera material.

On top of everything else, Katie had a few surprises up her sleeve. Only she and her producers knew when and how she'd dole them out. Every good journalist lived for moments like this. These sixty minutes were hers. This would be the show that propelled her, at light speed, from Katie Edwards, affiliate correspondent, to Kate Edwards, national anchor.

The first twenty minutes of the show were heavy on archive video and photo collages, backed by a compassionate score. Katie expertly navigated the viewing audience, with great sensitivity to the Wills, through the early days of the story: Mikki's kidnapping, the failed retrieval attempts, the trial, the pressures on their marriage and careers, and, eventually, Jaspar's decision to go to Morocco.

"We've talked before about your arrival in Marrakech. How you came to be deceived by a man pretending to be a taxicab driver," Katie recited. "A man who conned you into getting into his car. In your book, you describe in nerve-wracking detail those horrible moments when you first begin to realize that you aren't being taken to a hotel, but that something quite different— something unimaginable—was happening," Katie led.

"Yes," Jaspar responded, looking considerably healthier and more robust than the last time he'd appeared on camera with Katie, immediately following his return from Marrakech. "Even for me, a writer, someone used to expressing himself in words, I found this part of my story difficult to adequately explain in the book. There is a depth of fear to which a person plummets when you know, for certain, that you are truly, suddenly, unexpectedly, in great danger. It's nearly impossible to describe, even now.

"You're in a foreign country. You're exhausted from traveling for hours. It's hot. You can't speak the language. And then the unthinkable happens. At first you freeze. You doubt yourself. You doubt the reality of the situation. But when it hits you, when you know it's true, and it's happening to you, it's as if someone has pounded you over the head with a sledgehammer."

Katie visibly shuddered. "I don't even want to imagine it." She turned to the camera, somber eyes nakedly eliciting empathy from the millions watching. "I'm sure many of us know the experience of visiting a place we've never been to before. We might fleetingly think: 'what if something goes wrong?' But for it to really happen…" Back to Jaspar. "My God, Jaspar, it's terrifying to think about."

"Terrifying is a good word." He let out a half-laugh, half-moan. "You know, Katie, there've been times since when I've wondered whether it was a good thing the kidnapper knocked me out as soon as he did. At least when I was unconscious, I didn't have to live in the terror."

"Live in the terror," she repeated Jaspar's last words like a mantra. After a short pause, Katie moved on, elucidating for the audience's benefit: "It was when you began to register suspicion, and voiced your concern to the driver, that he knocked you out?"

"That's correct."

"You didn't regain consciousness until you were in the room where they first kept you?"

"Yes."

"Jaspar, I've never asked you this before…" Katie allowed a dramatic two-second delay. Enough time for the cameras to catch Jaspar's gape. "Did you ever wonder…did you…oh gosh, I don't know how to ask this…or even if I should." This hesitant uncertainty, Katie knew, was the kind of stuff audiences ate up—as long as you didn't do it too often.

Other than to close his mouth, Jaspar didn't respond one way or another. This apparent spur-of-the-moment, off-script diversion had not been part of the prep package he and Jenn had been given.

Seemingly resolved, Katie pushed on. "Have you ever wondered if your kidnapper, the taxi driver, targeted you specifically? What I mean to ask is: do you think he knew you were Jaspar Wills, bestselling author, renowned around the world? Or was this simply a twist of fate, or really bad luck?"

Jaspar nodded his understanding of the question. He hadn't expected it, but he was comfortable answering. "You know, Katie, I've spent hours wondering about that exact thing. In the many months of my captivity, I can't think of a single thing that would lead me to believe they knew who I was." Another short laugh. "Not that I expected them to produce a book and ask for an autograph."

With soft chuckles of their own, Katie and Jenn acknowledged the light moment—there'd been so few. Katie in particular was grateful for the reprieve. Nothing gave power and heft to drama more than a dash of counterpoint humor.

"Jaspar, as you know, I myself recently traveled to Morocco," Katie spoke in a way that indicated a shift in direction and tone. "To Marrakech. The same city where your harrowing kidnapping ordeal began. Of course I hadn't read your book, since it hadn't been written yet, but thanks to our friendship, I already knew a great deal about what happened to you there. I didn't go to Marrakech looking for that story. But," she quirked her head to one side, "I am a reporter, after all. I *was* after a story.

"I followed your footsteps in Marrakech because I wanted to tell the story of the place, to get a sense of the environment in which you found yourself. The extreme heat, the foreign languages, the strange foods, the smells...the sheer exoticism of it all. I have to say, I've rarely been anywhere where I've felt so out of place. Everything is drastically different from here at home. I wanted to capture that, to find a story that would do justice to your magnificent work in *Set Free*." The book's cover image flickered on-screen.

"Thank you," Jaspar whispered, nodding humbly.

"But I have an admission, Jaspar. I didn't come back with that story."

He gazed at her, uncertainty once again clouding his eyes. "Oh?"

"I came back with something entirely different." She steadied herself, like a bomber pilot about to release her payload. "Something that will surprise you, and everyone watching us tonight."

Chapter 39

Jaspar reverentially accepted the worn leather wallet, his eyes nearly bugging out. Katie knew she'd played the scene perfectly. The producers had wondered if he should be forewarned about the revelation. But she and the lead producer, Peggy Guttenberg—the only other person who knew everything that was going to happen today—had argued strongly against it. To tell Jaspar she'd recovered the wallet was to rob their viewing audience of a priceless moment. By the look on Jaspar's face and the way the cameras were zeroing in on it, Katie knew they'd made the right call.

Jenn leaned in to get a better look at the item in her husband's hands. "That's your wallet," she marveled in a hushed whisper.

"Yeah. They took it from me when…" Jaspar stopped, looking up from the wallet to glare at Katie. "But…how did you get this?"

"You're right," Katie said, ignoring the question for now. "Your kidnappers took this wallet from you while you lay unconscious in the back seat of their vehicle. I believe if you look inside, except for cash and credit cards, everything else is there. Driver's license, insurance card, family photos."

TV screens across the country flashed blown-up versions of the wallet-sized pictures Katie had found. Mikki as a baby. Mikki at about three. Mikki just before she was abducted and never seen again.

The cameras—and America—watched as Jaspar carefully withdrew the same photographs, one by one, and stared at them in amazement. When he was done with one, he'd carefully pass it to Jenn, who did much the same.

With the final photograph handed away, Jaspar was about to demand an answer from Katie about where and how she'd found the wallet, when she gave him more. First a set of keys. Then sunglasses.

"I believe these are yours as well?"

Jaspar massaged the keys in his right hand, as if attempting to force warmth into the cold metal. Gently taking hold of the sunglasses, Jenn studied them intensely, as if beholding a friend long believed lost forever.

"How did you do this?" Jenn marveled. "How did you get these?"

Katie nodded, as if hearing the question for the first time. "I know both of you must be shocked. I was too. To find something of yours, Jaspar, thirty-five hundred miles from home. It made your story all the more real for me." She smiled a sad, kind smile. "I'm just glad I could do this one small thing for you, to bring back at least a very small part of what you lost in Marrakech."

Jenn's thank you was tearful, her hands visibly trembling.

Jaspar nodded his gratitude. She'd not yet answered his question. He asked it again: "How did you get these?"

Sliding back into reporter mode, Katie faced the camera and told her well-rehearsed story. Low-quality video, taken with her own hand-held Sony, flickered behind her, its gritty inferiority adding a dark, grungy authenticity to the report and her investigative prowess.

The first images showed the immensity of Jemaa el Fna, all fine detail of the massive square lost in blaring, hot sun. Jerky shots of the *medina* aptly captured the frenzied activity and crowded maze of the marketplace. A long, lingering view of the Mattars' shop appeared as the camera meticulously panned the street where it was located. Although Katie did not specifically identify the store in her reporting—as advised by the station's legal department—her camerawork told the truth. She'd also included an artist's rendering of Mehdi Ahmadi, whom she identified only as a confidential source from whom she'd retrieved Jaspar's personal effects.

Jaspar and Jenn watched and listened, as enraptured and awed as any TV viewer. Immediately prior to announcing a scheduled break from the live telecast, Katie earned her keep by artfully ending on a cliffhanger: "When we return, you'll learn about my meeting with a man who went by the name of Tarek, and what he told me about what happened next to American detainee and bestselling author, Jaspar Wills." Concluding remarks done, she set her face in stone until the broadcast went to commercial.

"Katie, this is amazing!" Jenn exclaimed, jumping up. She made a stilted move toward the other woman. Given where they were, and the state of their recently-strained friendship, she decided a hug was inappropriate. "Why didn't you tell us about any of this?"

"Yes," Jaspar intoned, less enthusiastic, still fingering the keys. "And what else did you find? Who is this Tarek person?"

"Come on, Jaspar!" Jenn chided, attempting a cheerful tone. "Why so glum? Were you hoping your money was still in the wallet?"

At that exact moment, Peggy arrived, bringing the interaction to an abrupt end. The producer was demanding Katie attend to some urgent matter happening on her iPad. The diversion was planned. Both Katie and Peggy had agreed that it was important to keep the Wills from having too much chit-chat time with Katie during breaks, in the interest of maintaining the in-the-moment realness they were going for.

As Katie and Peggy stepped away, Jenn returned to her seat next to her husband. "Isn't this incredible?" She held up the sunglasses. "I remember when you bought these. I bet you never expected to see any of this stuff again." When there was no response, she asked: "Jaspar, are you okay?"

He nodded, eyes darting between his newly-returned keys and Katie's powwow with her producer.

"Oh, God," Jenn said. "I'm sorry. I didn't think. Is seeing these things bothering you? Are they bringing up bad memories?"

Their eyes met. For a moment it was just the two of them, husband and wife, the frenetic noise of the studio and hustle and bustle of the dozens of people who made the broadcast happen nothing but muffled background. Despite everything they'd been through and the difficulties in their marriage, Jenn knew this man.

She could tell he was uneasy, unhappy. But there was something else too: he looked worried. But what could he possibly have to be worried about? Wasn't the worst over with? Things were getting better between them. His book was an immediate bestseller. Wounds were healing. Weren't they?

"We can stop this anytime, Jaspar," she offered, her voice a gentle caress.

His head bobbed. "I think we sh—"

"Welcome back," Katie's voice boomed, sharp, powerful, at-the-ready.

Jenn tried to catch Katie's eye, to somehow communicate that maybe this wasn't such a good idea anymore. Maybe they could take a break? Something, anything, to avoid putting her husband through any more of this.

Immediately, Jenn realized it was too late. She also realized something else: at least here in the TV studio, Katie Edwards was not their friend. She was a professional newsperson, intent on doing her job at whatever cost. And then came one more hideous truth.

The surprises weren't over.

Chapter 40

"Jaspar," Katie began, full wattage on the author. She was bringing to bear her keen ability at making it seem as if there were no cameras, no millions of viewers on the other side of the lens, no collection of technicians, producers, social media managers, news directors, editors, camera operators, sound and audio engineers, hanging on to every word. "In your book, *Set Free*, you talk about the day it became apparent, to you and the kidnappers, that their demands were never going to be met. They decided to move you from your original location, which we now know to have been in the *medina* section of Marrakech."

Jaspar struggled to mentally pull himself out of the ugly place he suddenly found himself in. The camera showed him turning to his wife. Viewers would wonder what he was seeking. Comfort? Rescue? Benediction? But there was nothing Jennifer Wills could do. His gaze shifted back to Katie, questioning, as if he wasn't quite sure what she wanted from him.

"They moved you out of the city, isn't that right?" Katie asked.

Jaspar cleared his throat. "Yes. But I didn't know why. All I could think of was that whatever their original plan had been, it had failed. So they needed to make a change."

"You were right." Katie subtly shifted in her seat to concentrate on the camera. "We know from what officials are now making public about the case, that although the American government was fully engaged in discussions with the kidnappers, they were never in a position to obtain the release of Qasim Al-Harthi. We also know that international relations between the United States and Morocco have been—and continue to be—strained at best.

"Although we can't confirm their validity, for years there have been reports of prisoner release negotiations, such as this one, being successfully carried out behind-the-scenes, arranged privately, by non-government third parties. In the end, numerous questions still remain unanswered. Was everything done that could have been? Did Jaspar Wills' kidnappers simply give up and run scared? Or did something else happen to make them change plans?" Turning back to her guests, she asked: "Jaspar, is it your belief that, given the complexity of the situation, we may never know the real truth?"

Jaspar hesitated before haltingly agreeing. "I think I have to believe that. If for no other reason than to protect my sanity, and move on."

Katie nodded, as if never before having considered that point of view. Inside, she was smiling. He'd just given her the perfect segue. Choosing her words carefully, she asked, "Is it true then, that throughout your ordeal, and maybe since, you've feared for your sanity?"

Jaspar looked struck, not expecting the question. "I...I suppose in a way, yes. I talk in depth in my book about the times when I felt...removed from my normal self. As if my mind was taking me someplace else, someplace better, safer. If you want to call that insanity, so be it. But I certainly didn't fear it. In truth, I sought it out, in order to survive."

"I get it." She waited a count of three, then: "When the kidnappers moved you out of the city, was that one of the times?"

"I was gagged, tied up, thrown into the back of a van in the middle of the night. So, yes, I was probably a little cracked when that happened. You have to understand that by this point, I'd already been held for several days in a sweltering hot, dark, smelly room, with very little food or water. I was beaten almost daily. These were not good conditions."

The shake of Katie's head and grim repose of her mouth communicated sympathy. "I'll probably say this a dozen more times throughout this interview, Jaspar, but I just can't imagine what that would be like. No one watching tonight can. That's one of the reasons we're so appreciative of your willingness—and Jenn's—to be here today to share your story."

Jaspar and Jenn exchanged a not-so-private look that now questioned that decision.

"In the book, you state that on the night you were moved, you believed you were being taken out of the city, into the Atlas Mountains."

"Yes," Jaspar confirmed.

"It's astounding how, despite being battered, emotionally-overwrought, and frightened, you were able to deduce that."

Jaspar gave her a blank look.

"How did you deduce that?"

Jaspar cleared his throat. "Of course I couldn't see a thing. But I could hear traffic patterns, the change in sound the tires made when we moved from pavement to gravel. Based on how long it took us to reach the final destination, I made an educated guess."

"Well, you are a writer," Katie responded, her tone sunny and complimentary. "I suppose you're used to observing and researching and using clues to get at the truth."

"Uh, yes, I guess that's true."

"Of course, it wasn't until much, much later, when you finally made your escape from the place you've called 'the rectangle,' that you knew you were right?"

Jaspar shifted uncomfortably in his seat. Jenn laid her right hand over the fingers of his left, which were franticly at work on the keys Katie had given him earlier. "That's right," he agreed.

"You describe—in the book—the area as being remote, somewhere in the foothills of the High Atlas Mountains."

"Yes."

"After your escape from the rectangle, you wandered aimlessly until you found a small Berber village, is that correct?"

"Yes."

Katie inspected Jaspar with a keen eye, curious but not entirely surprised by the typically eloquent man's sudden lackluster ability to elaborate. She tried again with another leading question.

"You found help in the village and eventually hitched a ride back to Marrakech?"

"Yes."

"Jaspar, I know this may be difficult for you, but I wonder if you'd mind taking us back: to the time before you escaped, to the time you spent inside the rectangle. Why did you call it that, anyway?"

"The rectangle." Jaspar repeated the name, eyes and voice deadened, the only liveliness coming from his left hand as he manipulated the keys, threading them under and over his fingers like some kind of parlor game. "It was shaped like a giant shoe box," he finally uttered, "four walls with a metal grate for a lid. Like someplace you'd keep a hamster."

"Is that how you felt? Like a pet? Being kept in a box for the kidnapper's pleasure?"

"No. Pets are cared for, played with, loved. I was just...being stored. Until they could figure out what to do with me." Jaspar allowed Jenn to pull the keys from his hand. His eyes followed to where she placed them at rest on a side table.

"But things were different in the rectangle, compared to where you were held in Marrakech?"

"Yes. The rectangle was considerably larger. The grate roof allowed in light, sunshine, fresh air. My restraints were removed. I was free to walk around. The beatings stopped. There was more food and water. Eventually a lot more, as you'll read about in the book." *Why isn't she talking about the book?*

Katie referred to her notes and recited a list: "No TV, no internet, no books, no real bed to sleep in?"

"I had none of those things."

"For months." Katie's voice communicated her incredulity.

He nodded. "For months."

"Do you—and I'm sorry for having to ask you this—but you've talked openly about your battle with maintaining sanity in what, I know everyone watching tonight will agree, were dreadful circumstances," she said, wanting to circle back to the topic she needed him to talk about. "Jaspar, as you sat there—in the rectangle, day in, day out, waiting for who knows what, scared for your life, worrying about Jenn, about your friends and family back home, knowing they probably thought you were dead—do you believe this was when you slowly began to slip away from sanity? When you began to escape into what you've referred to as dreamscape reality?"

Having lost confidence in his responses, Jaspar considered his answer carefully before making a reply. "I don't know if it was an escape so much as a crucial mental adjustment. My dreamscape reality became a necessity of life. It was as essential as breathing and eating and sleeping. I needed to allow my brain to do what it needed to do..." Momentarily overcome, Jaspar swallowed hard, attempted to continue, swallowed again, then: "...so I could make it through another day."

Jenn watched her husband through silent tears.

Katie nodded. "So even though your physical body was healing, even though you were being fed more, you weren't tied up, you had more space and light, despite all of that, there really was nothing—other than being set free—that could even begin to heal the extreme emotional and mental damage that had been inflicted upon you. And I'm not just talking about the kidnapping and torture," Katie hesitated here to emphasize her point, "but *everything* that had happened to you. To Jenn. To your daughter. For months and months and months."

Jaspar kept his eyes on Katie, cementing them there, as if letting go would surely mean he'd be set adrift and forever lost. She was doing something to him, he knew that much. Either he needed to trust her, and hold on for dear life, or let go and get as far away from her as possible.

Chapter 41

"Do you believe your daughter is still alive?"

"I do," Jaspar announced without hesitation.

"Of course she is," Jenn forcefully agreed, frowning at the other woman as if to say: why the hell are you asking?

"I do too." Katie's words, without a hint of insincerity, instantly diffused the mounting awkwardness. "Jaspar, I wonder if you would tell us a little about the part in your book where you describe spending time with Mikki, while you were still being held in the rectangle."

A tremulous sigh escaped his lips. He nodded. But no words came out. Jaspar felt Jenn's hand land on his. He felt warmth, reassurance and—worst of all—trust.

"Are you alright?" Katie asked, laying her own hand on his free one, a striking pose the cameras were quick to hone in on. Before the moment was over, a screen shot of the devastated author, the two most important women in his life comforting him, all three faces etched in shared grief, began causing a sensation on social media.

Jaspar nodded. Simultaneously, the two women released their holds as he leaned forward to reach for a glass of water. He took two careful sips. When he was done, he began.

"She was never the same, on the nights she came to me," he recalled. "Sometimes she was exactly the girl I last saw. Grown up, a teenager, her hair carefully styled, her clothes perfect, wearing too much shiny lip gloss because we weren't letting her use makeup yet. Other times she was only a little girl, with pigtails that never kept their curl, and ice cream stains on her dress. Sometimes she was a baby, impossibly little, helpless, couldn't even talk yet. She would lay in my arms and gurgle and coo."

"You're talking about when you went to sleep every night, atop the pedestal? That's where Mikki would visit you?"

"Yes," Jaspar agreed, suddenly very aware of the audience on the other side of the question. "On the pedestal."

"You talk a lot about the pedestal in the book. I have a vivid image of what it must have looked like."

This time Jaspar didn't need further urging. "It was in the middle of the rectangle," he told her. "I don't know why it was there. I suppose it might have been some kind of support column, when there was an actual roof. It became a habit. Every night I'd crawl on top of it, to be as close to the outside world as possible. It's where I'd go to sleep. And every night, Mikki would…every night I'd *imagine* Mikki would visit me. Just like when she was a little girl. We'd curl up and I'd tell her a bedtime story."

"Is that what happened, when she'd join you on top of the pedestal: you'd tell her a story?"

"Sometimes."

"What else would you talk about?" Katie urged, wanting to go beyond what the book described.

"Sometimes we talked about everyday things. Sometimes we talked about what was happening…what had happened."

"To you, or to her?"

The unexpected clatter of keys falling to the floor was immeasurably louder than it should have been, reverberating through the room with startling intensity. They'd somehow ended up back in Jaspar's hands and now he'd dropped them. The jarring sound put everyone on edge, as if a bolt of lightning had cracked across their heads, highlighting the escalating tension in the room. No one bothered to pick them up.

"Both," he responded, as if further explanation was unnecessary.

"Did you talk about the eerie similarity between what happened to her and what was happening to you?"

"Yes."

"I know one of the most grueling parts about what happened to Mikki was not knowing how…how things turned out…not knowing what really happened to her."

"Yes."

"Incredibly, only months later you found yourself going through the same thing." She pushed harder. "What was that like?"

"What do you mean?"

"Did you find that going through the same thing Mikki had was helpful in dealing with what happened to her?"

"Yes."

Jenn gasped.

Jaspar did his best to ignore his wife's reaction. "Of course it was helpful," he hastily added, his manner showing signs of confusion. "Now I knew what she'd gone through. Now I could tell her not to worry, to not be scared."

Katie eyed Peggy, stationed behind the nearest camera. The producer was taut as a wire, arms tightly crossed over her chest, teeth biting into her bottom lip, face bloodless. She knew where Katie's questions were leading.

Katie pressed on. "When you and Mikki would talk at night, atop the pedestal, when she appeared to you as the little girl she was years before any of this happened, would you tell her about what was going to happen to her? About the kidnapping? You'd warn her?"

"Not warn her, just…try to explain…tell her not to be frightened. I, I suppose I was warning her in a way. I don't know," Jaspar said, sounding increasingly unsure of his words. "I just wanted to tell her how it would be. I wanted her to know that even though it would be really difficult at first, things would get better. That the people who took her would take care of her, and maybe…maybe even love her."

"Like Asmae cared for you? Like Asmae loved you?"

Jaspar flared: "How do you know about that?"

Katie eye's darted toward Jenn, on to Peggy, then back to Jaspar. Her words were gentle as she said, "You wrote about Asmae in the book, Jaspar."

Jenn let out a strangled sound. She had to intervene. This interview needed to stop.

Surprisingly, Jaspar shook his head and chuckled. "Oh, God, you're right. I didn't know what I was saying there for a second. I'm sorry about that. Of course, Asmae."

"Which isn't her real name," Katie said, visibly glad to see Jaspar recover his senses. It would make what was coming next easier. "It was a name you gave her."

"No. It's true she couldn't speak English, and I couldn't speak her language. But I did understand that much. She told me her name was Asmae."

"But other than that, you couldn't really communicate with one another, isn't that true?"

"That's true. Not with words. As you can imagine, like any writer, I love words. It's how we tell our stories. How we reveal ourselves. But we—Asmae and I—found other ways to communicate."

With an imperceptible nod from Peggy, the cameras panned out. A set worker rolled in a portable screen, setting it next to Jenn. The Wills stared at it, then at Katie. Instead of responding to the obvious question, Katie rotated in her seat to face the camera head on. "When we return, the woman who helped Jaspar Wills through his ordeal will join us, live from Marrakech, to tell us exactly what happened next."

With another anticipated nod from Peggy, who looked as if she was about to shed her skin, the cameras zeroed in on Jaspar Wills, his face blanching to deathly white.

Chapter 42

The moment the cameras went to black, Katie hopped off her chair and headed for Peggy, as if urgently needing to discuss something with the producer. But Jenn was too fast for her. Catching up, she grabbed Katie's arm and swung her around.

"What the hell are you doing? Why didn't you tell us about this?"

"Jenn, everything is going to be all right," Katie responded, her voice cool and soothing, as if applying aloe to a festering burn. "I'm sorry I didn't tell you, but we didn't know if it was really going to happen. We only received confirmation after we went to broadcast. Frankly, I'm as surprised as you are."

Jenn stared, doubt painting her face.

"It's going to be okay, Jenn. Really."

Something new began to replace the doubt on Jenn's face. Katie stepped back. Was it suspicion? Realization? All she knew for certain was that it was something potentially dangerous.

"I don't believe you," Jenn murmured, more to herself than Katie. "Why would you invite this woman to be on the show? To shame Jaspar? To embarrass me? You want to see what happens when I come face to face with the woman my husband slept with while he was kidnapped? What next? Are you going to trot Scott Walker out here?"

Not a bad idea, Katie thought to herself as she squared her body and braced, as if waiting for impact. Over her shoulder she could see Jaspar, still seated, eyes dazed, looking like a wax replica of himself. Cautiously she placed a hand on each of Jenn's slender forearms, and fixed her with a serious gaze. "Jenn, I would never do that. I would never intentionally hurt you. You have to trust me on this. I know it may be uncomfortable, and it might even hurt a little, but this *needs* to happen. You have to believe me. It's for the best."

Jenn pulled back, attempting to break free of the intense connection. "What are you talking about? Why does this need to happen? You told us this interview would be simple and straight-forward. Us telling our story. Promotion for Jaspar's book. That's it. But you're turning it into some kind of exposé."

"You're wrong. I'm simply telling the story. The *true* story."

Jenn's head moved slowly, side to side. "You were my friend. Our friend. But now I think…I think Jaspar was right. You're just using us. You don't want to help us. The only thing you want to help is your career."

Katie looked stricken. "You don't know what you're saying, Jenn. Believe me, when this is over you'll thank me. Please. Just take your seat and stick it out. It'll be over sooner than you think."

Peggy, watching the exchange from nearby, stepped between the two women and announced: "We're back in less than a minute."

Imploring the other woman, Katie said: "Jenn, don't you think Jaspar would want the opportunity to reunite with the woman who saved his life? To say thank you?"

Jenn's beautiful mouth curled into snarl. "As long as it's on TV, sure, why not?"

"Oh crap," Peggy groaned.

Katie and Jenn turned just in time to see Jaspar stumble as he lurched out of his seat.

Jenn dashed to her husband's side as he unsteadily made his way off set. He didn't get far, collapsing into the nearest chair, head in hands.

Alarmed, Jenn knelt next to him and cried: "Jaspar, what's wrong, honey? What is it?"

"Thirty seconds, Katie," Peggy anxiously announced, tapping her bare wrist where a watch should have been.

Quickly assessing the situation, Katie hissed instructions to Peggy: "We keep going. Confirm the live feed is cued. Reposition camera two on Jaspar. And for God's sake, make sure his mic is still functional."

Peggy nodded and rushed off. Katie took her place just as the camera's "on" indicator light beamed red.

Katie's mellifluous voice filled the studio. After a brief recap of what had transpired so far in the broadcast, she flawlessly moved into new territory. "While investigating in Marrakech, a mysterious man by the name of Tarek made himself known to me. He introduced himself as an agent for the people who owned the building where Jaspar Wills was first held captive." Behind Katie, an illustrator's rendering of Tarek-as-super-villain glowered at the viewing audience with malevolent eyes.

"Eventually, information provided by this man, Tarek, took me to the small Moroccan village of Asni, high in the Atlas Mountains," Katie reported to viewers, doubtlessly breathless, as the special broadcast continued. Refraining from looking at anyone or anything but the eye of the camera, she chose her next words carefully. "Although we will likely never know exactly why, with hopes of having their demands met by the American government dashed, the kidnappers decided to move Wills out of Marrakech. It was here, near Asni, where acclaimed author, grieving father, and kidnap victim Jaspar Wills was taken. It is here where most of *Set Free*, Jaspar's bestselling account of his ordeal, takes place. It is here where Jaspar first met a woman by the name of Asmae. A woman who, in his estimation, saved his life. She cleaned him, fed him, cared for him, and loved him...until the day she set him free."

Undetectable to all but those watching the closest, Katie's eyes flew off camera for a millisecond. Long enough to confirm that Jaspar and Jenn, although not returned to their seats next to her on set, were still in the studio, and that camera two had moved into position to capture their presence. Complexion wan and eyes devoid of life, Jaspar appeared to have fallen into some kind of stupor. Jenn was frantically whispering into his ear, anxiously attempting to figure out what was wrong with her husband and how she could help him. Katie took little pleasure in knowing that soon it would be Jenn who would need help. For she, and the rest of the world, were about to get the shock of their lives.

Chapter 43

"In his new book, *Set Free*, Jaspar Wills shares with us the nightmare of being kidnapped while visiting a foreign country, mercilessly beaten, and nearly starved to death. He recounts the terrifying night when he was bound, gagged and blindfolded, then forcibly moved from the prison where he'd been held captive for several days."

Katie recounted all of this, judiciously choosing each word and moderating her tone with great care. She knew that history would reveal what she was about to do as either cruel or compassionate. Her future depended on which. One wrong move and the audience would turn against her. No one would care that truth was on her side. In a situation like this, emotion reigned supreme, truth be damned.

"Jaspar," she said, intentionally switching to his first name, "believed he was being taken to his death. Instead, he was moved from one prison to another. One he came to call 'the rectangle.' We now know he was transferred to a location near the small village of Asni, in the Atlas Mountains—a barren, rugged, remote place.

"Then, in heart wrenching detail, at times almost too difficult to read, Jaspar describes his late night conversations with the ghost of his daughter. With a father's gentle hand, he attempted to guide his child toward what he knew to be her dark, dreadful, but ultimately inescapable future. He hoped to soften the blow of fate's harsh reality. For some, this may be difficult—if not impossible—to understand. But for any father or mother out there tonight, any parent who's been worried about a child, you'll know exactly what Jaspar was trying to do.

"Before any of this happened, he was like any other parent. He lived with constant regret: for things he'd done, and things he'd failed to do. He worried about making mistakes in raising his child. Like any parent, he sometimes wished he could go back and do it again. Like any parent, he promised himself he'd try harder, do better in the future. But there was no future. For Jaspar, all the typical worries and regrets of a parent were multiplied by a million the day his daughter was taken from him."

Katie's eyes moved purposefully toward her guests. Having seemingly snapped out of his daze, Jaspar was staring at her, taking in every word, deep, blue eyes glistening. Lines that had permanently etched themselves into his face over the past, tragic-laden months had somehow dissolved. He appeared nearly beatific.

Jenn, however, was frowning heavily. Obviously, she was not nearly as taken with the soliloquy. Katie didn't care. Right now, it was all about her and Jaspar. And she knew Peggy was enough of a pro to catch the silent communion on camera, for all the world to see.

Suddenly, the portable monitor, set next to where Jaspar and Jenn had been seated, came alive. Everyone watched in fascination as an umber-skinned woman with a thin, wizened face and large, brown eyes materialized, staring out of the screen as if from the bottom of a deep well.

"Kwella," Katie greeted the virtual newcomer. "It's Kate Edwards. I'm happy to see you again. Can you hear me alright?"

"I can hear." The elderly woman spoke in rutted but comprehensible English.

"I know it's very early in the morning there, so I want to thank you for agreeing to speak with us today."

"I work always. No problem for me."

"I'm glad to hear it."

Katie shot a curious glance Jaspar's way. His eyes were glued to the woman's face, looking as if his life depended on remaining perfectly still. Jenn was once again vigorously whispering something into her husband's ear, but his attention was lost to her. Katie suppressed a wholly inappropriate grin, as she imagined how discomfort and confusion were likely exploding in Jenn's brain as she wondered if this nearly toothless woman, more than twice her age, could possibly be Jaspar's Moroccan lover. Just as quickly, she realized that if she was thinking it, so was the TV audience. That, most definitely, was not the tone she wanted to set.

"This woman is not Asmae," Katie promptly announced. Looking first to Peggy for encouragement, then at Jaspar, she decided to take a risk and try for engagement: "Isn't that right, Jaspar?"

Katie counted off the seconds. More than five and she would switch tack.

At four-and-a-half: "No," he uttered. "It isn't."

"But you and Kwella do know one another, isn't that correct?"

Hearing her name, Kwella said loudly: "What is it you say?"

Katie felt frightened and excited at the same time. Her cheeks reddened as she realized that one false move in her delicate maneuvering of this increasingly complex and fragile interview would cause it to collapse...in front of millions. The sensation was nothing short of thrilling.

"Kwella," she addressed her new guest, "I'm talking with Jaspar Wills. He's here with me, in Boston."

"I'm happy to hear."

Making a snap decision, Katie asked the screen: "Kwella, can you tell us how you and Jaspar first met?"

"Ohhhhh, dear, well it was a bad, bad time. Very sad time. For him and for me too. It was very sad to see him that way."

"What do you mean by that?" She hoped the woman told the story just as she'd told it to her the day they sat together over tea in her home in Asni.

"The man was very skinny. With many pains and, how do you say it...woundings...from beatings. And hungry. So hungry. And mostly sad. Sad like death."

This wasn't quite what she wanted. "How did this happen? Where did you meet Jaspar?"

"My house. He found my house."

"He came to your house in Asni?"

"Yes. He came to my door. There he was."

"When was this, Kwella? When did you first meet Jaspar?"

"Ohhhh, a very long time now. Long, long time when he found me. Then he stay with me for long, long time more."

Katie let the words sink in. She knew most viewers would not yet have begun to comprehend the implications of what Kwella was telling them. Their minds wouldn't let them go there. They couldn't believe it. They wouldn't want to believe it.

She turned to Jaspar, wordlessly agog as he continued to stare at Kwella's kindly face. *He* had to be the one to do it, Katie knew. *He* had to hammer it home. "Jaspar, would you tell us about when you first met Kwella? Was it before or after your time with Asmae in the rectangle?"

"Katie, this is over," Jenn abruptly announced, anger seething through her teeth, her right hand rubbing a hole in Jaspar's back. "I th—"

"Jenn," Katie countered, admirably holding back her irritation at the interruption. "I think we should give Jaspar a chance to answer the question."

"No, he needs—"

"Jenn, it's okay," Jaspar declared, suddenly come back to life. Tortured eyes moved from wife to interrogator. His voice barely more than a croaked whisper, he said: "Just say it."

Katie held the gaze with all her might. With lips quivering, she returned the challenge: "Say what, Jaspar?"

And then he did it. He spoke the words Katie had been waiting to hear since the interview began. "There is no Asmae."

Chapter 44

For an electrifying moment, no one in the studio spoke, moved, or even breathed. Katie exchanged a satisfied look with her producer. Only she and Peggy knew what had been coming.

Beyond everything else, Katie also knew that *this* was the moment. This was the grand pay-off. Every camera was focused on Jaspar Wills—guilt-ridden, lips grim, jaw muscles strained, slumped in his chair, looking like a boy caught doing something naughty. Frozen at his side, was the speechless, disoriented, misled wife. This was the splice of film that would play over and over again, on countless newscasts in countless countries the world over, for days and maybe weeks to come, as the story was retold and sensationalized for a public in love with controversy and spectacle. From now on, this would be the centerpiece whenever stories surfaced denouncing author Jaspar Wills…or celebrating investigative journalist Kate Edwards.

Katie knew, in the days to come, viewers would remember this moment for two things: Jaspar Wills admitting his grand deception, and Kate Edwards revealing it. The next seconds were crucial. Of any point in the interview, Katie was now the most vulnerable. Public opinion was at the apex of being swayed. The tipping point was here. Katie did not want to become the newest incarnation of James Frey and Oprah Winfrey: author caught lying in his autobiography, interviewer outraged by the deception. Jaspar wasn't Frey. Jaspar was beloved, not only for his books but for being a father torn apart by his daughter's disappearance. And Katie was not Oprah. Oprah hadn't done the catching. All she'd done was be hoodwinked.

Katie had a rare opportunity. Today she would shape how she'd forever be defined as a journalist.

And that definition was going to be epic.

Her next move was another bold one, another first. With all cameras swiveling to follow her, Katie abandoned her post on set. She walked the short distance to where Jaspar and Jenn were now seated, near the camera line, an area typically out of view to the TV audience. She pulled over a nearby folding chair for herself, positioning it perfectly to allow the cameras unobstructed views of all three faces. This was even better than before, she decided. Without professional lighting and expensive on-set furniture, the look and feel of the interview had been transformed, grown perceptibly less shiny, less produced, more…real. It was just them, three old friends, who'd been through hell together, facing this latest bombshell. In front of millions.

Jenn was the first to break the reverie. "You lied?" she uttered, bloated with tears, looking as if she'd just woken up from a long, fitful sleep. "None of what you wrote in the book was true?"

This was perfect, Katie realized. Let Jenn instigate the blame game, rally the outrage of a public led astray and fooled into paying good money for fiction disguised as truth. Nothing made people angrier than thinking they'd been defrauded of their hard-earned cash.

Katie waited a moment to let the question resonate. She was, after all, still the interviewer here. She couldn't entirely step out of the picture. She needed to direct the conversation, drive Jaspar to say what everyone wanted—needed—to hear. "Did you lie, Jaspar?" she asked, keeping her voice low, almost reverential.

Ignoring her question, Jaspar had eyes only for his distraught wife. "Jenn, I'm so sorry."

Not good enough, Katie knew, not by a long shot. First, he needed to own up. Then he could apologize. To everyone. "What are you sorry for, Jaspar?"

It was no use. The couple were intent only on each other, disregarding the suddenly-gone-crazy world vibrating around them like a high tension wire about to snap.

"Why?" Jenn wanted to know. "Why would you do this?"

Now it was Jaspar's turn to be speechless. He tried to spit out a word or two, but couldn't, only managing to shrug and shake his heavy head.

Katie was not giving up. "You've admitted Asmae never existed. Isn't it true you also made up the entire time you claimed to have spent in the rectangle?"

From behind the eyes of the camera, Peggy began to move closer, looking worried.

Katie could read the signs too. Jaspar's hands were quivering. The skin around his usually firm jaw had grown slack and sprouted pinpricks of angry red dots. His breathing had grown shallow and he was continuously licking his lips and swallowing hard. The man was either about to go into a full blown panic attack or keel over. She had to move quickly.

"When the kidnappers took you to Asni, it wasn't to lock you up again. They knew their plot had failed. They'd wanted Qasim Al-Harthi released. But after days of threats and beatings and failed negotiations, they knew the American government would never give them what they wanted. Fortunately, killing you was never in their plan. But they couldn't just release you in the middle of Marrakech where you'd immediately be recognized or run to the police. Instead they took you into the mountains and dumped you there. They hoped that by the time you found your way back to civilization, they'd be long gone.

"They had no interest in keeping you captive. Why would they? You were no good to them. You were a liability. A liability who needed to be fed and cared for and could potentially put them in jail one day. It wasn't in their hearts to be murderers, so they let you go. Isn't that the real truth?"

Jaspar pulled his aggrieved gaze from his wife to behold this brand new torturer. Although Katie appeared just as she always had, he now knew he was looking into the face of a dangerous stranger. "I don't know what they were thinking, or why they did what they did."

Katie was impressed with the answer. Despite the tense circumstances, despite his physical symptoms and what must be excessive distress in the face of being caught in a lie, this was still Jaspar Wills. This was a man long used to being in the public eye, familiar with interviewers, and how best to manipulate them to his advantage. She'd do well to remember that, Katie inwardly warned herself. She wasn't dealing with a helpless, broken man. At least, not yet.

"You're right, Jaspar. We can only guess at the reasons for the kidnapper's actions at that point. These men have not been apprehended nor identified, as far as we know. But Jaspar," she paused dramatically and arched an eyebrow. "Let's talk about what we *do* know. Let's talk about the truth. The truth is that after they brought you to Asni, they let you go, didn't they?"

"Yes."

"There was no rectangle?"

"No."

"There was no pedestal?"

"No."

"There was no Asmae?"

"No."

"There were no late night talks with your daughter Mikki?"

Tension crackled like a tumbleweed of thorns in a blender set to 'destroy.'

Very slowly, Jaspar said, "Keep Mikki out of this."

"But you're the one who brought her into this. By writing about her in your book. A book which we now know is less autobiography and more...well, what is it, Jaspar? Creative fiction? Dreamscape reality? Filled with whatever you believe bestsellers have to be filled with these days?"

"Katie!" The shout came from Jenn. "Stop it!"

Katie bit her lip. Had she gone too far? As upset as Jenn must be with her husband, she was still his wife and, at least for the time being, still in love with him. But Katie was representing the people now. It was the people she wanted to please—her viewers, her fans—not Jaspar and Jennifer Wills. It was hard-hitting questions like this that people wanted answered. It was getting those answers that would keep them on her side.

"This is over," Jenn declared, abruptly standing up.

Cameras scrambled to reposition in order to catch the action.

Jenn held out her hand to Jaspar. He stared at it. He was surprised at the kindness of the act, given the atrocity of his own. So were viewers, watching from all corners of the country, mouths no doubt agape.

"Coming?" she whispered.

He nodded and stood.

Together, Jaspar and Jenn Wills, hand in hand, microphone cords trailing behind them, left the studio.

When they were gone, every camera turned to Katie. The interview had gone on far longer and delved much deeper than she or Peggy had ever dreamt it would.

Not the least bit fazed, Kate Edwards moved on. "What we do know is this," she reported in a disturbed voice, perfectly matching the expression on her face. "From my recent investigations in Marrakech and Asni, I discovered that after being dropped off in the mountain village by his kidnappers, Jaspar Wills inexplicably decided not to come home. He did not inform officials in either Morocco or the United States, or even his wife, parents, or other loved ones, that he was alive and set free. Instead, he decided to live a lie.

"From where he was abandoned by the side of a road, Jaspar Wills eventually found his way to the village of Asni. There he met a woman named Kwella, who we talked to earlier this evening via satellite. Unaware of who he was or what he'd been through, Kwella took pity on the stranger. He was wounded and bleeding, half starving to death, and in desperate need of help.

"Kwella admitted to me that Jaspar Wills had convinced her that he was a foreign traveler who'd been mugged while hiking in the mountains. He told her that after the muggers had taken all of his belongings, he'd been beaten and left for dead. She agreed to take him in. She fed him, clothed him, and gave him a place to recuperate.

"Over the next months, Wills did recover. Eventually he was well enough to work in Kwella's gardens and do odd jobs for her friends and family in the village, in exchange for his remaining in her home. She told me the only time Wills ever asked for money, was to buy paper on which to write. It was while living in Kwella's home that Wills first began to write the words that would one day become *"Set Free,"* a book which begins with fact—his kidnapping in Marrakech—but quickly devolves into what we now know to be a fictional tale of a fantasized, imagined captivity."

Katie paused for an uneasy breath. She allowed her gaze to momentarily drift from the camera, her expression communicating sadness, betrayal, pity, disappointment in a friend. "It was only when he was finished with the manuscript," she kept on, "after six months of hiding—six months of allowing his wife, friends, family, all of us, to believe he was dead—that Jaspar Wills finally came home...and sold us his book of lies."

PART III

Chapter 45

Excerpt from the novel Truth Be Told, *by Jaspar Wills.*

Leaving the studio after the Katie Edwards interview was more ambush than media scrum. The crazy scene brought us back to the awful days following Mikki's abduction. Except now there was a notable difference in how the rampaging newshounds jockeyed for pictures and juicy sound bites. Last time, they'd maintained a respectable distance, kept their enthusiasm in check behind a veil of compassion, shared humanity, and joint dismay over a child gone missing. We were part of a team, undoubtedly on the same side, rallying against an evil, unknown enemy. It was as if Mikki was everyone's child, a daughter of Boston, a city willing to do whatever it took to bring her home. Now the tone was changed, grown adversarial, jeering, ugly. Our team had fractured, with me, alone, standing against all others. Now I was the enemy.

"Why did you lie?"
"Will you give back the money you earned from book sales?"
"Do you still dream about Asmae?"
"Was Kwella your lover?"
"Do you feel guilty for lying to your fans?"
"Jenn! Are you relieved Jaspar's affair was a fake?"

Mercifully, a security guard, as surprised by the onslaught as we were, helped shield us as we struggled to reach our car. Through it all, Jenn squeezed my hand with fierce determination, like she'd never let go. I returned the favor. In the crazy, noisy mess that our lives had suddenly become—again—this was our only way to communicate, to say: no matter what, I am here for you.

As soon as we were in the car, I locked the doors. Simultaneously, we exhaled. It felt as if we'd been holding our breaths forever. Talking was still impossible. Reporters were falling on the car like a horde of locusts. I reached for the iPod connected to the car's stereo system, found a Joni Mitchell song, hit repeat, and blasted it. My brain was a jumble of emotions as I kept asking myself: "What the fuck just happened?" I relied on muscle memory to shift the car into drive and get us the hell out of there.

For the entire ride home, even after there was nothing left of the jilted reporters but bad memories in our wake, we spoke not a single word. Instead, we listened to Joni telling us "*…we are stardust, we are golden, and we've got to get ourselves back to the garden…*" We stared straight ahead, the power or our eyes fastened to the road the only thing keeping the vehicle from veering out of control.

Pulling into our empty driveway, we were relieved to see that our sudden infamy had not beaten us there. We rushed to get inside, knowing the peace wouldn't keep.

Without consulting one another, we instinctively knew what to do next. We set off on our tasks like well-trained robots. We extinguished all exterior and interior lights, lowered blinds, closed curtains, powered down phones. While I searched for candles, Jenn retrieved spoons, napkins, and two pints of ice cream: Vanilla for her and Rocky Road (how fitting) for me. In pitch dark, we headed upstairs in search of sanctuary.

It was only when we were seated, cross-legged atop our bed, facing one another, surrounded by a nest of thick blankets and pillows, three spoonfuls into our ice cream, that we first spoke.

"Why?" Jenn repeated the same question she'd asked what seemed like eons ago, in that stiflingly claustrophobic, aggressively lit, scorching hot TV studio in the city. "Why did you do it?"

I'd never loved this woman more. After all the world had thrown at us, after all we'd put each other through, after what we'd just experienced at the hands of our supposed friend on live television, with Katie basically telling millions of viewers what a horrible person I was, how I'd lied to them, and betrayed Jenn in countless ways…after all of that, this woman, my wife, was sitting across from me, knees touching, ice cream in hand, asking me "why?" with nothing but compassion written across her beautiful face.

I set aside my ice cream. Who cared if it melted and turned to goop? I wanted Jenn to know she had my full attention as I laid bare my truth. Yet even as I did, even as I prepared to come clean to my wife about what I'd done, I wasn't one hundred percent certain I understood the reasons myself.

Not until the instant I realized Katie knew the truth, and was about to reveal it to the world, had I allowed myself more than a moment of conscious thought about it. I knew I'd done it. I knew it was wrong. I knew I'd gotten myself in too deep to ever dig myself out. I knew that I wasn't absolutely sure I even wanted to.

Never in my life had I felt so comfortable in a lie. Which is a huge thing for me. As a writer. As a father and husband. As a person. I'd never been good with lying. I rarely found reason or rationalization to use one. And when I did, I was lousy at it, and gave it up pretty much before it was out of my mouth. But not this time. This time, it felt…right. Like it wasn't really a lie at all, but something much, much different. Someone better versed in human psyche than I would have to explain to me exactly what that something might be.

"You and me, Jenn," I tentatively began, "we're in a unique position. Only we know what we've been through since Mikki was taken. I know people sympathize with us: parents, friends, complete strangers too. But they don't really know how this feels. Only you do. And I do."

"I know that, Jaspar, I do," she said with tenderness. "But what does that have to do with any of this?"

"Even with our common bond, even as parents, as two people who have loved each other for a long time, even with all of that, you're you and I'm me. We're different people. We can't help but deal with all of this in our own way."

As she listened to me, Jenn's hand had frozen on its way to deliver a lump of Vanilla. Now she lowered it, carefully, but unable to avoid creamy splats landing on the blanket. I pulled the spoon and container away from her. I placed them next to mine, leaving us both free to act and react without the encumbrance of messy props. I dabbed up the drips of vanilla with a napkin, grateful for a respite from having to keep talking. Then it was over.

"In Marrakech...no, before Marrakech, long before Marrakech, ever since Mikki...Jenn, I was so fucking lost. So fucking sad. I hated waking up every day because I was sure something else horrible was going to happen. That was our life. Waiting for horrible shit to happen. And I knew it was my fault. I knew I'd done something wrong. I'd made a mistake I could never fix."

"What are you talking about?"

"I'm talking about Mikki. The only job I ever had that meant anything to me, was to be Mikki's father. Do you remember how panicky we were when we first realized that she was coming? That we were going to have to take care of a real, live, human baby? Remember how we read all those books, hoping they'd tell us step-by-step how to do it? But none of them helped. So we asked people's advice. They all said the same thing: don't worry about it, you'll know what to do when it happens. And then we finally had her. She was so tiny, so helpless, so frail-looking. I was afraid to hold her. And everyone said the same thing: don't worry about it, you're not going to break her.

"They were wrong, Jenn. There was plenty to worry about. I thought I knew what I was doing with her, but I didn't. I *did* break her, Jenn. I broke Mikki. I let her down. *I allowed someone to take her from us.*"

I felt Jenn's hand land on my knee. "Jaspar, you can't do this. We've talked about this. It wasn't your fault. Or mine. It happened. It's the most terrible thing in the world. But it wasn't our fault."

My head nodded a slow lie. "I can tell you I agree with the words coming out of your mouth all night long, but I don't believe them. At the end of the day, Jenn, we're two parents without a child. Nothing is right about that. If you're a parent, you should have a child. If you don't, then, what are you? There isn't even a word for it. At least when you lose a parent, you become an orphan. If you lose a spouse, you become a divorcée or a widow. But we…we're nothing.

"I couldn't stand it. I felt so horrible. I literally thought I might explode. So when what happened to me in Marrakech happened, do you know the first thing I thought?"

"What?" She sounded afraid to ask.

"I thought: good. Take me. Beat me. Kill me. Punish me."

Tears popped out of Jenn's eyes so suddenly it was almost cartoonish. "God, no, Jaspar," she pleaded, "don't say that."

"And then the assholes didn't kill me!" My rage reverberated through the room like an earthquake's tremor.

Jenn readjusted to bring her body closer to mine. She wanted to comfort me, but all it did was give me a better view of the pain and grief living on her dampened face, having settled there long ago for—I feared—forever.

But there was no stopping now. I powered on like a locomotive fresh out of brakes. "There was a moment," I shuddered, the memory disarmingly fresh and raw in my mind, "right after the van stopped and they pulled me out, still blindfolded. I was certain: this is it, I'm going to die. I was ready. I wanted it. I was finally going to stop hurting all the time. But when it didn't happen, when all I heard was the squeal of tires as they left me there on the side of the road, I think…I think that was the moment I finally broke."

Jenn made snuffling noises, but said nothing. I kept on.

"I have no way of knowing if it's true, but what I felt at that moment, it must be how people feel when they've leapt off of a building or taken pills, ready to end it all, then they wake up and realize they didn't die. Somehow they're still alive, and they hate it. They hate that they failed. All they can think about is how and when to try again.

"When I first met Kwella in the village and asked for her help, it wasn't because I thought: hey, I'm going to pretend I'm dead, write a book about what I *wished* happened, then pop up alive and become Jaspar Wills, bestselling author, all over again. I didn't tell anyone I was alive because I didn't plan to stay that way much longer. I was going to stay with Kwella long enough to say my goodbyes through letters—to you, my parents, to Mikki for when you found her—then figure out how to end myself."

"I'm glad you didn't," Jenn struggled to speak. She'd stopped trying to resist my story; even the tears had dried up. She was worn out, limp, with only enough strength left in her body to keep upright. But her eyes, ears, mind, and heart were open.

"So why didn't I?" I shouted the accusation, the sudden intensity surprising neither of us. Then, quieter: "Why didn't I kill myself? Instead I got better. Before I knew it, I started writing. But not the letters. I started writing this other thing, this other reality. One where I could be a father again. One where I could take care of my daughter, warn her of all the danger I knew was coming her way. I created Asmae in desperation, I think. I wanted to believe that even though we had no idea where Mikki was, who had taken her or what happened to her, there was a chance she was being cared for and looked after and even loved by someone as wonderful as Asmae."

"I get it," Jenn said very quietly.

"What?" I couldn't believe what I'd just heard. How could she "get it" when I barely could?

"Knowing the worst is better than knowing nothing," she said, her voice growing in strength with every syllable. "They all say it. I've been reading these books, about people who've gone through what we did, losing a child. When parents know their child has died, or been killed, or whatever, of course it's devastating. But at least they can deal with it, begin to heal. But it's parents like us, the ones who don't know what happened, who can't move on. They can't get past it. They can't figure out how to live again. Without the truth, their imaginations take over. They come up with all kinds of possibilities. And it ruins them, Jaspar, the not knowing. It slowly destroys them.

"So I get it. In order to survive, we have to replace the not knowing with something else. So why not make it something good? It's like all those people who suddenly come to believe in God when they've sunk to the lowest point in their lives.

"I suppose, in a way, it's selfish," she kept on. "Without knowing what really happened to Mikki, it makes me feel better to let myself believe that maybe, just maybe, it's not something horrible. When I heard what happened to you, about the rectangle, the pedestal, the visits from Mikki, even everything about Asmae, I went there too. I wanted to believe that someone like Asmae might be with our child, watching out for her. If I didn't, I don't know how I could have made it through another day. So, yes, I get it, Jaspar. I get it."

I reached over, my hands enveloping hers, surprised by how cold they were. Then, as couples sometimes do, we did each other a great kindness by telling a necessary lie, followed by an indisputable truth.

"Maybe there is someone like Asmae with her," I said.

"Maybe there is," she repeated, managing a feeble smile.

"Jenn?"

"Yeah?"

"I hate Katie."

Her smile dissolved. "So do I."

Chapter 46

The days and weeks that followed the Katie Edwards interview were unlike anything I'd ever experienced. Back when *In The Middle* first hit bestseller lists and movie screens, I was catapulted into a rarified stratosphere of literary stardom. Overnight, I was on everyone's nightstand, e-Reader, and favorite talk show. The world knew who I was. Of course there were critics, mostly contrarians, who claimed to hate the book. But no one hated *me*. They did now.

Writers—especially writers who've been fortunate enough to experience even a taste of success—can find it difficult to grasp that not everyone is infatuated by every word they write. Going a step further is even harder. To realize that people hate you as a person—so much so that they call for boycotts of bookstores that sell your books, demonize you on social media, and egg your house—is about as devastating as it gets. It's like having a statue erected in your honor, then pulled down, pulverized, and pissed on, all to the ravaging cheers of rejoicing detractors.

Jenn had an escape route all worked out. Whenever she went to work, she handily avoided media scrutiny by moving directly from our house, to her car in the garage, to the garage at work, to her office—all without having to step one foot outdoors. I, on the other hand, was a prisoner inside my own home.

On day three, I shut down my Twitter and Facebook accounts. On day four I stopped reading newspapers, watching TV, or listening to the radio. I only turned on my phone to make outgoing calls. Anything else was simply too damaging to my psyche. I was being painted a monster and—maybe worst of all—I wasn't entirely convinced the description was inaccurate. I'd done something bad, inexcusable even. To me, my actions had been unconscious, unplanned, non-self-serving, delusional, foolish, perhaps bordering on insane. But in the mind of the public, what I'd done was evil, calculated, and narcissistic.

I needed to re-focus, to find a way to think about or do something else—anything else—or risk combustion. I concluded the best thing was to retreat to my comfort zone: writing.

If you're reading this and haven't spent the last few months living on a different planet, you already know how it all turned out. You know how my decision changed everything. How it rocked the world—certainly mine. How by saving one life, it ended another.

What I chose to do next might not have been the healthiest thing to do. But from the outset, it felt damn good. And the feeling only got better the farther along I went.

I think of myself as a good man. A responsible adult. A person who lives his life by a defined set of moral and ethical codes. I cannot—even for a second—recommend, celebrate, or defend what I did to Katie Edwards. But as a father, husband, and someone who values justice and rule-of-law by a fair, policed system of reward and punishment, I admit this one thing: revenge tastes good.

Chapter 47

In the beginning, the best thing about my plan was that it got me out of Dodge. The storied rise and fall of Jaspar Wills was sensational and scandalous, but not quite big enough news to rationalize reporters chasing me beyond city limits. Which was why, after a pleasurable night of tender lovemaking with my wife— who wholeheartedly supported me, if not my purpose—I found myself on a Greyhound bus, fisherman's hat lowered over sunglasses, with a ten-day-old beard, rumbling cross country to Lake County, Indiana.

I hadn't bothered to contact my agent or publisher about the idea. They were busy enough, pulling books from shelves, battling lawsuits and demands for refunds on previous sales of *Set Free*. Our relationship, if not yet adversarial, had grown awkward to say the least. With absolutely no proof or even mild indication there was anything to expose, to tell them I wanted to write an exposé on the woman who, in one fell swoop, had taken my life, shit-kicked it, and ripped it to shreds on national TV, seemed foolhardy and pointless. Besides, I was going to do it with or without their support.

With no rumors to investigate, mysteries to debunk, theories to flesh out, and nothing but gut instinct propelling me, the only reasonable course of action was to start at the beginning. I was on my way to Katie Edwards' hometown of Hobart, Indiana. The strategy was to begin there and dig my way back to Boston, barehanded, nails cracked and bleeding from the effort if necessary, until I found something—anything—to use to my advantage. I'd gotten a peek behind Katie's bright and sparkly exterior, where lay menacing, dark shadow. I was going to prove to the world that the slick reporter with the upmarket-salon hair and chic designer suits—a woman they'd come to trust—was actually someone quite different.

My suppositions were weak, my purpose bordering on absurd. No agent, publisher, or editor would have a single sane reason to support my mission. So why undertake it? I knew what I was doing was irrational and most likely futile. But it fed me, fueled me, kept me alive. It kept me from contemplating worse alternatives for how to get away from a life that lay splattered on the ground around me.

Although I didn't admit it to myself at the time, if at the end of this road I found nothing to write about, nothing to justify my vendetta against Katie Edwards, then at the very least time would have passed. I would have gotten through the first days, weeks, months of what had become the next worst part of my ruined life. I'd have survived a little longer. Maybe by then I could think of something better to do. Because right now, there was nothing— *nothing*—I could think of that I wanted to do more than this.

And sometimes, wishes actually come true.

It was like striking gold in a potato patch. I'd dug down expecting clods of dirt, maybe a worm or two, some spuds. Instead I hit upon a gleaming, glittering nugget.

"She was an ugly duckling, turned swan, turned ugly duckling," Nancy McCraig philosophized as we sat on her creaky back porch, overlooking a yard of well-tended flower beds.

The small-town principal had the look of a good teacher at the end of a long, tough school year. The haggardness, earned from ten months of worry, devotion to students, scraps with parents, hard-won battles and demoralizing losses, was just beginning to smooth out beneath a layer of fresh summer tan. After a visit to Hobart Town Hall where I'd learned that any remnants of the Edwards family had long ago disappeared from town, I turned to Katie's high school for information. It didn't take long to track down McCraig. It took even less to bring a frown to her face. All I had to do was mention Katie Edwards' name.

"How do you mean?" I responded to her surprisingly maligning statement.

She chuckled. "I'm sorry. I know it sounds dramatic. I shouldn't be telling tales out of school, literally. But you caught me at a good time, Mr. Wills. School's out, it's a sunny day, I've got my cats, a jug of iced tea, and a handsome, world-famous author in my backyard. I'll tell you anything!"

I gave her a TV-ready smile. "Call me Jaspar," I buttered the other side of my bread. "I'm sure you watch the news, so you know I'm not so much famous anymore as infamous."

Her laugh petered out. "I suppose that's true. But don't they say in your business: any publicity is good publicity?"

I picked up the laughter. "I suppose so. But from where I'm sitting today, I don't know if I quite agree with the adage."

"I know who Katie's become," McCraig admitted. "Everyone in town does. We've watched her career with…interest." She sipped her drink slowly, taking time to think about what to say next. "And I know who she is to you. Everybody does. That last interview? Ooo-eee, that was a doozy, wasn't it? I hear she's planning to write a book about all that business now—about you mostly."

"Is she?" I'd heard the news.

"That's why you're here, isn't it? You're doing the same in reverse."

"I know it doesn't sound…"

She stopped me short with a 'don't say another word' kind of gesture. "You've come to the right place, Mr. Wills…Jaspar. I don't know how long you've been here or who you've all talked to, but I can tell you right now, nobody in this town is going to take her side over yours. Not after what she did to Hobart."

One by one, the hairs on the back of my neck began to stand up.

"You're looking for dirt, isn't that right?"

God, I hate that term. But—petty and cheap as it was—it was also entirely accurate.

"You're hoping to find something shady in her past, something you can use against her. You don't have to admit or deny it, sugar. But I didn't just fall off the turnip truck. Why else would you be here, in her hometown? Especially now."

The best I could do was a nudge of my chin.

"What she did to you, Jaspar," she said, eyes burning into mine, "well, let me tell you, it's not the first time."

If my ears could have exploded into flames and shot out fireworks, this would have been the moment. Was this woman saying what I thought she was saying? It's what, in my wildest dreams, I'd hoped to hear. But expected? No way. "What do you mean, it's not the first time? Are you telling me she did the same thing to someone else? Who else did she…" *How to describe it?* "…lethally embarrass?"

McCraig nodded her appreciation of the term, her worn face elegiac. "Take your pick. Katie Edwards…she pretty much screwed every single person in Hobart. That girl destroyed this town. So believe me when I tell you, Jaspar, you are among friends here."

Chapter 48

"Katie was born here. Everyone in Hobart knew her and her family. They were nothing special. Her dad, Vern, was an accountant. He had a small office downtown; he did pretty much everyone's taxes. Liz, Katie's mom, was a nice woman, quiet, never saw her out too much." Nancy McCraig tittered. "I heard she started the first Weight Watchers club in town. She never lost any weight, almost no one did because of the snacks she'd serve, and coffee with cream. But she just kept having the damn meetings anyway.

"Katie was their only child. About what I said earlier, funny thing is, I don't think anyone thought of her as an ugly duckling, until the swan appeared. I mean, she wasn't an overly pretty little girl, but certainly not what you would call ugly. She was quiet like her mom. Skinny as a rail though, smart, and a bit of a loner. I don't think I ever saw her with any other girls, or really anyone, except her parents. She wasn't disliked or bullied or anything like that, but she never seemed to quite fit in. More than anything, she was ignored. The other kids—most people actually—just didn't really notice her.

"It was in her grade ten year that she took over the school newspaper." McCraig chuckled. "I suppose 'newspaper' is a bit of an exaggeration. It was really nothing more than a photocopied one-sheet that someone sent around whenever there was a bake sale or school dance. But Katie liked to write. She wasn't part of any extracurricular groups so she had the time. I think it was Helen—her homeroom teacher that year—who encouraged her. It was the best thing to ever happen to that girl. And to the newspaper. Within three months, she turned that bird-cage liner into something that was actually interesting to read."

This didn't surprise me. "How did she do it?" I asked.

"First off, she got rid of the bake sale and recital announcements. She redesigned it so it looked more like a graphic novel than a cheap flyer. It was flashy, modern, young. She started writing short pieces that were aimed more at students instead of teachers and parents. She was smart about it. She knew exactly where the line was, where she could appeal to kids without pissing off the adults. It was, frankly, a shock to most of us teachers. This kid who we barely noticed not only had book smarts, but a savvy awareness of youth culture, loads of creative talent, and a darn sharp sense of humor."

"So what happened? It sounds to me as if everything was turning out okay for her."

"Well, I can only guess at this," McCraig said with a thoughtful look. "But after all the years I've been doing this, I'm pretty good at reading kids. Deep down, I think Katie thought that if her paper was popular, so would she be. Of course, that never happened. The students liked what she was putting out there, but they were too busy with their own teenage shenanigans and petty dramas to care about who was behind it. Katie pretended it didn't bother her, that she didn't want a bunch of girlfriends to hang out with, or a boyfriend to take her out on weekends. She was all about that paper. 'Who has time for friends?' was her attitude. The paper got bigger and more popular, and she got busier and lonelier.

"It was the summer between her grade eleven and twelve years when the transformation happened. It happens to every girl, every kid actually. But the change in Katie seemed more abrupt and dramatic. She was tall and gangly and physically awkward before, but come the fall of her final year, everything was exactly where it needed to be. Breasts, waist, hips, hair—all of it was working."

"And people took notice," I made the easy deduction.

McCraig refilled our iced tea. "Uh-huh. Everyone either wanted to be her friend or get in her pants."

"And did they?" I cringed as I asked the predictable follow-up question, not sure I wanted the answer. Is this what I'd really come all this way for? A story about how the toast of Boston's airwaves had once been a small town Lolita. Nothing about that appealed to me.

McCraig carefully considered her reply before continuing. "Well, sort of. It would have been a heady experience for anyone. But Katie was smarter than that. She didn't go overboard. I think she did her time with the bimbo Barbies and dumbbell dickheads..." She stopped there and nearly choked on a chortle. "Oh dear! Sorry about that. Believe me, I love those kids, all of them. Thoughts like that *never* cross my mind when I'm at school. But here, at home on a summer day..."

"Don't worry about it," I quickly assured her with a smile. "I understand. That was just between you and me."

"Thank you." She fanned a hand across her face. "I'll admit to you though, Jaspar, if I was her, oooooh, boy, I would have dropped that paper like a hot potato! I'd have accepted every one of those invitations to go shopping and join clubs and make out at the movie theater. But Katie was judicious about what she did and with whom. Aside from class, I rarely saw her. She never loitered in the hallways or outdoors like other students. She mostly hung out in the closet-sized office we let her use. That's when it must have started."

"When what started?"

The principal shifted in her seat, an uncomfortable look clouding her face. "Turns out, a few weeks of basting did not a juicy turkey make of our little Miss Edwards. All those kids who were suddenly being nice to her or trying to feel her up? Well, she played their game, but not because it felt good. No sirree. She was using those kids."

I didn't get it. "Using them how?"

"That's just it. None of us knew it was happening. Until we all found out at the same time. On the last day of classes. And then: KABOOM!"

Chapter 49

Note to self: stay clear of teachers in the heady, first throes of summer holidays. I suspected Nancy McCraig, Hobart High School Principal, was getting a kick out of entertaining the renowned author sitting in her back yard. She was doing a good job of it too. I was literally on the edge of my seat.

"What happened on the last day of classes?" I wanted to know.

"Katie's final edition of the school newspaper was circulated."

"Let me guess," I said. "It contained a message to the student body telling them exactly what she thought of them?"

McCraig sucked in her cheeks and shook her head. "Oh no. Not a message. This was a full blown report. Unbeknownst to everyone, at the same time as she was enjoying her newfound popularity, Katie was also collecting information…no, not information…secrets about her classmates. Dark secrets. Dirty secrets.

"Katie had the skinny on every girl who'd lost her virginity but claimed she hadn't, she knew every boy whose penis was under five inches long, she knew about same-sex dalliances behind the gym, kids who'd had sexual relations—consensual or otherwise—with adults. She knew the identity of every peeping tom, bed-wetter, and kid who'd cheated on an exam or was strung out on meth. All of it was fodder for her swan song edition. She exposed pretty much every student embarrassment, every illegality, every moral weakness, every clandestine assignation, every sweet, innocent indiscretion.

"And this wasn't just a quick hit-and-run. Quite obviously she'd been working on it for months. This was her own hideous version of the school yearbook, complete with photographs and snarky captions. Mary Beth Garner: Most Likely to Swallow. Allen Dalhousie: Most Likely to Wear Women's Panties." McCraig shuddered as she uttered the distasteful words. "It was, quite honestly, the most disgusting thing I'd ever laid eyes upon. In part, I blame myself."

Reeling with the revelations of teenage Katie Edwards' destructive, journalistic sledgehammer, millions of questions popped into my head, topmost being: do you have a copy? Instead I went with: "Why blame yourself?"

"By then Katie had been running the paper on her own for three years. None of us were paying attention. She'd been doing a good job. The kids liked it. The teachers and parents were amused by it. Everything seemed to be okay. I had no idea she was creating this, this, scathing scandal sheet. In my school. Using school resources. No one was watching her. No one was monitoring her activities or acting as an editorial board. The other students weren't the only ones who'd ignored Katie Edwards for all those years. The staff, me—we were guilty of it too. And we came to regret it. As adults, as teachers, we failed her. Me most of all. This was my school. I was the leader. The responsibility fell on me to protect my students and my teachers. I didn't do that."

All I could do was shake my head. The story was fantastical, epic even. If it was a movie, who would the audience cheer for? The besieged student body who'd had their grungiest laundry hung out for all to see? Or the long-suffering mouse of a girl, who'd finally gotten revenge for how she'd been treated?

"That day," McCraig remembered, a grimace distorting her face, "I'll never forget it. My first indication that something was wrong was when a teacher came rushing into my office to tell me a student had collapsed in the hallway. A girl named Lilly Kemper. Katie's paper had included before and after photographs of her nose job. And that was it. That was the last moment of normalcy any of us would know for a very long time. After that, everything happened fast, like a blur. It was like a bomb went off. The school exploded, and kids came crashing out of classrooms screaming or crying or just trying to get away so they didn't have to face anyone.

Bedlam is not a word I use lightly. But, Jaspar, let me tell you: that day was bedlam."

"What happened to Katie?"

"Before anyone came to their senses and put two and two together, we barricaded her in my office. We worried that once students stopped thinking about themselves and realized who'd done this, they'd start thinking about how to get back at her. And while all this hell was breaking loose on the other side of my door, she just sat there, hands folded on her lap, completely calm. It was really strange. Once we fully understood what had happened, we asked her why she'd done it. All she would say was: 'Everything I wrote was true.'

"I sent teachers and administration staff to scour the school top to bottom to collect every copy of that paper. But we were too late. It was a lost cause. Pretty much every student had already read it. Even worse, copies had left school grounds. It spread throughout the community faster than a brush fire on a windy day. Everybody knew about it. Everybody had either read it or heard the stories.

"Of course, there were those who thought it was funny, or harmless. Some thought it was nothing more than titillating gossip. Most saw it for what it was: pure poison. You cannot even begin to imagine the anger and frustration and accusations and threats and even fear that began to spread throughout Hobart. It tore this town apart. Everyone was affected in one way or another."

"That's why the Edwards family left town," I stated flatly, beginning to comprehend the widespread and shattering implications of Katie's actions.

"Yes," McCraig confirmed. "Vern's accounting office, those Weight Watcher meetings, the family house—all of it was gone by summer's end. And so was Katie."

Chapter 50

I spent four days in Hobart, Indiana, documenting the trail of destruction left by hurricane Katie: divorce, mental break down, incarceration, drug busts, firings, and a fifteen-year-old boy whose outing as homosexual led to unspeakable consequences—at home, at school, and finally, eighteen months later, at the end of a noose.

There were some who couldn't quite remember the name of "that girl" who'd started it all. A few even defended her, saying it was nothing more than an innocent teenage prank gone too far. But everyone remembered the long, devastating aftermath. It was like talking to survivors of a particularly ruinous tornado, who, years later, were still picking up the pieces. But instead of recovering from physical destruction, they were rebuilding broken relationships, pulling together destroyed families, healing emotional annihilation. The experience left me shaken, and I couldn't wait to go home.

I was grateful for the long bus ride back to Boston. I used the trip's monotony to focus on a single burning question: now that I had this dirt on Katie Edwards, what was I going to do with it? I'd had no idea what I was looking for when I'd first begun this crusade. All I knew was that I needed to get away from the venomous atmosphere of Boston. I needed to revive myself through writing. That Katie Edwards' obliteration of her entire hometown by the prick of her poison pen would end up being my antidote, was a surprising but much-needed boost to my spirit. As I traveled those long miles home, I felt that familiar fire-in-the-belly sensation I've always gotten when I know I've hit upon a winning topic for a new book.

Deep down, I never once truly believed I would actually write this book. It's like when a therapist tells you to compose a letter to an ex-lover, ex-best-friend, ex-boss—whoever it is who's betrayed or hurt you. You write it, get out all of your frustrations, recriminations, blame and pain, on paper. But never, ever, under any circumstance, do you send it.

As the bus rolled across the country, I was oblivious to alternating instances of great beauty and tedium on the other side of the window. I furiously scribbled notes. I organized, re-organized, and categorized fact, fiction, rumor and supposition. I gathered and structured my thoughts about what to do next. I read, then re-read, what I'd written, in the hopes of coming to a rational, intelligent, professional conclusion about whether or not there was a story here to tell, and if I was the one to tell it.

While still in Hobart, I'd made scores of inquiries, called in favors, and let my fingers do the walking until they were limping, all without finding a single lead to tell me where Katie Edwards' family had gone. No one would admit whether they'd left of their own volition or been run out of town. When I put my mind to it, my ability to dig up evidence—even the kind that's been deeply buried for years and never meant to resurface—is not inconsiderable. Still, I found nothing. Except for Katie, the Edwards clan had simply disappeared, never to be seen or heard from again. Had they left the country? Taken on new identities? Both options seemed excessive to me. But who can say what drives people to extremes? The answer is different for each one of us. My only move was to return to Boston. I hoped to pick up Katie's trail from when she first arrived in the city, following her graduation from journalism school. I knew exactly where to start sniffing.

"I shouldn't do this."

We were in a familiar setting. Living room. Lighting too dim. Jenn on the couch, sitting on her feet, laptop on her thigh. Me in the chair next to her. Blinds drawn, just in case some reporter had nothing better to do than swing by for a visit. Phones off.

"You're not," I countered. We'd discussed this. She'd agreed. "All you're doing is reviewing an old file, out loud. I happen to be in the same room."

She ignored my less-than-airtight reasoning. "Jaspar, are you absolutely certain you want to do this?"

"Are you kidding? After what I found in Hobart? It's more obvious than ever that there's more to Katie than meets the eye."

"And it's just as obvious that she's somebody we have to be very careful of."

"She doesn't scare me."

"Well she scares me."

"Have you talked to her? I mean since the interview?"

"No. She's been texting and calling. I think she thinks she did me a favor."

"She thinks she did the world a favor."

"Maybe we should just let this go, Jaspar. Move on with our lives."

"Haven't you already done that?" I regretted the comment as soon as I made it. Blame, accusation, hurt, all rolled into one stupid collection of words and petty inflection.

"You're the one who's always saying everyone deals with things in their own way," she flared. "How dare you act like I don't care about what's going on? Or what happened to you? To us! I go to work to make myself feel better. I work to forget."

"Jenn, I'm sorry. You know I am. I'm doing the exact same thing. I'm working to forget."

"No, you're not. Your work is writing thoughtful, entertaining, beautiful words that make people feel good. What you're doing now is mean and ugly and vengeful and…"

"…and true."

"The truth doesn't always have to be told!" she proclaimed. "Sometimes allowing a lie to exist is the better, smarter choice."

I lowered my eyes and considered this. Was she right? She often was, about many things. I've always fully admitted that the mind of my wife is substantially more logical and pragmatic than my own. And over the past months, I'd been making mistakes. Huge ones. I used to be a man who trusted his gut instincts. Now I'd grown to doubt them. It didn't feel good.

"I don't know what's driving me, Jenn, I really don't. But I just…I have to do this. Something inside of me is making me do this. I don't know where it's coming from or where it's going to lead or what it'll end up being, but I just know I have to do it. But I can't without your help."

She expelled a deep, troubled sigh. We looked at each other for a full minute. Me, laying bare my need, my fear, my anxiety, my uncertainty. She, considering what to do with it.

"What do you want to know?" she asked.

Chapter 51

Jenn scrolled through several documents on her computer before beginning her report. "The first time I met Katie, she had come into the office looking for a lawyer. It looks like that was in March of last year." She read a bit further to remind herself of details. "She wanted to know what her options were in forcing an ex-boyfriend to return some items he'd taken when their relationship ended. Most importantly their cat."

"Name?"

"Fluffy."

I stared at her. "The boyfriend."

"Also Fluffy."

We laughed. We actually laughed. It felt strange, but good, like something we hadn't done in ages and had forgotten how much we liked.

She searched and came up with a name. "Calvin. No last name. It was a non-starter anyway. There wasn't much she could do. Not much I could do. You know, come to think of it, that was probably the reason we ended up becoming friends. Within ten seconds I knew there wasn't a case. But I felt sorry for her. I wanted to help her. She was very friendly, easy to talk to, and funny. Despite the circumstances, we laughed a lot in that first meeting. It felt like we'd known each other forever. So when she called a couple of days later and asked to meet for drinks, I said yes. I remember thinking about the last time I'd had a girlfriend, or spent time with someone who wasn't from work or you. I couldn't come up with an answer."

"I remember you telling me how guilty you felt the first time you went out with her. Because you weren't at work or coming home to me and Mikki."

"You're the one who made me understand just how badly I needed the diversion, that Katie might actually be good for me."

I cracked a weak, apologetic smile. "Sorry 'bout that."

"Oh, you were right about the concept," she was quick to say. "I was the one who picked the wrong person. Before I knew it, we were seeing each other at least once a week."

"What did you talk about?"

She gave me a look.

"You can skip the descriptions of my awesome lovemaking skills. What I want to know is what you found out about her. What did you learn about her family, her background? Did she have other friends? Did you meet any of them? Where did she live? That kind of thing."

"Jaspar, you know nothing about girl talk."

"That should be a good thing in a husband, no?"

"I have her home address and where she was working at the time in the file, but other than that we weren't exchanging biographies. We talked sex, shoes, and salad dressing."

"That doesn't sound like you."

"Which is why I loved it. It had nothing to do with me being a lawyer or a mom. It was just about being girls."

"Really?" I liked it, supported it, hell, I even pushed her into it, but I still found it difficult to picture this puerile side of my wife.

"Really. And I know this is going to sound crazy," she read my mind, "but I miss it."

I set aside my nearly blank iPad on which I'd meant to take notes.

I got up, stood before my wife, legs slightly apart, hands at my sides. My eyes languorously roved her body, halting momentarily on her breasts, before moving lower.

She stared up at me, her beautiful face at first curious, then softening as she understood my intentions.

I slowly began to unbutton my shirt.

She pushed aside her laptop, swung her feet to the floor and subtly parted her thighs.

"I can't help with shoes and salad," I said, my voice barely above a whisper, "but I can certainly talk sex."

Her deep blue eyes sparkled in the shadowy light. "Is that all you want? Talk?" Her voice had taken on a low, syrupy quality that never failed to entice me.

"You know me," I responded, "I talk a lot with my hands." My shirt slipped to the floor.

In one fluid motion Jenn repositioned herself, fingers moving to the top snap of my jeans. In seconds I was standing entirely naked in front of her. I can't remember that happening ever before. Like many couples who'd been together for multiple years, we'd developed a routine: a well-honed sexual ballet that worked for us. In the past, I'd be on her like she was a picnic and I was a big horny ant. My wife is a stunning woman with a gorgeous body. Whenever I saw an opportunity to see it unclothed, I was on the job in an instant. Oftentimes, by the time I'd enter her, she'd be stripped bare and I'd still be fully clothed. She'd have worked me into such a frothing lather, the best I could manage was a quick unzip.

This time would be different.

Chapter 52

My life had become a schlocky detective novel. By day I was an intrepid investigator, ferreting out pieces of the puzzle that was Katie Edwards. By night I sat in surveillance—at her office if she was working late, or outside her home.

Since first undertaking the scheme to expose Katie, I'd discovered an important distinction: as an author, people generally like your attention; as a detective, people do their best to hide from it. Which makes finding stuff a lot harder. Turns out, I'm a rotten detective. So far, I'd turned up nothing useful. Tonight was no different.

Most of the people who'd worked alongside Katie on her rise to TV stardom had pretty much the same thing to say: she was driven, worked hard, was single-mindedly career focused, rarely socialized. There were neither warm fuzzies nor cold denunciations. They didn't outright like her or hate her. They simply didn't know her very well.

One thing kept me digging: Katie's friends. Other than my wife, I couldn't find a single one. When people would tell me she didn't socialize, I thought to myself: she doesn't socialize with *you*. A lot of people keep their personal and professional lives separate. But that was the problem. If Katie had a personal life, I couldn't find it. No pals she'd hang out with on weekends. No boyfriends. No bars or restaurants she frequented. From what I could tell, Katie got up every morning, went to work, worked hard—I had to give her that—then, except for regular errand type stuff, she returned home and stayed there until it was time to do it all over again the next day.

On nights when Jenn was working late, and some when she wasn't, I'd taken to grabbing a sandwich or takeout sushi and having dinner in my car outside of Katie's apartment. Once again, I found myself having no clear idea of what it was I was looking for, other than some sign that she had a life outside of work.

Katie was nothing if not consistent. If the people of Boston knew her history, they'd be wise to be concerned about her spending all her time alone doing nothing but concentrating on work. The last time she'd done that, she'd gutted me on national television, and the time before she'd destroyed an entire town. A frightening resume. The big question: was she preparing to do it again?

By nine o'clock, food gone, iPhone and iPad batteries dying, and absolutely nothing happening, I was fighting the temptation to nod off. It was time to go home. And maybe, I was beginning to seriously consider, it was time to stop this altogether.

I was about to reach for the key and start the engine when the passenger side door opened.

She got in.

"H-hi," I stuttered, stunned.

"Hi, daddy."

Chapter 53

Eleven Months Earlier

"Hi, who's this?"

"Mikki, it's Gail Dolan. I'm Melissa's mom."

"Oh...hi." Mikki frowned, surprised. How had Melissa's mom gotten her number? She and Melissa Dolan hadn't hung out since grade three.

"Listen, Mikki, this is so last minute, but I know you girls are always looking for extra money to buy make-up and stuff and I'm in a real bind. I've got a slight emergency and I need someone to look after Gavin, Melissa's little brother. It's just for a couple of hours, right after school today. You get off at three, right?"

Mikki checked her watch. It was nearing two o'clock and she was walking to her last class of the day. "Yeah. But I usually go right home after school."

"Of course. I know where you live. I could pick you up in front of your house at four. If you give me your mom or dad's number, I'll call and ask them if it's okay. I can have you back no later than six-thirty. That sound alright?"

"Can't Melissa do it?"

"She's got some kind of student meeting thing after school. I'm really desperate, Mikki. I'll pay you double because it's so last minute. It would really help me out."

"Uh, sure." Mrs. Dolan was right. The extra cash would come in handy to supplement her unfairly austere allowance. Mikki knew both her parents would be home late that evening, so she could probably get away with the babysitting gig without either of them knowing about it. But, they'd just had the "trust talk." Her parents had agreed to loosen the reigns a bit on things like allowing her to stay in the house alone. She didn't want to screw that up. So she gave the woman her dad's cell phone number—he was more likely to pick up—and agreed to the job.

At four o'clock on the nose, a small brown car pulled up on the street outside the Wills' house. Mikki waved from where she'd been waiting on the front steps. She'd had to rush after last period. The walk home from school was only a few minutes, but she needed extra time to drop off homework for her best friend who'd been sick and missed school that day. Grabbing her things, she dashed down the path and into the back seat of the waiting vehicle.

"Hi Mikki," Mrs. Dolan said, turning in her seat to fix her young passenger with a wide, sunny smile.

Mikki noticed the ridiculously big, way-out-of-fashion sunglasses and oversized, floppy hat. She wondered why one of the woman's friends didn't suggest a make-over.

"I got you this. I hope you like *Reece's Pieces.*"

Mikki accepted the *DQ Blizzard* with a nod. It was her favorite. She'd never actually met Melissa's mother before, but she was pretty sure her mom had, at some parent-teacher thing ages ago. "Thanks, Mrs. Dolan. Did you talk to my dad?"

"Yes I did," she said with a musical lilt, turning to face the road and slip the car into drive. "Don't forget to put on your seatbelt, sweetie."

By the time the car pulled into the carport attached to a small house in an older, rundown, East Boston neighborhood, Mikki was fast asleep. The drugs in the ice cream treat had done their job.

Gail took a minute to observe the activity level on the street. It was typically quiet during the day, and thankfully today was no different. She knew her landlord, old Mrs. Wazlowski, would be out, attending her weekly bridge game at the community center. Not that any of that mattered. The distance between the car and the private entrance to Gail's basement suite apartment was less than five feet, and at this time of day, all in shadow. No one would see her helping the droopy girl inside.

Gail had Craigslist to thank for her new home. She'd been renting a perfectly respectable apartment closer to downtown. It was small but cute and she was sorry to have to give it up. But the tenancy agreement precluded having a pet, never mind a thirteen-year-old girl held hostage for a few weeks. And Gail needed extra space for that second person. A person who needed to be kept quiet, or more accurately, couldn't be heard. She'd searched the online classifieds website and found exactly what she needed.

The house wasn't in her favorite part of town, and now her commute to work was longer, but in all other ways she couldn't have asked for a better set up. Mrs. Wazlowski was an elderly widow. Her son, long moved on and disgracefully neglectful of his mother, had been one of those kids who was always in a band or practicing to be in one. She and her husband, being the type of parents who did whatever they could to encourage their child's developing talent, had refitted a room in their basement to make it soundproof. It was a place where little Wazlowski junior could drum, or strum, or screech his head off, without disturbing the rest of the family or eliciting complaints from the neighbors. Once the son moved on and her husband died, Mrs. Wazlowski wisely decided to convert the basement into a rental property, from which she could make a few extra dollars.

Mikki Wills was pretty, popular, and purposeless. Exactly the kind of girl Gail Dolan detested. Even so, she'd sacrificed her own lifestyle and committed a significant chunk of her savings to setting the girl up in teenybopper heaven. Except for the part about being kept under lock and key.

The room in the Wazlowski basement had been repainted bubblegum pink, the single bed outfitted with matching sheets and covered with stuffed animals. There was a flat screen TV, Blue Ray player, and large stack of movies Gail believed any thirteen-year-old girl would enjoy. There was even a small selection of makeup, lotions, perfumes, and hair care products. If that wasn't enough to keep her busy, Gail stocked the room with books, and a selection of magazines she planned to refresh every week. Most young girls like Mikki were happy as clams, so long as they could keep up to date on every piece of breaking news in the world of celebrity gossip and fashion.

Gail was quite certain the one thing Mikki would not be happy about was having to give up her phone. Before destroying it, Gail would check the roster of calls registered the day of the abduction. Most would be to and from her school chums. There would be at least one call from an unknown number. Not so unusual. But even if investigators did follow it up, all they'd learn is that the call originated from a disposable phone, now swimming with the fishes at the bottom of the Charles. Yes, Mikki Wills would be upset at being completely cut off from the cyber world. But there was no reason the child shouldn't have to make a few sacrifices of her own. It's not like she was staying in the apartment as a paying guest. Well, not exactly. If all went to plan, Gail certainly expected to benefit greatly from the girl's presence.

The room had its own bathroom. And Gail had hired a handyman to build a swinging flap at the bottom of the door—like a pet door—through which meals, magazines, and whatever else the girl might need could be delivered. Although she'd made some effort to disguise her look and voice, Gail did not want her new "roommate" having any more opportunity to look at her face than was absolutely necessary.

Even before the teen arrived, Gail had prepared the first note. It had been strangely enjoyable. Planning for and creating the ransom letter, cutting out letters and phrases from newspapers and magazines, fashioning the message: it was kidnapping-arts-and-crafts.

By the time Mikki Wills woke up that first day, dazed, confused, and scared out of her mind, she was fully ensconced in Junior Wazlowski's former music room. Neither she nor her captor knew it at the time, but it would become her home for considerably longer than either ever imagined.

Chapter 54

After Katie Edwards revealed the lie, *my* lie—about being held prisoner in the Atlas Mountains—everything I'd written in *Set Free* was tainted, soundly derided, discounted, then promptly forgotten.

Yes, I'd lied. Eventually, I came to understand I'd done it to protect myself, to make myself feel better, to heal. I know none of those are good reasons or apt excuses. I should have damn well kept whatever I needed to say, in whatever way I needed to say it, to myself. At the end of the day, I lied and it was wrong. But along with the lies, truth had also been tossed away.

The truth is that I was never in a Moroccan prison shaped like a rectangle. I never slept atop a pedestal to be closer to the sky and fresh air. I was never cared for and loved by a woman named Asmae. But the descriptions of my daughter coming to me at night, our conversations, our comforting one another…nothing was closer to the truth than those moments. They didn't happen in a rectangular cell atop a pedestal. But they did happen. In a miniscule back room of a red clay house, in a village inconspicuously built into the side of a mountain. I can still feel the wisp of my daughter's warm breath against my neck as we hugged, the softness of her face as it pressed against mine, her golden curls tickling my nose. I remember the fresh, clean scent of her that reminded me so much of home I thought my heart might break in two.

People will think it was a dream, a hallucination, or the desperation of an emotionally wrecked man, that brought Mikki to me during my self-imposed exile in Morocco. And they'll think it again, to hear of her sitting next to me in my car, outside of Katie Edwards' Boston apartment.

But they're wrong. It wasn't any of those things. It was the unbreakable bond between parent and child. One born of relation, bred of time spent together, cemented by steadfast, unwavering love. A father's most important job is to look after his child: to protect her, teach her, ensure she knows every second of every day that she is valued, and loved, and special to him. But I've learned this connection is not a one-way street. A child can do all those same things for a parent. It's a role that grows and develops as the child does, the tables slowly turning until one day, the parent is old and feeble and unable to care for themselves and the child takes over.

But when the natural progression of life is interrupted—by circumstance, by the retarded development of one of the players or, as in our case, by unimaginable tragedy—an imbalance develops. The one left behind—parent or child—is left reeling, incomplete, searching for something to fill the unfillable gap. But here's where the unthinkable comes into play. Something which, had I ever considered it before all of this happened, I would have never believed. Sometimes, the impossible *can* become possible. The unfillable *can* be filled. I know Mikki didn't miraculously appear to me in Morocco like some kind of divine apparition. But she *was* there. She *did* comfort me. She *did* allow me to comfort her. She *did* guide me back to sanity. She saved me. She set me free and sent me home.

We'd always been connected, Mikki and I. So why is it so impossible to believe, in the absolute worst moments of our lives, each of us experiencing similar hells simultaneously yet separately, that we'd need each other's help? Desperately so. Who's to say that we didn't, somehow, do exactly that? Who's to say it wasn't I who helped my daughter survive, and she who helped me?

In the darkened interior of the car, parked next to Katie Edwards' apartment, although I was not entirely surprised to see my daughter because of our past history of visitations, something was notably different. In Morocco, Mikki had always appeared to me as a child. Sometimes she was a helpless infant, sometimes a little girl of three or four, sometimes a teen. But never was she older than when I'd last seen her, when we'd lost her at the age of thirteen. Tonight, Mikki was a young woman, maybe twenty-one or twenty-two. I'd never seen her at that age, of course. But there was no mistaking who she was. She had the same warm, friendly eyes, glowing face, and a pink barrette holding back her hair.

For a full moment I simply stared, saying nothing. She too was silent, endlessly patient, as if knowing this is what I needed. Like the times before in Morocco, I was inexplicably calm, not at all shocked to see her. But I was taken aback by her mature appearance. As I took in this older version of my child, a bloom of pride began to swell inside of me.

Suddenly I knew what she was there to tell me.

I'd done it. I'd protected my child. I'd somehow kept her safe into adulthood. Not only that, but I could tell by the set of her kind face, the gentleness of her smile, that she'd grown into a good, compassionate, generous human being.

Silly thoughts began to race through my mind. Like how, even though I'd owned this same car for most of her life prior to the kidnapping, this new, adult Mikki had never been in it. I hoped she wasn't upset by the mess in the backseat—her usual spot. I glanced down at her hands, looking for a wedding ring, but saw none. I assessed her clothing, the healthy color of her cheeks, the light in her eyes. I was relieved to see laugh lines, the same ones her mother had.

"How are you, sweetheart?" I finally found my voice.

"Daddy, I'm fine."

"You're fine?" My heart fluttered with the hope that it was true. In all the time we'd spent together in Morocco, she'd never said those words.

"I am now."

I felt myself welling up, but resisted the impulse to cry. I didn't want to waste one second on tears. "You don't know how happy that makes me."

She laughed, a marvelous sound. "Oh, I think I do."

I released a colossal sigh and grinned at her. Inside I was feeling something I was certain I'd abandoned long ago: contentment.

"I need something from you, Daddy," she said.

"Anything."

"Go inside."

"What?"

"Dad, I need you to go inside."

Chapter 55

The plan had come to Katie late on a dark, rain-soaked Friday night. She was alone, as usual, in her one-room studio just off downtown, eating flavorless Thai takeout. She was at her wits end, and having to admit something she never thought she would: she missed her one-pony, Hicksville hometown.

No one could ever claim that her high school "stunt" had resulted in anything less than a mighty uproar. Within hours, everyone in town knew who Katie Edwards was and what she'd done. It all happened a long time ago, but she'd bet her bottom dollar—which was pretty much all she had left in her bank account—that the residents of Hobart, Indiana still talked about her to this very day. But here in Boston? Not a peep. She might as well be invisible. To her great irritation, she was living the same dismal life she'd had as a "pre-stunt" high schooler. No one noticed her. No one knew she existed. No one cared.

Katie'd had enough. She'd fixed the problem before; she could do it again. This time, though, she'd need to think bigger. Right now she was a nobody, staring at the bottom from underneath. This was war. She was meant to be a frontline hero, not a measly foot soldier. Everyone knew, when it came to war, it was the foot soldiers who were the first to end up in a pile of dead bodies—a fate Katie Edwards simply refused to accept.

To make a name for yourself, a journalist had to be top dog on a big story. The first one on the scene. The one people turned to when they wanted information, or had it to share. No one bothered with a no-name reporter who couldn't see the door, never mind get her foot in it.

Katie had given the issue considerable thought. She concluded there was only one way to get the jump on a story before anyone else did. She had to be the only one who knew about it. Or, at the very least, the first to know about it with as much lead time as possible. The only way that was going to happen was if she created the story herself. Which was pretty much what she'd done in Hobart. Sure, it was the kids who got pregnant and stole sports equipment from Walmart, but it was Katie who'd found out and made it newsworthy.

The idea was big. Ballsy. Alarming. Almost too daunting to contemplate.

Almost.

If she was really going to do this, Katie knew she'd have to go all out. She had to come up with something that was going to enthrall every last person in Boston and beyond. She considered the options. Human interest stories weren't big enough and had short shelf-lives. Crimes stories were good, but Katie wasn't into committing petty crime. Robbing the corner Chinese store was too small, too boring. No, this had to be something with teeth. Shark teeth. Maybe a crime of passion? That was better. Something that not only interested the masses, but titillated them. Or made them mad. Or sad. Something with children in peril was always a winner.

Concept in mind, Katie set to work with the same fervor and dedication she'd applied to her Hobart High exposé. But this time, her end goal was considerably more grandiose than breaking free of her mind-numbing hometown. This time she had an even bigger break in mind. Katie was going to orchestrate her coming out party, as Boston's newest star journalist.

The more Katie thought about it, the more excited she became. A huge story was about to hit the city.

And it was all hers.

Although it would have certainly added juice and gravitas to the story, Katie adhered to one steadfast rule in planning her next career move: thou shall not kill to get ahead. She just couldn't see herself doing that. She might be capable of ending someone's life—she believed most people would in the right circumstance—but why take the risk if you didn't have to? It hadn't come to that yet.

Besides, she had ingenuity and tons of smarts. All she needed was to put her prodigious creative juices to work.

Katie knew the answer was the kid angle. Madeline McCann. Elizabeth Smart. Caylee Anthony. JonBenét Ramsey. Jaycee Lee Dugard. Right back to the Lindbergh baby kidnapping. Any story with a child in danger captured the public's attention, and—best of all—kept it, sometimes for decades.

She could snatch a child from a playground or someplace like that, ask for ransom. Of course she'd keep the kid blindfolded so she'd never be recognized once she'd wrung the story dry and let the kid go. And she *would* let the kid go. She wasn't *that* kind of monster. In the meantime, she'd be the lead reporter on the biggest story in the city. That kind of exposure could bring her to the precipice of the type of career and recognition she'd always wanted and definitely deserved.

The idea was sound. But it needed something more. Something that would get her play outside of the city, outside of the state, on a national stage, maybe even international. Unfortunately, kids were being taken and having their faces plastered on milk cartons all the time in this country. The tale was sure to be harrowing, but not unusual. It was just too white bread. She needed a story with more oomph. Something exotic but not too exotic. Something with widespread appeal that not only piqued curiosity but held it.

A rich kid?

Still not good enough. Being rich didn't make a missing child more interesting unless…unless they were already famous.

Katie felt a trilling in her stomach. Neurons fired in her brain as she considered the new notion. She could kidnap a famous kid. A Justin-Bieber-ten-years-ago type.

Definitely better. But riskier. Certainly more difficult to pull off. Famous kids came with security and entourages and constant media attention. There'd be all kinds of challenges to overcome.

Then it hit her.

What if the kid wasn't famous, but the parents were? Justin Bieber would be impossible to take. But if he had a kid out there, and of course he must by now, that would be much easier pickings by a mile. Less risk, easier access, but with the reflected benefit of being tied to celebrity; it would be a story *everybody* wanted to hear about.

Katie smiled.

Chapter 56

For weeks, Katie Edwards mulled over her plot. Hours of research resulted in a list of potential targets. Of course, nothing was as simple as it might have seemed on a depressing, rainy Friday night after one too many glasses of cheap, red wine. Even the child of someone famous was not going to be an easy grab. It's not like they were a pair of boots left unattended for too long on the front porch. And the list of celebrities who: (a) lived in Boston; (b) were big enough names to elicit the kind of attention Katie was after; and (c) had a child she could finagle reasonable access to, was pitifully short. But one name continued to pop up at the top of her list: Mikki Wills.

My daughter.

What had started out as an incredible turn of professional good fortune for me and my family, was about to become the cause of our greatest nightmare.

I had somehow become Boston's—and really the country's—flavor of the year. I'd written one of those books that, for reasons baffling to most—like *Fifty Shades of Grey*, *Gone Girl*, *The Fault in Our Stars*, *The Da Vinci Code*—hit the zeitgeist in just the right way. Suddenly a mostly unknown author—me—was a huge celebrity, and everyone was reading my book and clamoring for a new one.

While I was not the biggest star on the horizon by anyone's estimation, and my five minutes were already running short, I was the perfect target for Katie's scheme. I was a native son to the Bostonians, and in their typically exuberant and generous way, they loved me. Thanks to nature's grace and prevailing trends, I had the right "look" and, whenever it was needed, I could pour on the charm. All forms of media ate me up, as did their viewers and subscribers.

Katie, no slouch when it came to figuring out what the public hungered for, knew that if something bad happened to me, people would care. They'd be rapt, and rapturous with attention, on both the story and the person who told it. I had a child about the right age, who hadn't yet morphed into a rebellious teen or gotten into trouble with drugs, the law, or the wrong paramour. I'm probably the only parent in history who ever wished for the opposite to have been true. Any of those things might have made Mikki less sympathy-inducing, less relatable, less saleable to the masses—and therefore less attractive to Katie Edwards.

In so many ways, Mikki was the perfect mark. With me being a relatively new celebrity and only modestly well off, my daughter still went to a public school. She had nary a bodyguard, guardian, or paparazzi trail of any kind to get in Katie's way. And she was local, which made logistics, planning, and implementation much easier.

Once she had the "who," Katie turned to the "how." She was clever. She knew she couldn't just nab Mikki and hope for the best. She needed to plan two dozen steps ahead. Long before Mikki was ever taken, Katie had to be cemented in position as the most likely person Jenn and I would turn to, and trust, to tell our story. She concluded that a friendship with my wife was her best hope of slipping into our circle of influence.

Jenn was a busy lawyer, working long hours. She had few friends outside of the office, something Katie could definitely relate to. And, Jenn had a secret. Something no one—not even I nor our daughter—knew about. A secret ripe for exploitation.

Every so often, Jenn would leave work early under the guise of having to meet a client or attend to a fictional private matter. Regularly maintaining an eighty-to-ninety-hour billing week, it wasn't her professional responsibilities she was short-changing. It was her personal ones. The associated guilt was why she kept this from me.

On these occasions, still rare by most anyone's standard, Jenn would leave her office and, instead of joining a client or carrying out a family errand, she would indulge in what could only be described as "me time." She'd window shop at a mall, visit a spa, or take in a movie. She always did these things by herself, never veering off radar for more than a couple of hours. A little slack in the self-awareness department, Jenn was a woman screaming out for a BFF. Long before she began playing hooky, even I knew she needed to. I just didn't know what to do about it. Katie Edwards did.

Reporters and lawyers can be formidable adversaries or staunch allies, depending on who needs what, when, and how badly. Katie wasn't taking any chances. She'd pull the "reporter" card much later in her game. Her first priority was to develop a friendship with Jenn. One based, in part, on the simple supposition that women need time together, to the exclusion of the men in their lives.

Reporters and lawyers also share a tendency towards a sort of God complex, characterized by the firm belief that they alone can solve people's problems. A reporter does it by digging up and disclosing the unknown, a lawyer by wielding the strong arm of the law. To kick-start this new friendship, Katie knew she'd have to temporarily allow Jenn to play God, leaving her the role of a troubled woman in need of help.

Katie knew that in Massachusetts, common law relationships are legally recognized only if created outside the state. This fact was essential to her plan. She needed to present Jenn with a problem she'd want to fix, but couldn't. This would allow the relationship to move from professional to personal more quickly than might otherwise be the case. The story of an abusive boyfriend who'd left her, taking their beloved cat with him, was pure fiction. Unless the fake boyfriend had done something out-and-out illegal, Katie knew Jenn would be forced to tell her there was little she could do.

That was the easy part.

The difficulty for Katie was playing her role well enough, and subtly enough, so Jenn would like her, but not be suspicious of future overtures of friendship. Katie immediately sensed that my wife was starving for female companionship. She also knew Jenn was whip-smart and not easily fooled. In the end, all it took was a "chance" run-in at a local lunch spot, a follow-up phone call suggesting a quick drink after work, and the strategy was a success. Katie was in, and Jenn, taken in.

Oddly enough, the most important part of Katie's plan was also the simplest: the kidnapping of my daughter.

Chapter 57

Katie Edwards—or as my daughter knew her, Gail Dolan—never wanted money. Money was how kidnappers got caught. Either when they picked it up, or when investigators later tracked it down. The fact that Katie never intended for the ransom demand to be met, freed her of any sense of worry about whether or not the scheme would be successful. It allowed her to ask for a ridiculous sum of money—ten million dollars—and threaten we'd never see Mikki again if she didn't get it.

She made no demand that police not be involved. In fact, she wanted them all over it. Once police were involved, the media were involved. Once media were involved, Katie Edwards was involved. No, Katie did not want money. She wanted attention. And a starring role in a career-making story.

The outrageously excessive ransom demand was perfectly designed to force our hand. Katie knew we couldn't afford anything close to ten million dollars. If we could have, we might have decided to keep the story quiet, make the payoff, and get our daughter back. None of which did Katie any good.

Jenn had confided in Katie during a girls-night-out that our financial situation, although good, was not ten-million-dollars-good. Yes, sales of *In The Middle* had gone through the roof. But that was a while ago. Much of the royalty payout had been sucked up by debt we'd accumulated while allowing me to stay home to pursue a writing career (no one's idea of a get-rich-quick scheme), raise a child, and have a nice home in an expensive city. Because I'd been foolish and blindly rushed into signing a contract without proper advice, the movie option money wasn't the windfall everyone assumed it to be either. The movie did well, but my share of the notoriously stingy, nebulously-defined "Producer's Net Profits" was spectacularly chintzy.

As Katie hoped, the police were called. Unlike how it's often portrayed in movies, a command post is typically set up away from the kidnappee's home. Only a small team is stationed at the residence to coordinate with lead investigators. The off-site team consisted of a supervisor, investigative coordinator, search coordinator, media specialist, communication specialist, logistics specialist, and various administrative personnel. Because of the "Lindbergh Law"—which immediately gives the FBI jurisdiction to investigate any reported mysterious disappearance or kidnapping involving a child of "tender age," usually defined as twelve or younger—the team was ultimately under the control of a cadre of FBI agents.

Whether real or perceived, as the parents, Jenn and I believed we had some say in what was being done to save our daughter. Knowing that, Katie moved swiftly. She subtly and skillfully pushed the right buttons and yanked the perfect chains to encourage us to insist that she should be the lead media contact, all the while making it seem like it was our idea.

In the blink of an eye, we'd found ourselves trapped inside our own home, under siege by a press corps ravenous for information, Katie right there with us. Her strategy was a bit of brilliance. She played us like a virtuoso. At first, her sole purpose in the house was to bring us hot tea, run bubble baths for Jenn, deal with incoming casseroles and platters of cold cuts delivered to our door by neighbors and friends, screen phone calls, and selflessly carry out all the mundane chores we just couldn't think about. Every so often she'd make a passing comment about the reporters outside, sometimes even mentioning that she knew one or two of them, reminding us that she, too, was a journalist. Subliminally, the idea was planted. Without us knowing, we'd been force-fed in itty bitty, nearly imperceptible pieces. To this day, Jenn insists the idea of using Katie as our mouthpiece was hers. But she's wrong.

Katie had the goods, which made the whole notion simpler and smarter. She was a damn good reporter. She was comfortable in front of the camera. She was instantly relatable, oozed compassion, and was trustworthy. Whatever she reported, people believed they were getting it from as near to the horse's mouth as they were ever going to. And they were right. Katie told our story from inside the bunker that was our home. She alone held the ticket that allowed her access across enemy lines, with impunity. She quickly became the bridge between the famous author and his grieving wife and the viewers. What we didn't know, is that we'd fallen for the oldest trick in the book: Katie Edwards was a modern day Trojan Horse.

Chapter 58

Like a maestro conducting her greatest composition, Katie knew just how to manipulate her audience into wanting more. First withholding, then giving—just a little, then a touch more, hitting them with a high note, taking them down with a low. Over the months of our ordeal, Katie's career would follow the same dramatic path. From unknown freelancer to byline reporter to TV correspondent to on-air personality and eventually, national affiliate anchor.

I'm sure local law enforcement and the FBI agents involved in our case still ask themselves the same question I do: how could we not have known that Katie Edwards was playing both sides of this opus? Whenever she sensed public interest was about to wane, she'd find a way to ratchet up the volume. Kidnapper Katie sent another note, reporter Katie put us back on TV. Kidnapper Katie arranged another failed ransom pickup, reporter Katie interrupted scheduled broadcasting with a breaking newsflash.

Authorities were frustrated by many aspects of the case: the length of time between notes, the use of snail mail as the delivery system, the lack of opportunity to negotiate with the kidnappers, the lack of contact with Mikki or proof of life. For them—and the rest of us—the entire ordeal was taking way too long. For Katie, however, the longer this played out, the better. While every passing day brought us greater woe and deepening despair, Katie benefited from increased exposure and offers of employment.

Who stands to benefit? That's the question seasoned investigators repeatedly ask themselves while attempting to solve any crime. If only one of us had thought outside the box. The scenario was casebook archetypal, and therefore so were the suspicions. Everyone assumed the benefit was money, the benefactor unknown kidnappers. In reality, the benefit was fame and a fat salary bump, the benefactor a friendly wolf in designer sheep's clothing.

And then the maestro did what all good maestros must: bring the score to its inevitable, triumphant conclusion. The final money drop was a bust. Ransom notes stopped coming. We never heard from Mikki or the kidnappers again. By this point, the story was such a sensation around the country and beyond that Katie couldn't help herself: she continued to orchestrate the final dying bars for several more weeks.

In time, attention moved away from the mysterious kidnappers who'd vanished into thin air and descended upon people closer to home. In one way or another, everyone became a target. Speculation, rumor, and gossip ran rampant throughout the city, filling tabloid papers, choking social media sites. *Had police dropped the ball? Had something happened to the kidnappers? Was the FBI keeping secrets? Did Jaspar and Jennifer Wills use kidnapping to cover up murdering their own daughter?* Katie Edwards reported on every morsel of it—fair, professional, empathetic. Viewers gobbled it up.

The wisdom of keeping the case in the news for as long as possible had been thoroughly drilled into us. The longer the story stayed alive in the public's eye, the better chance we had of someone, somewhere, seeing something or hearing something or knowing something that could help bring Mikki home. But, eventually, we had enough. More than enough.

Katie whole-heartedly agreed. She suggested an exit strategy that would satisfy everyone. A final interview, with Katie, in our home. Jenn and I would tell our story one last time. We'd end with a public plea for peace and privacy, and thereafter refuse any further public statements or appearances.

That night, when the ratings-blaster interview was over, cameras and microphones and cables packed up and sent back to the studio, Katie put a homemade pizza in the oven, opened a bottle of red wine, and quietly left us alone to grieve and recover, the ever-caring friend.

And then, unbeknownst to us, her perfect plan fell horribly, terribly, irreparably apart, and our daughter's fate was forever sealed.

Chapter 59

The plan had always been to let her go.

The original kidnapping story had morphed into a mystery. Everyone wondered where the kidnappers had disappeared to, and why. What had they done with the famous author's daughter? Could the girl possibly still be alive? But even with fascination at this high level, sustained interest eventually ran its course.

Katie expected this. Her initial plan was to wait until the public had pretty much forgotten about the story. Then, just as they glanced away, looking for something new to discuss over coffee or on Facebook, she would release Mikki. She'd probably do it the exact way she'd taken her in the first place, only reversed: drugged and dropped off on her own front lawn. Mikki's reappearance would set off a brand new tornadic media windstorm, with Katie its calm, well-informed center.

My intent is not to blame my wife by saying this, but it was Katie's continuing friendship with Jenn which gave her the idea for her next strategic move. As often happens with couples who've lost a child through tragedy, we'd grown apart. Not Jenn's fault, not mine. It just happened. Somewhere in the muddle of our grief, loneliness, and anger, Jenn began her affair with Scott Walker, our neighbor. He was also the father of Mikki's best friend—the same friend whose house Mikki had briefly stopped at prior to being kidnapped.

During the same muddle, punctuated by guilt and remorse and coerced by several glasses of wine, Jenn admitted the affair to her sole confidante. Katie played the understanding best friend, but inside she was thrilled by the development. It was perfect. Not only could she use this to once again reenergize the story and her career prospects, but within Jenn's infidelity lived another golden opportunity to take advantage of. She could deflect suspicion from ever falling on her by doing what all good defense attorneys do: point a finger at someone else.

Although, God knows, I have no love for the man, Scott Walker never stood a chance. Once Katie called upon her impressive research chops, it didn't take long for her to figure out when and how to break into Walker's house and where to plant the pink barrette—its importance gleaned from Jenn—so that my wife was likely to find it.

The idea was far from foolproof. But when it worked, Katie was ecstatic. It was an unexpected bonus in the bonanza she'd created for herself. She'd proven, once again, that single-mindedness and exhaustive planning reap endless rewards.

Overall, Mikki's kidnapping was paying off handsomely: trust and respect of an ever-growing audience, healthy paycheck, network broadcasters scrambling to grab onto the tail of her rising star. This was Katie's ransom—not some dirty sack filled with millions of marked dollar bills.

It had been surprisingly easy to keep Mikki hidden in her basement apartment's soundproof room. Being a loner had its benefits. Katie had no nosy friends or interfering relatives to dissuade from coming over. Her landlady only cared that she paid rent on time, which she always did. Colleagues at work didn't know her well enough to expect an invitation. Even if they had, no one was jumping at the chance to visit dodgy East Boston for a cup of coffee. Katie was also discovering something else: besides the cost of a few boxes of cereal, Hamburger Helper, and some chocolate, it wasn't that hard looking after a teenager—at least not one behind locked doors.

It was a moment frozen in time. A pair of eyes looking up, a pair looking down, the owner of each knowing that everything was about to change.

Aside from the day she actually took Mikki from the front of our home, Katie never again donned the disguise she'd used as Gail Dolan, the desperate mom in need of an emergency babysitter. The floppy hat, over-sized sunglasses, and messy red wig were one-time props. There was no reason to wear them again; Mikki lived on one side of a door, Katie on the other. Their only contact was through the pet flap, where Katie passed food and other items. In the beginning, Mikki had tried to engage her captor in conversation, but eventually gave it up.

The one thing Mikki did not give up on was trying to find a way to escape. The only obvious access in or out of the windowless room was the door. The only tool she had was a nail file found in a makeup kit Mrs. Dolan had provided. It would be useless against the door, but Mikki hoped for better luck against the swinging mechanism of the pet flap.

She could only work on the escape project when she was absolutely certain Mrs. Dolan was away—usually during the day—making progress painfully slow. Months passed. She couldn't count the number of times she hurled the file across the room, smarting from painful nicks and cuts to her knuckles, crying with frustration at the hopelessness of her plan and inadequacy of the nail file against the flap's hinges.

Then, unbelievably, it worked. Sort of. Her efforts had successfully dislodged the swinging door from its moorings. The resultant open space, however, was much too small for her to squeeze through and free herself. The best Mikki could manage was to press her face against the floor and take her first glimpse into the room on the other side.

When Katie walked into the apartment that evening and switched on the light, there they were. Eyes. Mikki's eyes. Staring straight at her, from the floor level opening where the pet door used to be. For ten interminable seconds silence boomed, captor and captive bonded together, both shocked at what was happening. Mikki had no idea who this woman was. She'd never met her mother's friend Katie, and reporter Katie Edwards hadn't become "recognizable" until after the kidnapping. All Mikki knew was that this was not the same woman who'd picked her up for the fake babysitting job.

"Noooooo!" Katie suddenly wailed, rushing the door like a madwoman, arms flailing, scrambling to find something, anything, to block the opening. She grabbed the first thing she could find, a cardboard box full of old magazines, and pushed it over the hole. Immediately, she realized it wouldn't be heavy enough. With a bit of manipulation, Mikki could easily push the box clear. Eyes wild, she searched the room for something of greater weight.

Summoning brute strength born of adrenaline, Katie huffed and puffed and shoved until she'd positioned a heavy bureau in front of the missing flap, effectively covering the offending gap.

When it was done, Katie collapsed on the floor, her back against the wall. Only then did she notice her labored breathing, as if she'd just run a marathon, and a nail broken so close to the quick it was bleeding.

"Why did you do that, you…you…you stupid girl!" she hollered, fury and a dawning horror at the implications of what had just happened, tearing at her voice.

"I have to get out of here!" Mikki cried. "Please, you have to let me out. I can't stay here anymore."

Katie listened to the pleas, pitiless.

"Please!" Mikki tried again. "I'll do anything you want!"

"Well then, you're just going to have to die, aren't you!" Katie harshly shot back.

Mikki was stunned to silence by the ugly words, gagging on thick tears and mucus.

"It's your fault, you know," Katie bellowed. "I was going to let you go. Soon."

Mikki would have had little reason to believe the woman. In the past, each time Katie would begin to think it was time to end the imprisonment, a new wrinkle would appear in the story. There'd be charges of police blundering. Suspicions of wrongdoing thrown onto me, Jenn, or others close to us. Rumors of Mikki-sightings around the world. Jenn accused of attempted murder. Scott Walker's trial. My own abduction and eventual return home. Each of these events unwittingly conspired to keep Mikki in captivity, as Katie held off on letting her go in order to capitalize on career-bolstering developments. By the time Mikki had managed to loosen the pet door, she'd been in the room for nearly a year.

"Now I can't. I can never let you go," Katie railed on. "You've seen my face." She was still breathing heavily through her nose while sucking on the bloody finger. Katie Edwards hated surprises. She was a person who strategized meticulously. Carried out plans to exacting precision. Considered every possible eventuality. Katie rarely had to deal with the unexpected.

Now what?

Katie Edwards had done horrible things to meet her end game. She'd committed crimes, lied, cheated, taken advantage of others. But she was not, in her heart, a cold-blooded killer. But how could she allow Mikki to live, when the girl could now identify her? A conundrum. Katie hated conundrums even more than surprises.

Sitting there on the floor, battling to catch her breath, Katie regarded the bulky piece of furniture she'd nearly sprung a hernia to move. A useless gesture, she grimly realized. It wasn't as if by blocking the opening, Mikki could miraculously un-see her. Not only that, her own easy access to the opening had been blocked. Without it, she couldn't pass the girl the things she needed. Without them, the girl would…

…starve.

Starvation.

Katie knew little about it.

How long would it take?

She'd read somewhere—*where was it?*—that after a while, a starving person will no longer feel their own hunger pangs, even refusing food when presented with it.

Chapter 60

"Dad, I need you to go inside."

The hand pounding on the scarred wooden door of Katie Edward's apartment didn't look familiar. My hand.

"Jaspar?"

She sounded surprised. And looked it too. Why wouldn't she be? I'd never been to her apartment before. I doubted Jenn had. And we hadn't exactly been on friendly terms recently. I hadn't seen Katie's face—other than on TV—since our final, explosive interview.

She recovered quickly. "Are you okay? You look terrible."

Never moving from the doorway, she glanced over my shoulder and asked if Jenn was with me.

"No," I said. "It's just me."

Her eyes warmed and her sympathetic tone was almost a coo. "Oh Jaspar, do you need to talk? I'm glad you came to me. We can talk about it, whatever it is."

"Sure," I replied, trying my best not to plough her down on my way inside. I didn't want to 'talk about it' with Katie Fucking Edwards! She was the last person I'd go to for anything. The fact that she didn't know that, reinforced my belief that she was more than a little delusional. "Let's do that."

"Okay." She glanced at her watch. "Tell you what, there's a great little place around the corner. It's called Sam's. I'll meet you there in ten minutes. Order me a beer." She stepped back and made a move to close the door.

"Why don't I just come in?" I said pleasantly. "We can talk here."

She seemed to consider it for a millisecond, then responded with a practiced chuckle: "Believe me, you don't want to see what's behind this door. It's an unholy mess."

She was wrong about that. I very much wanted to see what was behind her door. "That's alright. I don't mind a bit of dust or empty food cartons or kitty litter." I was being as accommodating as I possibly could, biting the inside of my cheek the whole time, resisting what I really wanted to say: "*Step aside, you crazy bitch. I'm coming in.*"

Another of her fake laughs. "Kitty litter? Are you kidding me? I hate cats. And I'm allergic."

That's when I knew for sure.

Katie Edwards was lying to me. Katie Edwards had been lying to us since the very beginning.

"It's just that I haven't cleaned up in weeks…it's been so crazy at work and…really Jaspar, I've been so worried about you and Jenn. I've been trying to call."

I nailed her with cold, hard steel in my eyes. "You told Jenn you wanted to get your cat back from your ex-boyfriend."

It was barely there: a first peek as the metamorphosis began. Tightness around her mouth. Wariness in the eyes.

"Wh-what?" she stuttered.

"When you first met Jenn, in her office, you told her you wanted help getting your cat back from the boyfriend who'd just left you."

The hesitation was barely there, then: "Oh no, that's not right. She must have told you the story wrong, or forgot what I said. That was such a long time ago, wasn't it?" She made a sighing kind of noise, as if to communicate how pleasant it was to reminisce about her and Jenn's long friendship. "Can you believe it? We've known each other for over a year. We've been through so much together, haven't we?"

"Let's talk inside." I moved closer.

The face grew colder. "No. I'll meet you at the bar." Firmer.

"I'd like to come in."

"Jaspar, I said no." Her eyes flickered with malcontent.

"I'm coming in."

"Fuck you!" She was lightening quick, throwing both the curse and door in my face with matching force.

But I was a father sent on a mission by the ghost of his daughter. Nothing trumps that.

I charged forward and fell into the room like a drunken sailor, nearly tripping over my own feet. Katie was thrown to the floor by the force of my attack on her door. She screamed at me to get out of her home. The whole scene sounded like crazy-town. And it was. If anyone lived upstairs, they'd hear the commotion. I didn't care. I was barely registering her ravings anyway. Everything was muffled, as if we were playing out the bizarre scene underwater.

The apartment was small and cramped. Overhead lighting from two bare bulbs was exceedingly bright and the room was too warm and stuffy, as if fresh air was a rarity. Some kind of rose-petal perfume or air freshener overwhelmed the space with sickly sweetness, as if being used to cover up another smell.

The kitchen, dining room, living room, and bedroom were uncomfortably squeezed into one room. A door at one end opened to a bathroom. Along one wall sat three cheap-looking wardrobes, no doubt containing the sharp outfits and shoes and accessories that turned mild-mannered Katie Edwards by night into super-journalist Kate Edwards by day. Every free surface and most of the floor were covered with loose paper, magazines, books. It wasn't surprising to me that a news person would bring work home with them, but this was more like the remnants of a tornado than a collection of reference materials. Was Katie some kind of hoarder?

My eyes landed on a second door. A large shelf of drawers was pushed up against it. "What's in there?" I asked, my voice menacing.

Katie, making it to her feet, reached for her iPhone. "If you don't leave right this second, I'm calling the police."

"Do it." I said as I stepped toward the door.

Then something stopped me.

I turned and looked at the woman. Katie's trademark fearlessness, known by scores of television viewers, was gone. The storm of fury mixed with self-righteousness had suddenly dried up. All of it replaced by something I did not want to see.

Stone. Cold. Fear.

It could only mean one thing.

Oh, God.

No.

"Mikki!" I howled, sounding more like a wild animal than a man who feared he'd found his daughter…too late. "Mikki!"

I threw my weight against the shelf and started shoving it away from the door as if it was made of nothing more than feathers.

I felt a body land on top of me. Katie.

I heard another voice, a new voice. It belonged to a woman, shrieking from the open front doorway of the apartment.

Crying. Scratching. Wailing. Threats. Punching. Pushing.

Police sirens.

More voices. Different voices. Loud. Aggressive. Challenging. Warning.

I didn't care. I kept pushing.

Finally, the bureau was clear of the doorway.

I yanked open the door and looked inside.

And then it was all over.

Jenn was in her usual seat in her usual pose on the couch, legs tucked under her, laptop resting on her thigh, the room's lighting too dim. Carrying a carton of *Reese's Pieces* ice cream and spoons in one hand, I flicked on a couple of lamps as I made my way to my usual spot in the armchair next to her.

"Find anything?"

Jenn answered without looking up, intent on her screen, the off white glow brightening her pale cheeks. "I can get us from Boston to San Francisco, and San Francisco to Auckland. It's the flight from Auckland to Rarotonga on the date we need that's proving elusive."

"Need more time?"

"No, that's okay. I'm beat. I'll try again tomorrow," she said with a lazy smile. Thwacking shut the computer, she caught sight of the ice cream. "Mmm, hand it over."

I handed her a spoon and laid aside another. Holding a third in the air like a talisman, I yelled: "Come and get it!"

Book Club Addendum

Over the years, I have had the privilege to be invited to a great many book club meetings. I quickly learned that no two are alike, varying in size, organization, membership, mandate, programing, and desired author interaction. Discussions have ranged from serious, light-hearted and spirited, to the esoteric and philosophical. In one case the group never once mentioned my book, but the wine was excellent. I enjoyed every experience.

In appreciation, I've prepared this short list of questions as a guideline when discussing *Set Free*. Some of the questions contain details which lead me to issue this **SPOILER ALERT**. Only read further if you've read the book or don't mind a few spoilers.

Let's begin with the burning question on everyone's mind when they read the last page of *Set Free*:

1. Is Mikki Wills alive or dead? Why do you think so?

2. *Set Free* is about being physically imprisoned and the desire for freedom. Beneath the surface, *Set Free* is also about the many ways people can be imprisoned—physically, mentally, spiritually—the many ways they seek freedom, and the many kinds of freedom. In what ways have the three main characters (Jaspar, Jenn, Katie) been imprisoned? What costs were paid for their freedom? Were the costs too high?

3. Have you, or has anyone you know, experienced a type of imprisonment? How was freedom achieved? Was it worth it?

4. Jaspar created an elaborate lie about what happened to him after he was abandoned in the Atlas Mountains. Why did he do this? Was he successful? Were there other possible reasons for him to do what he did?

5. Which is the more powerful emotion: grief or guilt? Why? Would you prefer to feel grief or guilt?

6. What are the lies told by the three main characters?

7. Did the main characters lie for the same reason? How are their lies similar or different? Are some of their lies more obvious than others? Are some of their lies more acceptable than others? Are some of their lies more successful than others?

8. Which lie do you relate to (if any)?

9. Is lying ever acceptable? If so, under what circumstances?

10. Being kidnapped and held for ransom is nearly unimaginable, but if you could put yourself in Jaspar's place, how would you feel and what would you have done? How is the situation influenced by his mental state before being kidnapped?

11. In times of extreme mental stress, what best describes your go-to first reaction? (For example: hope, despair, disillusionment, anger, fatigue, acceptance, accusation)

12. What are typical responses to being caught in a lie? Did the main characters react to being caught in the same way? (For example: acceptance, denial, escalation, apologetic). Were any lies left un-revealed?

13. Faced with certain death, how would you react?

14. As a reader, did you find your sympathy (or lack of sympathy) for each character shift throughout the book? When did your feelings change?

15. Were there parts of the story where you secretly rooted for Katie Edwards to be successful even though you'd begun to suspect her motives?

16. Can you rationalize any part of Katie's actions? If so, at what point did she cross the line into unacceptable behavior?

17. How did Jaspar and Jenn's marriage survive? At what point was their relationship most vulnerable? At what point was their relationship the strongest?

18. What methods of revenge are used by each of the main characters? Were they ultimately successful?

19. Is seeking revenge ever a good thing?

20. Jaspar Wills is the author of four books: *"How to Travel with a Two Year Old and Survive"*, *"In the Middle"*, *"Set Free"* and *"Truth Be Told"*. Which of these books (if any) would you read and why?

CPSIA information can be obtained
at www.ICGtesting.com
Printed in the USA
LVOW11s0934290517
536165LV00002B/394/P

9 780995 229211